MISTLETOE AND MURDER

THE FOURTH PETE CULNANE MYSTERY

S.L. Smith

SIGHTLINE PRESS

Cover photo by Matthew Gorrie

ISBN: 978-0-9964640-5-5

Printed in the United States of America

Published by
Sightline Press
Alachua, Florida 32615
www.sightlinepress.com

To Ruth and Stan Krueger, Tom Motherway, Gale Hawkinson, Tara Kennedy, and Rick and Judy Winter for supporting me throughout the creation and publication of each novel

One

Tonight, Colette rang in the New Year like there was no tomorrow. Little did she know that, for her, that was indeed the case. Had she known, she would not have spent her final hours this way. She loved her brother, and she loved to party. Just the same, she had a long list of things she intended to see and do before exiting this life for the something … or nothing … that lay beyond. She had her heart set on traveling to Australia and New Zealand to bask in the lingo and marvel at the scenery. She intended to walk at least a mile on the Great Wall. She planned to learn to play the violin.

She knew not the day, and she'd never have pegged these as her final hours. Confident she'd be on this earth for at least a few more decades, she spent little time thinking about, fretting over, or preparing for an afterlife. Some time down the road, perhaps. For now, she needn't worry—or so she thought.

Momentarily, the consequences of her procrastination would be between her and her maker. She'd planned this party. Did that mean, in some perverse way, she'd planned her demise?

Unwilling to risk a no go at Christos Greek Restaurant, Colette called in a lot of favors. Actually, this time her brother got his way. All of this was about and for him.

Beverages flowed freely before, during, and after the meal. Colette kept up with the best of them. Even so, she'd noticed the volume of voices grew with the consumption of alcohol.

She'd beamed when the smells and appearance of food hushed the din of conversation, confident it signified an endorsement of the dinner selections. With a large helping of assistance from the manager, she had planned the menu. Dinner began with Saganaki—an appetizer of melted kasseri cheese with brandy. Flamed tableside, the delivery silenced most of the chatter. Fresh-from-the-oven pita bread made the perfect accompaniment. Colette selected her all-time favorite, Mousaka, as the main course. Reactions exceeded her hopes and expectations.

During dinner, little more than the click of a utensil on a plate or serving dish broke the silence. Colette reveled in the fact that, true to her expectations, partaking of this feast took priority over conversing.

Most nights, including New Year's Eve, Christos stopped seating by nine o'clock, and the last diners departed by ten or ten thirty. Tonight, thanks to Colette's connections, this catered event provided an exception. The party goers celebrated her brother Demetrius's wedding. He'd scheduled the wedding on New Year's Eve, hoping to ring in the New Year at Christos. He loved the setting and the authentic Greek food. His Greek heritage played a part in the selection of this venue. His and Colette's parents were more Greek than not, and proud of it. Son and daughter inherited that sentiment.

Situated in the Great Hall in St. Paul's Union Depot, Christos encompassed the original waiting area in this Greek, neoclassical landmark.

Construction of Saint Paul's Union Depot began in 1917, but World War I intervened. The Spanish influenza pandemic of 1918 to 1919 wreaked havoc with the labor force and no doubt also played a role in delaying the completion until 1923.

The depot's Great Hall radiated a palatial look and feel. Fifty-two-foot ceilings demanded deference. The iron chandeliers sought favor by gushing light and flaunting the highly polished floors. The floors rebuffed those advances, returning the light to the source. Thanks to their warm pink color, these Tennessee marble floors provided a gracious reception to visitors. Classical columns and clerestory windows delivered an aura of elegance rarely captured by current architecture. Holiday garlands, along with poinsettias large enough to hold their own when pitted against the columns, enhanced the flair and festive mood.

In addition to celebrating Demetrius's wedding, guests spent tonight preparing to ring in the New Year. Some used this as an opportunity to drown regrets about a year of failed attempts to better themselves, while preparing for another shot at the golden ring.

This was Demetrius's second time around. Colette believed he'd regret this marriage as much as the last one. Just the same, she knew sharing that opinion wouldn't change his mind. It would, however, change their relationship—at least in the near term. For that reason, she set aside her feelings and helped with the arrangements. She always did that. Nothing, not even a gold digger, could come between her and Demetrius.

During the final seconds before midnight, Colette took center stage. Ordinarily, she reveled in the attention. Not tonight and not this type of attention.

For the last few hours, Colette danced and drank, but not in that order. Shortly before the crowd commenced singing "Auld Lang Syne," she began slurring her words. Soon her words became unintelligible.

Most of the guests pretended not to notice. Many observed that Colette seemed unusually thirsty tonight, so this didn't shock them. Unfortunately, what followed raised greater concern, but failed to set off any alarms.

Colette began nodding off. Repeatedly, her chin sank and rested briefly on her chest. That would have been surprising if she was seated at the time. She wasn't. She did it while standing and talking with several people. Suddenly, without warning, she teetered and slumped to the marble floor.

To her immediate left, wide-eyed and paralyzed by disbelief, Demetrius observed all of this.

"I'll call 911," a gruff voice shouted, sounding as drunk as Demetrius felt.

"Hold on. She'll be fine. Get some coffee," Demetrius shouted. He thought, but didn't say, *it's the alcohol.* We just need to sober her up. She'll kill me if we send her to the hospital at a time like this. They'll take her straight to detox. She'll never speak to me again.

"Fine, but if a little coffee doesn't do it, I'm calling 911. You can drink enough to kill yourself, you know."

"Of course I know that. I'm not a blooming idiot," Demetrius snarled. "And I know she drank a lot. I also know she didn't drink enough to kill herself."

In a swift, fluid motion, he swept his sister off the floor. After gently placing her on a chair, he positioned himself to guard against her return to the floor. *Why tonight, Colette?* he wondered.

"Could someone please get a pot of coffee?" he asked loud enough to be heard by everyone in Christos.

"I'll get it," a voice answered from the direction of the kitchen.

Oblivious to those around him, Demetrius spoke calmly to Colette. He did his best to elicit a response—any kind of response.

In keeping with St. Paul Police Department policy, a uniformed officer stood at the ready during this catered event. Before long, this officer recognized the indications of a problem.

"What's up, folks?" she asked, pushing her way through the crowd gathering around Colette and Demetrius.

"She passed out. Drank a bit too much, Officer. You know how it is, right? New Year's Eve and all? She's my sister. I got married today. She's thrilled. In fact, *s*he's responsible for all of this."

He raised a hand over his head and made a circular motion. "Planned the whole thing for me, including the menu." Demetrius smiled nervously, aware that he needed to stop yammering.

"I don't like her color," the officer said. Working her way through the guests still separating her from Colette, she lifted one of the collapsed woman's eyelids. Then she placed two fingers on the unconscious woman's jugular.

Two

Wait here, everyone," the police officer ordered, sounding calmer than she felt. "I'll be right back."

Withdrawing far enough to prohibit being overheard by the party goers, the officer called it in.

This abrupt halt to the festivities dismayed Demetrius. With only a few minutes left until midnight, why would Colette ruin his party—not to mention New Year's Eve for all his guests? Feelings of disbelief, then irritation accosted him.

Pushing her way back through the crowd, the officer told Demetrius, "Help me lay her on the floor."

Looking puzzled, he shrugged and did as instructed.

Without another word, she began doing chest compressions.

"That's not necessary. I told you, she just drank a bit too much. You're ruining her dress. She's going to be furious if I don't stop you."

The officer's look silenced him.

This should be his night. How could Colette drink herself into a stupor? Why do this to him? He'd reluctantly turned over the planning, including the selection of Christos, to her. *That should have sufficed, right? Now this?*

His irritation festered as two uniformed police officers muscled their way through the circle of friends surrounding the other officer, Colette, and him. Why did they come? Talk about an overreaction!

Demetrius opened his mouth, intent on regaining control. Much to his chagrin, he only managed an emphatic, "Hey!"

That's all it took for one of the cops to look him over.

The officer's stare locked the remaining words in Demetrius's voice box.

"You the brother?" the cop asked.

"*Ahh*, yeah," Demetrius stammered. Regaining a modicum of self-confidence, he added, "She's fine. I'll handle this. You're not needed."

"If you value your sister's life, back off. Second thought, just back off," the cop whose look had intimidated him said. "This is out of your hands."

"All of this is overblown … unnecessary!" Demetrius's attempt at sounding authoritative failed a second time in as many minutes. Disheartened but still determined, he continued, "She just needs some coffee. I can handle it!" He tried to insert himself between Colette and the cop doing CPR.

"Get out of my way or I'll have you escorted out of here," she said.

"That's crazy! She just passed out. How many times do I have to tell you that all she needs is coffee? Why won't anyone listen to me? I'm her brother. I know her better than any of you."

Demetrius hated the uncertainty invading his words. He did know, didn't he? Of course he did. But if he couldn't convince himself, how could he convince these cowboys?

Why did Colette pull this tonight—his wedding night? He and his bride had reservations to fly out early tomorrow morning. No, they had reservations for this morning. Midnight had come and gone. Happy New Year. Great! Colette better not screw up his honeymoon, too.

"C'mon, Colette," he moaned, leaning in as close as he could get to her ear. "Wake up. You've got to wake up right now! You're going to be sorry if you don't. I guarantee it."

Colette failed to react to his words—or the CPR.

A thick blanket of despair descended over Demetrius, isolating him from everyone and everything in this crowded room.

Having stepped away from Colette, Demetrius stood on the sidelines, moping. He continued doing so until the paramedics arrived.

By then, Colette lay on the pink marble floor, reduced to a disheveled heap. The color of the floor accentuated the absence of color in her face. Her hair bore little resemblance to the hairdo her hairdresser spent hours creating. Clumps of bottle-brown hair stood out as wildly as Colette had danced just a short time ago. Her gold, lamé, sheath-style dress looked crumpled. One of the seams that previously displayed the curves coveted by many of her friends failed to withstand the incident. Now it disclosed a peep at the girdle she swore she never wore.

As soon as the paramedics reached his sister's side, Demetrius backed away even further. He wanted to run, but quelled the instinct. He watched as the pros took his sister's vital signs and looked beneath an eyelid. Too far away, he couldn't hear the results. He did see them inject something into her arm, continue chest compressions, insert an IV. What the hell? The insertion of a subtracheal tube almost sent Demetrius into shock. All of this hubbub threatened his ability to continue believing Colette suffered only from a simple case of overimbibing.

A guest he'd previously considered a dear friend took it upon himself to paraphrase the results. Blood pressure? Alarmingly low. Heart rate? Distressingly high. Breathing? Shallow.

Unable to believe what transpired, Demetrius watched the paramedics lift Colette onto a gurney and rush her from Christos.

He stood by, dumbfounded, while the manager pleaded for details. He maintained his silence, while his friends and his bride assured the manager he needn't worry. What happened had nothing to do with Christos. Colette would be fine.

The two officers who'd recently arrived, apparently in response to the call made by the officer doing CPR, photographed the scene and obtained information from everyone present. They documented what each person observed in the period leading up to Colette's collapse. They gathered contact information for everyone present, including Christos employees. They relied on those present for contact information for the few who cut out early. They also worked on a blow-by-blow account of Colette's actions for the entire day.

So much for the party. Some of the guests went home—earlier and far less euphoric than they'd anticipated. A few, including Demetrius and his new wife, followed the ambulance to Regions Hospital. He intended to take Colette home the minute the hospital released her. If necessary, he would intercede on her behalf, waylaying any attempts to send her to detox.

An emergency room nurse glommed onto Demetrius.

He became her vehicle for acquiring Colette's medical history. Mind racing and heart throbbing, he answered what seemed like enough questions to write her biography. Unwilling to share some of his sister's escapades over the past few years, he carefully considered and skipped over details about which he'd later be forced to plead ignorance. He knew this could bite him in the ass, but he did it for Colette. Her indiscretions didn't matter at a time like this, right?

Despite the quick actions of the police and paramedics, and in spite of heroic efforts in the Emergency Department at Regions Hospital, Colette's death certificate documented her time of death as 12:46 a.m. on New Year's morning. The fact that Regions was a Level One trauma center made no difference. She was gone.

Hell of a way to start the New Year, and now I have to spoil it for a lot of other people, the charge nurse thought as he notified the Ramsey County Medical Examiner's Office. "I have a woman who died shortly after being transported from the Christos Restaurant in Union Depot," he told the on-call investigator at the ME's office. "She was there for her brother's wedding reception. The brother said he's her closest living relative. Also said she was fine until just before she collapsed. She has needle tracks on her lower arms. Her brother said she's never abused drugs."

"We did a urine analysis. Found opiates. Based on the presentation, she died of an overdose."

The on-call investigator, in turn, notified the watch commander at the St. Paul Police Department.

The watch commander shook his head and called the two homicide investigators lucky enough to be on-call tonight. For very different reasons, he hated contacting both of them. After taking a deep breath and exhaling slowly, he made the first call.

Meanwhile, unable to delay the inevitable any further, the charge nurse walked to the waiting room. On the way, he prepared himself. Second only to losing a patient, this qualified as the worst part of his job.

"What do you mean she's gone?" Demetrius asked, getting in the charge nurse's face. "No way! You've got to be talking to the wrong guy."

"I'm sorry. We did everything possible."

"But she was fine an hour ago! We all ate the same things. She wasn't allergic to anything on the menu. She eats that stuff all the time. No one else got sick—unless that's why Hank left so early."

"I'm sorry. Determining the reason for your sister's death is in the hands of the Ramsey County medical examiner."

THREE

Pete Culnane and Katie Benton welcomed in the New Year with Pete's family. Four generations gathered at his sister's home in South St. Paul. The four-season porches built by Pete's brother-in-law added the space and ambiance and made this the ideal venue. The walls, consisting of sliding glass doors, opening onto wraparound decks, provided an unobstructed view of everything up to and beyond the cliff that marked the property line.

In the distance, along the Mississippi River, a blanket of snow highlighted the black skeletons of trees. Amber lights illuminated the footbridge, connecting Simon's Ravine, Kaposia Park, and Thompson Park to the trail along the river. In honor of the season, white lights formed stars on this bridge. Other white lights broadcast the location of the runways of the St. Paul airport, Highway 61, and the swing bridge that carried trains across the Mississippi River. Far beyond glowed the lights of 3M's corporate offices.

For months, Pete's relationship with Katie had qualified as a favorite topic of discussion in the Culnane family. Could Katie cope with the demands of his career? His family stood evenly divided over that question. These days, the rash of police shootings and anti-police sentiments put everyone in Pete's family on edge. Long term, could and would Katie deal with it?

Pete's cellphone vibrated as he bent to kiss Katie good night.

"Great timing," she shrugged. "Please, tell me it doesn't mean you're going to work."

"I hope it is work. Anything else would probably be bad news."

"Such as, you forgot your leftovers?"

"Oh no! Think of it. The implications are profound." Pete smiled and took the call.

Katie watched him absorb and memorize the details.

"Gotta go. Turns out my night is just beginning," he said as he disconnected and slid the phone back into a trouser pocket.

"Can you hold on just long enough to tell me when you got to be such a pessimist?"

"Meaning?"

"Your reaction to late-night phone calls."

"Can't tell you in ten words or less, so I'll wait until the next time we talk."

He gave her an abbreviated good-night kiss and turned to leave.

"Pete, please be careful."

"Always." He smiled and nodded.

Pete drove as fast as road conditions permitted, bent on arriving at Regions before the dead woman's family departed. The ED staff regularly went through this drill, so they knew the cops assigned to the case needed to talk to the family. Even so, they couldn't force the family to stay.

His thoughts boomeranged back to Katie's last remark. He hated the way current events put her and his family on edge. Their heightened concern for his safety bothered him almost as much as the events precipitating it. Katie's parting words provided another indication of her newfound, or previously undisclosed, apprehensions about his life's work. What did that say about their future?

When he answered the call that sent him running, Pete wore his standard work attire—a suit and tie. If he was a betting man, he'd bet Martin Tierney's call dragged him out of bed. At least he hoped so. For months, Martin had rarely gotten sufficient sleep. So much so, he frequently looked half-dead.

The problem began when Martin's wife, Michelle, contracted a mysterious illness. After months of appointments, it remained undiagnosed. In this age of medical miracles, both he and Martin had difficulty comprehending this.

Pete wished the watch commander could drag his feet for several hours, before notifying Martin. He'd like to tell his friend not to report in until daybreak, but Martin would rail against that. Although he sometimes convinced Martin to hang it up early, in favor of a few extra hours with family, Martin never wavered in his commitment to the job.

Not quite halfway to Regions, a traffic light turned yellow too soon for him to make a run for it. His distance from the intersection, combined with the ever-present threat of black ice, decided it. He eased to a stop. While he sat there, tapping impatiently on the steering wheel, his cellphone pinged.

He wanted to know what the text said and debated with himself. The light was red. The message could be time-sensitive. Reading it would take only a second or two. However, making this exception meant, inevitably, there would be others. Each time would require a bit less justification, until the exception became the rule. He'd traveled this road before. In college, he'd earned a master's degree at it—with honors, much to his chagrin.

Besides, making this exception would turn him into a phony whenever he lectured anyone else about texting while driving. That decided it. He ignored the phone's second signal.

The light changed, snapping him back to the present. He proceeded through the light and pulled over to the curb. Yup, it was Martin. "En route," it said.

Pete multitasked all the way to Regions Hospital. In addition to thinking about the dead woman and her family, he evaluated the drivers in the few vehicles he encountered along the way.

Those drivers were stone-cold sober or doing a passable imitation.

Thinking about drunk drivers often brought back memories of his wife and their unborn child. Both died when a drunk who didn't have enough sense to take a cab T-boned his wife's car.

Pete bit his lower lip and strove to clear his mind of the fury he experienced whenever he thought about this. Driving drunk qualified as stupid … and so human. The "it'll never happen to me" mindset survived past the teen years for far too many adults. Some degree of it is essential. Too much is destructive. With a total absence of this trait, no one would dare leave home … or return home. When carried too far in the other direction, you had those confident of their indestructibility, regardless of the circumstances or indications to the contrary. Thankfully, assuming they survived their teen years, most adults occupied the space somewhere in the middle—and stayed there most of the time.

After parking in the lot adjacent to the emergency department, Pete sprinted to the entrance. As he neared the door, a man and woman dressed to the nines exited. Both heads hung low. The woman had mascara smeared around her eyes.

Unwilling to chance missing the people he came here to interview, Pete stepped in front of them, apologized for the intrusion, identified himself, and asked their names.

Striking out with them, he entered Regions, stopped in front of the emergency department receptionist, and asked if she knew whether Demetrious Brewster, the brother of a patient named Colette Hammond, was still there.

"Sorry, I have no way of knowing," the receptionist shrugged. "It's been a busy night. New Year's Eve always is, and people rarely stop to say goodbye. Guess they have other priorities when they leave, huh?" She shrugged and smiled up at Pete. "Want me to call the charge nurse?"

Pete nodded. "I'd appreciate it." While waiting, he called the Ramsey County Medical Examiner's Office. The effort paid off.

The on-call investigator told him the hospital sent the woman's purse, along with her body, to the ME's Office. "The paramedics took it with them when they transported her to Regions," he explained. "I logged the contents. No syringe or any other drug paraphernalia, and no drugs." The investigator estimated the autopsy would begin at nine o'clock that morning.

When Pete disconnected, the receptionist motioned him over. "Family's gone. Want to talk to the charge nurse?" She held out the phone.

Taking it, he asked, "Can you tell me when they left?"

"Fifteen, maybe twenty minutes ago. We tried to get them to stay to talk to you. The brother seemed pretty distraught. My guess is he needed some time alone to process all of this. Any time is a bad time to lose a sister, but on your wedding night? Wow! What a way to start a marriage."

"Her brother provided her medical information?"

"Yes. Swore she never used illicit drugs. Found evidence to the contrary. First, a urine analysis revealed opiates. Second, she had a fresh needle mark on her left forearm not attributable to the paramedics."

"Did anyone come from Christos with her brother or meet him here?"

"His bride, of course, and six friends. All left when he did."

"Did he say where he was going?"

"No, but I assume home."

Walking toward the emergency department entrance and keeping an eye out for Martin, Pete called the patrol sergeant.

Thanks to the sergeant, he obtained information from the reports filed by the officers who responded to Christos. This included the address and phone numbers for the victim's brother.

Then based on what he'd learned from the ME's office, Pete asked the sergeant to have patrol officers gather and mark the bags from all trash receptacles within two blocks of the Union Depot. Due to tonight's temperatures and windchill, Pete decided that distance more than sufficed.

"I'll get a warm reception when I issue that order," the sergeant said.

"Glad I could help, Sergeant. You should welcome anything warm on a night like tonight."

"Not just any warm thing will do. I prefer something with a heartbeat."

Pete laughed.

Martin arrived, panting, as Pete ended the conversation.

"What took you so long, Martin? Did you have to sober up before you could drive?"

"Sure did! Apparently Marty's grape juice sat in the refrigerator much longer than I'd realized. Didn't discover it until I found myself weaving as I made my way from the living room to the bedroom. Guess I better start paying more attention to the contents of the fridge! Had to drink twelve cups of coffee, before I could head over."

"Got a mayonnaise jar? We're going to be on a stakeout for the rest of the night."

"You're kidding, right?"

"Right." Pete smiled. "The brother left. Just got the numbers. I'll call him."

"He left? Go figure. Needed time to construct an alibi?"

"Possibly, but the charge nurse provided an excuse. She also said track marks on the woman's forearms indicate prolonged use, but the brother swears she never touched the stuff. Let's go find him. See if he's more forthcoming, or enlightened, when he talks to us."

"Don't you think it unlikely she could hide it from him, Pete?"

"Perhaps they didn't spend much time together. Otherwise, I agree."

Pete called the brother's home. His effort met with a greeting from the answering machine. The next call, to the cellphone, went immediately to voice mail. "He lives five minutes from here, Martin. Should be home by now. Either didn't go home or isn't answering the phone. It's understandable if he doesn't want to talk to anyone. I'd probably feel that way.... Have felt that way."

Martin grimaced, aware of the situation referenced.

"Let's knock on his door," Pete said.

"If he isn't answering the phone, what makes you think he'll answer the door, Pete?"

"He may not. If he doesn't, I'll have an opportunity to test my creativity."

"Oh, like breaking down his door?"

"No. I could injure my shoulder. That might mess up my downhill skiing. I'm thinking about going this afternoon, after we wrap this up."

"Fess up, Pete. Your New Year's resolution is to function in a world divorced from the impediments of reality."

"And yours is to earn a PhD in psychology?" Pete quipped as they stepped from the frigid wind tunnel on the corner of Sixth and Jackson into the welcomed warmth of Galtier Plaza.

"Correct, but I'm more realistic. Unlike you, I know I can't complete it today. I figure it will take me until Valentine's Day."

"Such pessimism, Martin. It doesn't suit you."

Demetrius Brewster did as Martin expected. He didn't answer the call, so he couldn't give Pete and Martin access to the elevators to the condominiums.

"Now?" Martin asked.

Unfortunately, the listing of residents posted outside the door they had to enter to reach the elevators did not include their condominium numbers. Perhaps even more unfortunate, the manager wasn't on call 24/7.

Despite the hour, Pete selected a name and the related code from the listing. Out of deference, he selected a man, hoping it wasn't a widow who hadn't changed the listing. He entered the number on the keypad.

A minute later, a groggy, baritone voice said, "Who are you, and why are you calling me at this hour? This better be good!"

"Sorry if I woke you up," Pete said. "I'm a police officer. Do you know Demetrius Brewster?"

"Yeah. So?"

"He got married today. Did you know that?"

"What does that have to do with anything?"

"His sister died tonight. I called him. He didn't answer. He may be unconscious, suffering from the same thing that killed her. It's imperative I check on his well-being."

"How do I know you're really a police officer?"

"Are you able to see outside the security door from your condominium?" Pete already knew the answer. He saw no sign of a camera. Surprising for a pricey place like this.

"No."

"In that case, come down. I'll show you my badge."

A few seconds later, the lock on the lobby door released.

Simultaneously, the voice said, "No thanks. I'm going back to bed."

Martin smiled and shook his head.

Pete now had access to Demetrius's condominium door, but not to Demetrius.

If Demetrius was home, he ignored Pete's knocks … even when he banged on the door and shouted, "Police. We have some questions. Open the door."

After a minute, in a last ditch attempt, he added, "I have your sister's personal effects. Thought you might want them to insure nothing is misplaced."

That, too, failed, but Pete did succeed in opening the doors and raising the ire of several other residents. None admitted knowing whether Demetrius was home.

A few minutes later, Pete shook his head and walked back to the elevators.

Trying to keep up with Pete's stride, Martin said, "Noble attempt. Next?"

"Let's see if the manager or any of the help is still at Christos."

"Why? You hungry? My guess is the kitchen is closed."

Pete smiled. Thankfully, being woken up in the middle of the night hadn't hurt Martin's sense of humor. He wouldn't ask now, but hoped that also meant positive things about Martin's wife.

"What are we going to do if everyone's gone?" Martin asked.

"Find you an apron, so you don't get grease on your suit, while you whip up an omelet. I'd do it, but supper is my specialty."

Pete hoped this evening's excitement slowed the cleanup enough for the manager, for anyone, to be there.

FOUR

Let's drive to the depot, Martin."

"It's only three blocks. You *are* hungry."

"Doing it out of deference to you." Pete smiled. At the speed Martin moved, Pete knew they could both be in the throes of hypothermia by the time they reached the depot on foot.

"Not to mention your own fingers, toes, ears, and nose."

"My partner, the poet. I'd also prefer the ink in my pen remains in liquid form. Never can tell when I'll need to document a case-solving note."

The two investigators dashed to Martin's unmarked car. More accurately, Pete sprinted, and Martin moved as fast as his shorter legs and body mass permitted.

In the time it took him to get from Galtier to the car, Martin's face attained the color of a beet.

For three days running, winter had a death grip on Minnesota. Frigid temperatures brought more than a few folks relying on public transportation to their knees.

"How long are the sub-zero temps supposed to last?" Pete asked his panting partner, as Martin slid in behind the steering wheel.

Tucking his hands in his armpits, Martin said, "At least a few more days. I wonder if the governor will close schools again to protect the kids taking busses."

"I'll bet Marty will be furious if they extend winter break."

"That would require an extension of a year or two. These days, he's hypnotized by the LEGOS Mindstorms EV3 my parents gave him for Christmas. He spends his time building and programming robots. I'm happy to see him so absorbed but worry that it's an escape."

Pete bit his lower lip, fearing he knew what Marty needed to escape. He recognized Martin's comment as a signal. Martin needed to talk. Taking the lead, he said, "Escape?"

"Yeah. Same old same old."

"No change?"

"None. Later, okay? We're here."

Reaching the depot, Martin crossed the light rail tracks and drove along the sidewalk to the north entrance. Once there, he parked within spitting distance of the St. Paul PD Forensic Services Unit's white panel van.

Pete had requested the watch commander dispatch Forensic Services. Despite the likelihood of drawing a blank, he didn't want to risk overlooking anything. Thanks to Pete's track record, the watch commander did as requested.

Stepping inside the door, Pete did a rapid assessment of the restaurant and surrounding areas. That accomplished, he strode over to a friend whose hands moved with the speed of light, accentuating his words.

Either the sergeant didn't see Pete or he chose not to pause.

Averting any chance of an injury, Pete gave the sergeant wide berth as he made his way to stand alongside the sergeant's audience.

Noticing Pete, the sergeant stopped mid-sentence and said, "Lieutenant Culnane. This is Michael Pennock, the manager. Michael, Lieutenant Culnane, homicide."

"Finish what you're doing, then bring me up to speed, Sergeant," Pete said.

"I was just explaining we could be here for several more hours. Any other questions, Michael?"

"Just one. Can I get a business card from each of you?"

Cards in hand, Michael said, "I'm going to my office and try to calm down." Looking back over his shoulder, he added, "Please let me know when I can begin the cleanup."

"This won't go down as one of his or Christos top ten New Year's Eves, Pete. Liability, potentially some bad press, *yada yada yada*. Actually, probably not going to be a favorite for you or me, either."

"Depends on whether we solve it," Pete shrugged.

"It's a tough one. Nothing in any of the restrooms. Still scouring the skyways, garage, the waiting area, and the rest of the depot. A few other employees were still here when we arrived. They were pretty shaken up. One waitress, Elizabeth Frost, saw the victim go into the restroom back there," he pointed beyond and to the right of the bar, "shortly before midnight. Said she wouldn't have noticed, but wondered why someone would head to a restroom so close to midnight. Anyway, she wasn't alone. Unfortunately, her description of the woman accompanying the victim won't do much to narrow the field. And, like I said, we checked all restrooms. If that was the chosen location, they took everything with them."

"Actually," Pete said, "if the other woman was involved, she took it all with her, at least out of the restroom. I spoke to Ron from the ME's office. He inventoried the contents of Colette Hammond's purse. No drugs. No paraphernalia. So I spoke with the patrol sergeant. His people grabbed all the trash bags within a two block radius of the depot. Didn't mean to step on your toes. Requested it before I asked for your assistance. Decided it wasn't fair to leave you out."

"Got the word on that. My people were put out about having to concentrate their efforts indoors," he said with a grin. "Do you think we'll ever get out of the deep freeze?"

"I like this weather. When I go skiing, there's no waiting in line for the chairlift. I ski right up and get on."

"Did they have a piano player last night?" Pete asked, motioning with his thumb at the grand piano.

"Yes. The responding officers spoke with him. Said he didn't see anything suspicious or noteworthy. It's in the reports, along with his name and contact information. If you raise the lid and sit on the bench, you'll see the lid almost entirely blocks the view of the restrooms to the right of the bar, assuming that's relevant."

"Guess we should ask the management to reposition the piano, in case there's an encore, huh?"

"Have at it, Commander." The sergeant smiled and shook his head.

Pete saw Martin returning from the direction of the waiting room and wrapped it up, saying, "I'll be working on getting a search warrant for Hammond's home. See you there?"

FIVE

Martin drove Pete to Regions to retrieve his car. "Help me think this through, Pete," he said en route. "Her brother said she never abused opiates. He must either have his head buried in the sand or be a liar."

"Yes and no. Maybe they rarely saw each other. That seems unlikely, since the manager said she planned the reception. Said he never heard from her brother. You'd think she'd conferred with her brother over the details, but not necessarily. She may have had the connections to pull it off or maybe she was always the take charge one."

"If she drank heavily," Pete continued, "he could have mistaken the telltale signs of a heroin high for the indications of overimbibing. It wouldn't be the first time. People have fooled their spouses for years."

"I know that's true, Pete, but it's still hard to comprehend. Can you imagine shooting up at your brother's wedding reception? Doesn't that mean she had to be a hard-core user? Otherwise, wouldn't she wait an hour or two?"

"They call it addiction for a reason. If she needed a fix, getting one ASAP could become all consuming, her location at the time notwithstanding. We both know of instances of someone who would literally give their right arm for a fix. Consider this, a waitress said Ms. Hammond went with someone to the ladies room shortly before midnight. Assuming the waitress is right, it is likely when she shot up. If so, would she do it in front of the other woman, if that woman wasn't also using?"

"Unless she went into a stall for privacy."

"True, but we found no drugs and no paraphernalia in Hammond's purse. She didn't leave the restaurant under her own power, and by all indications went straight from the restroom back to the restaurant. The Forensic Services Unit found nothing in the restroom and, last word, nothing in the restaurant. Sound like the other woman brought or at least exited the restroom with the stuff?"

"Yes, so who is the other woman?"

"Well, Martin, that's the five-million-dollar question. The waitress wasn't able to tell Forensics much about her. Said she was too busy to pay much attention. Said she knows the victim. That and the time were the reasons she paid any attention to Hammond."

"Could she pick the other woman out in a lineup?"

"Hope we'll find out. Meanwhile, my car's right there. I'll meet you at headquarters."

Without waiting for a response, Pete exited Martin's car and sought refuge from the wind in his. After all this time, the seat in his car felt as stiff as a board, and its temperature could induce frostbite in minutes. Thankfully, that's all the time he required to reach headquarters.

At headquarters, reviewing the reports prepared by the responding officers became their first priority. While doing so, they obtained the names and contact information for the wedding guests and the Christos employees working the event. Then they constructed a timeline, beginning with the earliest accounts of Colette's day on New Year's Eve. The responding officer reports also provided insights, although potentially skewed, into Demetrius Brewster's personality.

"Says here Brewster was told not to leave town before he received the nod," Martin said.

"Does it say whom he was told to contact or obtain the nod from?"

"Yup. Homicide."

"Does it say how he reacted to that?"

"*Uh huh.* Started screaming that she only needed some coffee."

"It's six thirty-five," Pete said. "I'll see if he's now answering his phone."

While Pete tried to reach Brewster, Martin made copies of the contact information. Standing at the copy machine, he smiled when he remembered being told early in his career that, thanks to technology, they'd soon go paperless. For the sake of his children, he wished that would happen. He also wondered how he could function that way.

Six

Yes?" an out of breath voice interrupted the fifth ring of Demetrius's cell.

After verifying Demetrius Brewster was on the other end, Pete identified himself and added, "I want to meet with you *now*."

"I can't meet with you today. I'm trying to cope with my sister's death."

"It can't wait. I need answers. I assume you want answers, also."

"I don't understand. Answers about what? Was it the food? No one else got sick."

"I'll explain when I get there. Where are you?"

"My wife and I are at home. She's in the shower. As soon as she's ready, we're leaving for Keys Restaurant."

"You're at your condominium in Galtier?" Pete asked.

"Yes."

"Stay there. We'll be there in five minutes. This won't take long."

"How about meeting here, after we return?"

"I'm unwilling to put the investigation on hold while awaiting your return. See you shortly."

Pete heard a deep sigh followed by dead air.

Parking downtown presented no problem. Downtown St. Paul looked like a ghost town this New Year's morning. The sub-zero temperatures contributed, but without a Saints baseball game, a Wild hockey game or some special event, downtown St. Paul didn't bustle on Sundays or holidays.

Martin and Pete entered Galtier for the second time in five hours. This time, Demetrius answered when Pete keyed his code into the security panel. Pete identified himself, and Brewster released the latch on the security door, giving them access to the elevators.

"We're so much more efficient this way," Martin said, referring to their last attempt to meet with Demetrius Brewster.

The two investigators found Brewster in the hallway, waiting for them.

"Get the impression he's anxious to get this over with?" Martin muttered under his breath.

Brewster looked like he'd put in a rough night.

Pete introduced himself and Martin. "Sorry for your loss, Mr. Brewster," he added.

Martin nodded and said, "My condolences."

"Yeah. What a way to begin a new year. I still can't believe it." Brewster closed his eyes, drew in a deep breath, and exhaled loudly. He looked spent.

A woman joined Brewster. She kissed his cheek and rubbed his back.

Demetrius smiled at her and gave her a peck on the cheek. "Officers, this is my wife, Shelby." Demetrius introduced Pete and Martin. Then he led them to the living room. It provided an award-winning view of the State Capitol building.

Once everyone was seated, Pete pulled a notepad from a suit coat pocket. "Tell us about last night," he said.

Martin decided to leave this one to Pete. He felt depleted and happy to remain on the sidelines, unless Pete overlooked something. Fat chance.

"Where do you want me to start?" Demetrius asked.

"Who arranged the time and location for your reception?"

"Colette arranged everything. She fancies …," Demetrius bit his lower lip, "she fancied herself an event planner."

"Who compiled the guest list?"

"Colette. Then Shelby and I made some modifications. After all, it was our reception."

"How many people did you invite?"

"Seventy-four. That doesn't include Shelby, Colette, and me."

"Did you get a final count of the attendees from the manager of Christos?"

"I'm sure Colette would have done that. It never occurred to me. That wouldn't affect the cost, anyway."

"I need a list of all attendees."

"I'll get it, honey," Shelby said. "It's on the desk." Turning to Pete she added, "I'll be right back."

"I need a cup of coffee. Can I get you one?" Demetrius asked.

"That would be great," Martin said.

"Same here," Pete said.

Shelby returned and was reading the names on the list when Demetrius returned and gave a mug of coffee to each investigator. Before he sat down, he handed each a coaster, saying, "New furniture."

Pete checked off the names on his list, as Shelby read her list.

"Do you remember anyone else, Shelby?"

Shelby shook her head.

"Did anyone leave before the police arrived?"

"Hank is the only one I'm aware of," Demetrius said. "Did you see anyone else, dear?"

Shelby shook her head.

"Hank's last name?"

"St. James."

"When did he leave?"

"Way before Colette got sick. About eleven. Does that sound right, Shelby?"

Shelby nodded. "Definitely before eleven."

"I understand you told the folks at Regions that Colette didn't abuse drugs."

"Right."

"When did she stop?"

Demetrius licked his lips.

Pete waited patiently.

It took more than a minute, then Demetrius said, "She's been clean for almost a year. She had back surgery, took opiates longer than she should have. I blame her doctor. When she could no longer get a prescription for the opiates, she became desperate. Someone solved her problem by hooking her on heroin."

"Who did that?"

"She refused to tell me. I did everything I could think of to find out. I talked to all of her friends and employees. I promised to give a thousand dollars, then five thousand to the first person who got the name for me. I owed it to Colette. She would have done it for me. When I failed to get a name, I pleaded with Colette. For months, I did that every time I saw her. One day, we were talking, and I was crying. She grabbed me and said, 'Okay, okay, I'll quit. I'd planned to anyway.' I don't know whether or not she'd planned to, but she actually quit. She went to a treatment center. The people there did a phenomenal job. Somehow, they got her through it. She still missed the stuff. Told me that as recently as yesterday. But yesterday she also promised she would never use the stuff, again."

Demetrius's jaw dropped. "Is that what happened last night? Did she die of an overdose?"

Pete nodded.

"Then I may have killed her. I should have let a friend call 911 right away!"

"When did you first notice Colette had a problem?"

"Just before midnight. I mean, literally, one or two minutes before. I saw her sink to the floor. She didn't fall. She just sort of sank. She resembled a feather, floating from a standing position to the floor. I went right over and tried to help her. I thought it was the booze. She drank a lot last night. Almost immediately, a police officer took over, pushing me aside."

Pete knew from the reports that the officer on site called it in at two minutes to midnight.

"After she got clean, did she tell you where she got the stuff?"

"No. Initially, I think she worried about losing her source. Then, after she got clean, I think it was either loyalty or fear of retribution."

"Once she'd conquered heroin, did she consume a lot of alcohol?"

"Only last night. That's why I was so sure it was the booze." Demetrius closed his eyes and shook his head. "Well, actually, she started drinking heavily when she turned sixty. She went through a major identity crisis, due to that birthday."

"Who else went to Regions after the paramedics took Colette there?" Pete asked.

Demetrius named the people on Pete's list.

"Were any of them drunk or exhibiting signs of heroin use?"

"Not that I know of, but I was so worried about Colette, I wasn't really paying attention. What do you think, Shelby?"

Shelby shook her head.

"Did Colette have a significant other?" Martin asked, deciding to take a turn.

"Yeah, but she planned to send him packing," Demetrius rolled his eyes.

Shelby stuck her nose up in the air. "It was all part of the crisis she experienced when she turned sixty," she added.

"Tell us about him."

"He's a leech!" Demetrius said. "He was her boy toy. He was interested only in what she could and did do for him. It made me sick. It was a bad joke—on Colette. I can't believe she fell for him and his line. I can't believe she let him move in with her. He's a total loser. Without her, he's nothing."

"Then it behooved him to keep her around," Pete said.

Demetrius shrugged. "I guess."

"Did Colette have an ex?" Pete asked, looking for a motive.

"No, Gilbert died eight years ago," Demetrius said. "Great guy. Had cancer. What a crime. Bet he started rolling in his grave when she hooked up with Odin."

"Personally, I think she was working on becoming a cougar," Shelby said.

"I can't believe you said that! Shelby, she died this morning," Demetrius sighed.

"Any other siblings?" Martin asked.

"No. There were just the two of us."

"Children?" Martin asked.

Demetrius shook his head. "No. Not sure why. When we were kids, she said she wanted to have at least four. I don't know what changed that."

"Are your parents still living?" Martin asked, covering the last link in her immediate family.

"No. Father died five years ago, and Mother died three years ago."

"Can you think of anyone who might want to hurt Colette?" Pete moved back into the driver's seat.

"The only thing I can think of is possibly one of the authors with whom she dealt. You'll have to talk to her staff about that. If she ever mentioned a name, I can't remember it. She did say they are a temperamental and demanding group who blamed her if their books didn't fly off the shelf. She said few accepted or understood that the onus for marketing rested squarely on their backs."

"Were any of her authors at the reception?"

"Some attendees were her friends, but I don't know the connections."

"Did anyone crash the party?"

"Not that I noticed. Did you notice, Shelby?"

"Too many of the people were strangers for me to know that."

"Colette owned this business?"

"Yes."

"What's the company name and address?"

SEVEN

Delaying their return to the deep freeze, Pete succeeded in reaching the piano player. He lived in an apartment several floors below Demetrius and Shelby's condo.

Percy greeted the two investigators as they stepped off the elevator. Judging from the bags under his eyes, he'd slept little if at all after leaving Christos this morning.

"My wife is a light sleeper," he explained. "How about talking here?"

"Sure," Pete said, noting the empty hallway. "This shouldn't take long. I understand you played the piano at the Brewster wedding last night and into the early hours this morning."

"Correct. As I told the officers who came to Christos, I was busy playing the piano and talking to guests. I didn't have time to pay attention to what was happening around me."

"Understood," Pete said. "You faced the bar, correct?"

"Correct."

"That means you also faced the restrooms to the right of the bar."

"Correct, and if the piano lid was closed, I might have spent the night watching people dispose of the drinks many consumed at an amazing rate. I know that because I saw the wait staff running to keep up with the drink orders."

"Granted your view was obstructed, but you could see at least a portion of the ladies room door, couldn't you."

"If I had a strong desire, probably. I'm paid to look at the guests while I play, talk to anyone who walks over to the piano, know or have the charts to play requests, be attentive and welcoming. I'm *not* paid to monitor the restrooms."

"You met Colette Hammond, correct?"

"The groom's sister. The woman who collapsed. Yes."

"No doubt you were counting down to midnight, so you could begin playing 'Auld Lang Syne' at the appropriate time."

"Of course."

"Do you have a driver's license?"

"Yes. What does that have to do with anything?"

"When was the last time you took the vision test?"

"Last month. So?"

"And your license was renewed?"

"Yes."

"So there's nothing wrong with your peripheral vision."

"Correct."

"When you looked at the guests, the restrooms were a little less than ninety degrees to your right. Colette Hammond wore a shiny gold dress last night. I'm surprised a color like that didn't grab your attention as it passed through your peripheral vision."

Percy didn't bother to mask his irritation. "Well it didn't," he snarled. "I could have been talking to guests at the time. I could have been searching for a chart, that's the music for a song, in my three-ring binder. I could have been getting a drink. I never noticed a gold dress going toward or into the restrooms, if that's what you're asking."

"What time did you start playing?" Martin asked.

"Started at eight thirty. Scheduled to play until twelve thirty. That, of course, didn't happen. They wanted me to play during dinner. I'm a union musician. Can't work a six-hour gig, so I had to start after dinner."

"If I were you, Pete," Martin chuckled as the elevator doors closed behind them, "I'd think twice about asking him to play your favorite song the next time you're in Christos."

EIGHT

It warmed up a few degrees, during the time the two investigators spent with Demetrius and Shelby, but not enough to make a difference. The steam created by their breath still preceded them down the sidewalk. On the positive side, despite the foot of snow that fell in December, at least the sidewalks in this part of downtown were clean all the way down to the cement.

Martin moved unusually fast on their way back to the unmarked car. *Amazing what a little incentive accomplishes*, Pete thought and smiled.

Avoiding frostbitten fingers, Pete got in the unmarked car before looking up the number and calling Colette's boyfriend.

"Yeah?" Grayson Odin answered.

Pete confirmed the address.

Martin took Jackson north, then Twelfth Street west to I-94. By the time he reached the freeway, the vents pumped warm air. "Do you think Odin is actually a boy toy, or is Brewster jealous?" Martin asked.

"Could go either way—or both ways. A little less complexity in the human condition could make our jobs so much easier. Martin, how is Michelle? Any improvement?"

"No change. I'm not expecting her doctor to pull a rabbit out of a hat, but wouldn't you think they could find the right test and figure it out? It's going on five months. Why do they have to do a few tests, wait for results, do a few more, ad nauseum?"

"A matter of economics?"

"Right. Glad the patient is such a high priority." Martin scowled.

He took the Cretin exit and crossed the freeway. Cretin took him to Jefferson, which he followed to Mount Curve. The less-traveled city street still bore signs of the snow that fell with monotonous regularity in December. Despite the snow two days ago, dark patches marred the snow banks piled along the curbs. These vestiges of sand and salt represented efforts to keep the streets navigable.

En route to the Odin interview, they passed St. Thomas University. Until the late 1970s, it remained a haven for young men trying to occupy a space separate from the female persuasion—at least when it came to their living space. Beginning in the late sixties, women from St. Catherine's started invading the St. Thomas classrooms, and vice versa. Now, while St. Catherine maintained its exclusivity, St. Thomas was co-ed.

Colette Hammond lived in a gorgeous shuttered, brick, two-story home. It looked like a lot of square feet for a woman and her significant other. Conspicuous consumption? The snow hid a lot, but the shrubbery in the front yard looked like an obsessive compulsive kept it manicured.

As they pulled up to the home, Martin said, "Hey, Pete, are you and Katie still looking for a house?"

"Yeah. Looked at lots of them. Not impressed by anything in our price range. Doesn't help that the value of my home is still depressed."

"And you're depressed because the value of your home is depressed?"

"Not depressed, just unhappy."

"I imagine the family will put this house on the market. Wouldn't mind living here."

"Neither would I. Mine and Katie's budget, however, would have a fit."

Martin parked on the street, and the two investigators walked to the front door. The sidewalks had been shoveled, but not meticulously cleared like the ones downtown.

Martin rang the bell.

A man who appeared to be in his mid-to-late thirties opened the door. He wore plaid flannel pajama bottoms and a matching long sleeved T-shirt. The shirt, a size or two too small, showed off his abs. judging from his hair, he'd showered after Pete called.

Martin and Pete produced their badges and IDs.

Grayson stared at them long enough to chill the house several degrees, and the two investigators a like amount.

"Okay, come in. I hope this won't take long. I have a lot to do."

You're not alone there, Pete thought.

Grayson led them to the family room where a fire burned aggressively in a fireplace overloaded with logs. Dark-brown leather chairs crowded the room, and bookshelves populated with leather-bound books maintained the motif. An expensive-looking painting of a seascape hung on one wall.

Grayson sat in close proximity to the fire and motioned the two investigators toward a couple of chairs on the far side of the room.

"We have some questions about the events of last night," Pete began.

Grayson nodded.

"First, our condolences," Martin said. "I don't know if you're aware Colette died early this morning."

"No way!" Grayson jumped up out of the chair. "What happened?"

"We're working to determine that," Martin said and began with questions about the relationship. "How long have you been seeing Colette?"

"Three or four months, I guess." Odin eased back into the chair.

"Which is it, three or four?"

"Since Labor Day weekend. I met her at Lord Fletcher's on the Fourth of July. I worked there, and she came with some friends. We hit it off right away, but I didn't see her again until Labor Day weekend."

"You said you worked at Lord Fletcher's. Past tense?"

"*Huh?*"

"You don't work there anymore?"

"No. I quit when I moved in with Colette. The commute was impossible."

"What do you do now?"

"My main job has been helping Colette with whatever needed doing. At the same time, I've been looking for a job in the vicinity. Haven't yet found anything suitable. Guess I better kick it up a few notches, huh?"

Good idea, Pete thought. *I doubt Colette's family will support you in the manner to which you appear to have become accustomed.*

"So, what do you need from me? Like I said, my day is packed."

Packed or busy packing? Pete wondered.

Martin continued the questioning, knowing Pete would step in along the way. "Describe your night at Christos, before and after Colette collapsed," he began.

"Well, we ate, we drank, we talked, and we danced. She loved slow dancing with me. Up close and personal." Odin smiled smugly. "Out of the blue, she started falling asleep. Couldn't believe it. She had plenty of sleep the night before, and it couldn't have been boredom. After we ate, I asked her to dance. She said no, so I danced with a few of her friends. I refused to ring in the New Year watching her sleep. Next thing I knew, the paramedics rushed in. I went to the bar. Hung out there until the paramedics wheeled her out. I got my jacket and left."

"Did you go to Regions?" Pete asked.

"No. We took her car, and the keys were in her purse. By the time I thought of that, she and her purse were gone. Besides, I knew her brother didn't want me there," Odin said as an afterthought.

Lame, Pete thought. "Where did you go from Christos?"

"Came back here."

Pete took a turn. "How did you get here?"

"A couple of friends gave me a ride."

"What are the friends' names?"

"Kingstons."

"First names?"

"Meredith and Lyle. I don't know what she sees in him. He looks old enough to be her father."

Curious comment, Pete thought and asked, "Were they shaken up, by what happened to Colette?"

"Like totally. Thought Meredith was going to kill us. Didn't think I'd survive the trip. Offered to drive. She shut me down. Told me I could walk, if I didn't like her driving. I would have frozen to death before I got here. I had to take my chances."

And that has been the final decision for far too many people, Pete thought. "I understand Colette owned a business," he said.

"Yeah. She published books. Put in a lot of hours for the little she got out of it."

"Do you know of anyone who had a feud going with Colette? Anyone who might have wanted to harm her?"

"Yeah, her brother. He couldn't stand to see her spend so much money on me. Called me a prostitute. He didn't believe I loved her. He had no idea how much I did for Colette. He thought I was stringing her along. Jealous bastard!"

Pete changed the subject. "Do you know if Colette had a will or a trust?"

"Yes, a trust."

"Any idea about the beneficiaries?"

"Her brother, I think, but I'm sure that would have changed had she lived a while longer. I'm sure she'd have added me."

"Did she talk about changing it?"

"No, but she wouldn't use her money as bait. Didn't have to. She knew she had me hook, line, and sinker. I wasn't going anywhere."

This time, Martin changed the subject. "Did she have major problems with any of her employees or clients?"

"Don't know. Whenever she started ranting and raving about her company, I tuned her out. After all, it's not like I could fix it. Well, actually, I know some of the authors she published were a pain in the ass. Unfortunately, often she didn't discover that until they'd signed contracts. Then it was too late."

"How many employees did she have?"

"Five, I think. I'm not all that familiar with her business."

"Who are the five you're aware of?"

"Can't name them all. I believe there are two editors, someone doing layout, another person handling the marketing, and another managing distribution."

Again, Pete took the lead. "In addition to you, who was invited to the reception due to their connections with Colette?"

"I only know about Avery and her husband, Harper and Donovan, Meredith and Lyle Kingston, Rhina and her husband. After strumming his knee for several seconds he said, "Oh yeah, and Beverly and Adrian Atwater. There were probably others, but I don't know. What's going to happen with her company?"

"Did she invite any of her authors?"

"Got me."

"What's the name of her company?" Martin asked.

"Read Ink Press. That's r-e-a-d, not r-e-d. Turned out, r-e-d would have been more accurate." Odin shrugged.

"Did Colette like to gamble?" Pete asked.

"Must have. She started a publishing company when everyone and their brother were self-publishing."

"Seemed to be doing quite well," Pete said, looking around.

"She bought this house and the furnishings with money she inherited."

"Did she tell you that?" Pete asked.

"Of course not. She was bent on impressing me."

"We need the names, addresses, and phone numbers for all the people working for Colette," Martin said.

"I mentioned Avery Renner. She's an editor. I don't know the other names, any of the addresses or phone numbers."

"I bet she has that information somewhere around here," Pete said.

"She has it in her office, but it could take me awhile to find it."

"We'll wait," Pete said. He welcomed the opportunity to make a phone call without being overheard. Couldn't risk alienating the guy before they completed this interview.

Pete finished the call with time to spare.

Eventually, Odin returned with an eight-and-a-half by eleven sheet of paper. "Here, I printed it for you." Odin held the page out to Martin.

"Just a few more questions," Pete said, then broached a potentially touchy subject. "I understand Colette shot up …."

"She used to. I knew that, because I saw the tracks. Stopped before I met her. I would never have moved in if she still used."

"Did she ever talk about the way it felt, how she got into it, that sort of thing?"

"No. She refused to talk about it."

"Did she talk about her problems with staying clean?"

"No. I'm serious about her refusing to discuss it."

"Based on something you said earlier, it sounds like her company drained her financially," Martin said.

"Do you actually think she'd tell me if it did?"

Martin tried another subject. "Did she have a life insurance policy?"

"Yeah."

The tone of his voice and the way his eyebrows shot up indicated a substantial payout.

"Any idea of the value?"

"Two million, I heard."

"Who did you hear that from?"

"Got me."

The two investigators thanked Grayson Odin and left a warm house for a cold car.

Sitting in the car, Pete glanced back and forth between the side mirror and the list of Read Ink employees. Multitasking, he asked, "Why would a woman with no children, no dependent parents, and a brother as the sole beneficiary have a two-million-dollar life insurance policy?"

NINE

Before Pete had a chance to contemplate the life insurance policy, the Forensic Services Unit pulled up behind them.

Pete and Martin walked back to the new arrival, and Pete said, "Commander Lincoln must have rattled a few cages to get a search warrant so early on New Year's Day."

"Anything for you, Pete."

"A little background," Pete said. "Hammond's brother and live-in both insist she was clean. Brother said she has been for almost a year, and claims opiates served as the starting point."

"Not exactly a first," the same sergeant who handled Christos shook his head. "It's happening with monotonous regularity to people in all economic strata and all age groups."

"Yeah, and once the opiates are unavailable, heroin is a ready replacement," Pete said. "Due to the quality of the heroin on the street and the things being used to cut it, the number of accidental overdoses is shocking. Wish people understood it's different now. These days, it's a crap shoot. Experienced users die on a regular basis."

"You're preaching to the choir, Pete."

"I know. Sorry. I feel so powerless."

"Join the club," the sergeant nodded.

"Find anything at Christos or in the garbage hauled from the surrounding areas?"

"Nada. Are you going in with us?"

"Thought about it, but we should get to the ME's. They already started the autopsy. Didn't plan to spend so much time here. Call when you finish, okay?"

"That's the plan."

Grayson Odin looked puzzled, then perturbed the second time he answered the door that morning.

The officers of the Forensic Services Unit split up, working several areas simultaneously. They checked every imaginable place and many that amazed Grayson. They unscrewed the light switch and receptacle covers. They examined the underside of toilet tank lids, inside the tank, and under and behind the tanks. They unscrewed the backs of the stove, refrigerators, washer, and dryer and checked inside. They removed the cover from her computer. They stripped her cupboards and drawers and examined their contents. They checked for loose carpeting and loose bricks in the fireplace. They looked for an asbestos bag inside the flue. They removed all pictures from the walls and looked for modifications to the backing. They examined every inch of the pool table, including the pockets, ball returns, and underside. They unscrewed and checked for space inside the cues. They even removed the grips from the handlebars of the two bicycles in the garage and looked inside.

The outcome mirrored the one at Christos. They found nothing.

The autopsy was underway when Pete and Martin reached the autopsy room.

"Tell us what you have thus far," Pete said, motioning to the body of Colette Hammond.

"According to all of the reports, here's the puncture wound not made by the hospital or the paramedic responding to Christos."

The pathologist indicated a mark on Hammond's left forearm.

"It looks fresher than the other marks," Pete said.

"Yes. None of the others were recent. You can tell from the presentation."

"That's consistent with what her brother and live-in told us," Martin said.

"Did Regions check her blood alcohol level?" Pete asked.

"Yes. It was .15. Sent her clothing over to the Forensic Services Unit. Notified them of the location of the puncture wound. They may find some foreign DNA in the vicinity."

"If she self-injected," Pete said, "her clothing may provide little. If someone else injected her, that won't help us find the person. Too many people with nothing to do with her death might have deposited DNA there, through casual contact."

"Agreed. You're a good student."

"I'm gathering DNA samples from the area around the fresh needle track." The pathologist worked as he spoke. "That, of course, only helps if you have DNA to compare it to."

"When will you have the DNA results?" Pete asked.

"The usual. A couple of weeks, give or take."

"Figured that, but asked in case one of your New Year's resolutions was …."

"My resolutions, my friend, have nothing to do with it."

"Guess there are probably better ways to spend our time, *huh*?" Pete asked.

"Not anxious to get rid of you, but that would be my guess," the pathologist said.

"Please let us know if you come up with anything else," Pete said. "Meanwhile, we'll talk to more of the people who spent last night with her.

Ten

Now?" Martin asked as he started the car.

"I'll try to reach Avery Renner. Since she worked for Ms. Hammond, she must have known her for more than four months. She may have some insights into the victim, her company, and her finances."

A man answered, and Pete heard a football game blaring in the background. After a woman picked up the line, Pete arranged a meeting.

"What had you planned for today?" he asked as Martin drove to the Renner home in North Oaks, an exclusive, country club addition north of St. Paul.

"Planned to take Marty skiing until I heard the forecast last night. He was pretty bummed."

"Since when do you ski, Martin?"

"Today was supposed to be my maiden voyage. Marty talked me into it. I decided it would be a good opportunity to spend some quality time with him—assuming I didn't end up taking my first trip down the hill on a toboggan, behind a member of the ski patrol."

"Hell, Martin, you've already conquered the vocabulary. That's the toughest part."

"Right, and stringing up your skates is the hardest part of ice skating. How about you? Did you plan to spend the day planted in front of a TV?"

"No, actually, Katie and I hoped to ski at Afton Alps. With a name like that in Minnesota, do you think they have delusions of grandeur?"

"Hadn't thought about it but, now that you mention it, Afton Ant Hills might be more accurate."

"I won't tell the management you said that." Pete laughed. "When they changed the forecast last night on the six o'clock news, we decided we'd be crazy to stick with that plan. Didn't yet have another. What if this case, rather than the forecast, forced you to change your plan to ski with Marty? Would he have understood? Does he accept it as a necessary part of your job?"

"Sometimes yes, sometimes no. All depends upon how excited he was about our plans and whether or not he succeeded in coming up with a Plan B."

Avery, her husband, and two children lived in a four-gabled McMansion. Pete thought the roof must be a roofer's best friend and worst enemy. Best friend when it came to the price one could charge for the job. Worst enemy when it came to doing the work. Much of the landscaping lay buried beneath a layer of snow, but large trees seemed to insure the privacy of the inhabitants.

To avoid blocking one of the cars assumedly parked in the three-car garage, or perhaps to get a better look at the home, Martin parked on the street.

The volume on a television set located somewhere in the home provided a play-by-play to the two investigators as they approached the front door.

Pete rang the doorbell, doubting anyone inside would hear it. He was wrong. A bulky, fortyish woman wearing a Christmas sweatshirt, leggings, and fashion boots answered the door. "Police?" she asked.

Pete nodded.

"Come in. Come in. It's freezing out there. Hope I didn't keep you waiting. You could suffer frostbite in less than a minute in weather like this. Let's talk in my office. It's as far as we can get from our home theater. My husband and two sons plan to spend the day watching football. I have my hands full keeping them supplied with food." She sighed and shook her head.

Pete figured the furniture they passed on the way to Avery's office cost more than his house. Didn't matter. He had no desire to change places with this woman or her neighbors.

Avery settled in, behind the desk.

Even in this location, Pete had no problem understanding every word uttered by the play-by-play announcers. To close the distance between Avery and them, he and Martin moved a couple of Queen Anne winged chairs in front of the desk.

If that irritated Avery, she did a great job of hiding it.

Is that her poker face? Pete wondered. He opened with, "How long have you known Colette Hammond?"

"I met her when I interviewed for an editor's job at Read Ink Press, her publishing company. Liked her instantly. She's decisive and efficient."

"Let me back up a minute," Pete said. "You may not have heard. Ms. Hammond died early this morning."

"Oh my God!" Avery gasped. Her hands flew up and covered her mouth. "Are you saying she drank enough to kill herself? I know she drank a lot, but …."

"No, it wasn't the alcohol," Pete said. "I understand you and Colette went to the ladies room shortly before midnight. Did she have a problem? Did she ask you to accompany her?"

"I don't know who told you that. It isn't true." The shaking of her head accentuated her words. "I went to the ladies room once, at eleven o'clock, give or take a few minutes. Colette didn't go with me."

"Then she arrived while you were there."

"No, she didn't!"

Pete wondered why she was so emphatic. Did she know something?

"Are you certain it wasn't later than eleven o'clock? Say eleven thirty?"

"I'm positive. I glanced at my watch while there. It said ten fifty-eight."

Interesting she remembers the exact time, Pete thought.

"Did you see Colette go into or head in the direction of the ladies room any time around midnight, say after eleven thirty?" Pete asked.

"No, but I couldn't see the hallway leading to the ladies room from my table. Why are you so interested in when I went to the restroom?"

"Trying to figure out if Ms. Hammond felt ill before she collapsed," Pete said.

"Did you go to the hospital last night after the paramedics took Colette?"

"No. My husband felt exhausted. He started bugging me to cut out before it happened. I insisted we stay long enough to ring in the New Year. Besides, we couldn't see her at Regions or help her."

"Were all of Colette's best friends at Christos last night?" Pete asked.

"Everyone except Esther Lancaster. I couldn't believe she wasn't there. She's celebrated the New Year with us for the last four years."

"How about ex-friends?" Pete asked. "Have any of Colette's friends gone by the wayside?"

"I think most of us are in for the long haul. I don't know of any ex-friends."

"When did you interview for the job at Read Ink?" Martin asked.

"Seven years ago."

"Is that when she established the company?" Martin asked.

"Yes, I was the first person she hired." Avery smiled.

"Did Colette have any enemies?" Martin asked.

"She feuded with a few of our authors, but I wouldn't call any of them enemies. They owe us a lot. We get them in print. Oh my God, what will happen to the company now?"

"Did any of them ever lose it with her?" Martin asked.

"Not that I'm aware of."

"How many authors are you working with?" Martin asked.

"We have forty-six under contract. We published some of their books years ago, but their rights haven't yet reverted to them."

"Is anyone fighting to get the rights back?" Martin asked.

"A couple of authors are anxiously waiting for that to happen. No one is doing anything to push it or challenge the time frame."

"Might a Read Ink author benefit in some way from Colette's demise?" Pete asked.

"I don't know how. If the company now folds, and that seems likely without Colette, the authors with books in the pipeline will be delayed while they search for another publisher. For some, it might not happen at all."

"Why is that?" Pete asked.

"It depends on how long and hard they worked to find Read Ink. They may not have the energy to begin the process all over again or to self-publish as an alternative."

"Even after they spent all the time and energy required to write the book?" Pete asked.

"Many authors will tell you that's the easiest part. Most of them hate the marketing."

"Doesn't Read Ink handle that?" Pete asked.

"Only a small portion of it. If an author doesn't do their part, even a well-written book will sell only a few copies. And typically, those copies are purchased by friends and family. When that happens, Read Ink loses money on the book, and it's the last book we publish for that author."

"Does that happen often?" Pete asked.

"Yes. Despite the fact that Colette requires a marketing plan before offering a contract, more often than I care to remember." Avery shook her head.

"Were any of the Read Ink authors invited to Christos?" Pete asked.

"Just one."

"Name?" Pete asked.

"Dory Carlisle."

"Did Colette have any problems with her?" Pete asked.

"None that came to my attention. Dory's one of our success stories. Colette tried to get her to produce two books, rather than just one, per year. Dory insisted the quality would suffer. Both Colette and I disagreed."

"Did Ms. Hammond have problems with some of her authors?"

"Every publisher has at least one or two problem authors."

"Who were Read Ink's?"

"Minor issues are a part of the game. Only one significant problem comes to mind. That's K. C. Fisher. Her first name is Kara."

"How serious were the problems with her? Was Colette concerned? Was she afraid of her?"

"I don't think their disputes qualified as that serious."

"Did Colette have any enemies?"

"If so, I never heard about it."

"Did she owe anyone money?" Pete asked.

"All I know is she borrowed money to start Read Ink. I don't know what bank or person loaned it to her." Avery shrugged. "And, of course, Read Ink has all the costs of doing business."

"Why do you think a person, rather than a bank, may have loaned her the money for Read Ink?" Pete asked.

"I don't know why I said that. Guess it must have been a bank, *huh?*" Avery rearranged her position on the chair.

"Did you or your husband loan her money?" Pete asked.

"I invested in Read Ink when I began working there."

"How many shares of Read Ink do you own?" Pete asked.

"None. I have a note."

"What did she use as collateral?" Pete asked.

"Her house."

"So she owns the house free and clear," Pete said.

"I hope so. She did seven years ago."

"Did Colette have a life insurance policy?" Pete asked.

"I believe so."

"Any idea who she named as beneficiary or beneficiaries?" Pete asked.

"I'm not even positive she has a policy."

"Did Colette like to gamble?" Martin asked.

"I don't think she ever went to a Minnesota casino, if that's what you mean. Once she told me about shooting craps in Vegas. She said it's the only casino game where the customer had a reasonable chance of making money. Can't shoot craps at any of the Minnesota casinos."

"In the last few years, has she gone to a casino that offers craps?" Martin asked.

"I don't think so, but she wouldn't necessarily tell me. Why would she? We're friends. We aren't linked at the hip."

"You attended Demetrius's reception and regularly ring in the New Year with Ms. Hammond. Obviously the two of you are close," Pete said.

"She has a group of friends that are inseparable. I'm on the fringe. I'm included maybe a quarter of the time. A lot of it probably has to do with our working together. Some of it may be due to the loan. She may not want me to drift too far. You know, 'Keep your friends close and your enemies closer' or something like that."

"Was Ms. Hammond into sports wagering?" Pete asked.

"If so, I never heard about it."

"How did Ms. Hammond spend her nonworking hours?" Pete asked.

"For the last several months, she's spent most of them with Grayson." Avery rolled her eyes.

"Did you think that was a mistake?" Pete asked.

"Definitely. I don't know what she saw in the guy—other than a gorgeous body."

"Did that relationship bother Colette's brother?" Pete asked.

"She never said, but seeing them together last night gave me the impression it did."

"What gave you that impression?" Pete asked.

"Just the way Demetrius turned his back whenever Grayson approached."

"I understand Ms. Hammond got hooked on opiates," Pete said.

"Yes. The poor thing had unbearable back pain. She resorted to surgery. It made the pain worse. Her doctor refused to continue prescribing Oxycodone. Her pleas fell on deaf ears. It's unbelievable! She even tried a different doctor. That, too, failed."

"What did she do?" Martin asked.

"Used over-the-counter painkillers and suffered."

"Doesn't sound like much of a solution," Martin said.

"What else could she do?"

Pete couldn't help thinking Avery was playing dumb. Anyone who watched the news or read a newspaper knew what many people did. "Unfortunately, too many people turn to heroin," he said.

"I know. It's horrible! People who would never strike you as addicts are becoming addicted. Colette made that mistake, but only for a short time. A year ago, she stopped using it. Thankfully, I don't have to worry about my boys," she added.

Pete didn't ask her why she believed that. Too many other things on the docket. "We'd like to speak with your husband," he said.

Avery nodded. "I'll get him."

Martin watched her exit, then shook his head and said, "I'd rather be skiing."

"How can you say that, Martin? I think her husband is going to bring each of us a couple of beers and a plate full of chips and wings. Once that happens, I'll never get you out of here."

"Okay, I admit it. I can be bought," Martin chuckled, while watching the door for Avery or her husband.

They heard the approaching footsteps. The man walked with a heavy foot. When he reached the doorway, the two investigators understood why. Quentin Renner stood about five-feet-ten and had to tip the scales at three hundred pounds. The hair on his head fought a losing battle for dominance with his scalp. The hair on his face was more successful. To Martin's vexation, Quentin didn't carry any food or beverage.

"Sorry to hear about Colette," he said. "My wife enjoyed working for her. Wonder what will happen to Read Ink."

"Maybe her brother will keep it going," Pete said.

"That'll be the day."

"We heard Colette went to the restroom shortly before midnight last night. Trying to determine if something happened to her at that time. Did you happen to see her come out?"

"What time?"

"Between eleven thirty and midnight," Pete said.

"Sorry, can't help you there. While at our table, I had my back to the bar and the hallway leading to the restrooms. Only time I got up, from eleven on, occurred when Colette started having a problem. Went to see if I could help."

"Thanks for your time. Hope you didn't miss any key plays," Pete said.

"No problem. You have a job to do. Besides, I have TiVo."

ELEVEN

Read Ink could somehow play into this," Pete said, walking back to the car. "Another employee lives nearby. He didn't attend the party, but might have a different take on Hammond, the company, and its authors."

"Are you referring to the guy in Shoreview?" Martin asked.

"Do you have a photographic memory?"

"No, but I figured he'd probably be the next person we tackled."

"Martin, we aren't permitted to tackle people anymore. Someone might be recording it."

"How many people did you tackle before the world started crawling with recording devices?"

"How do you crawl with a recording device?"

"Google it," Martin chuckled.

"How many times a day do you use that line with your son Marty?"

"Never. He uses it on me."

Compared to the Renner family, Cohen Walters, Read Ink's interior designer, lived in a hovel. Looking at it another way, the price of this house compared to Pete's. The white, split-level had a tuck-under garage.

With hopes for children in the near future, Pete shied away from this floor plan. Despite the mandates for detectors, the dangers of carbon monoxide poisoning concerned him.

The idea of moving remained a mixed bag for Pete. Before proposing to Katie, he decided it would be unfair to ask her to move into the house where he'd lived with his deceased, first wife. In his mind, it would run a close second to giving her the ring he'd given Andrea. No way!

Ascending the steps to the front door, Pete heard another football play-by-play. "When you decided to go skiing with Marty, did you give any thought to how you'd keep up with me while on crutches, Martin?"

"Less consideration than I'm now giving to accidentally bumping you and sending you flying back down these steps."

"Such disrespect. Can't help but wonder about the quality of your upbringing."

Martin smiled and shook his head. After wiping the smile off his face, he stood alongside the front door and rang the doorbell. Then he placed his gloved hands over his ears. After a brief respite, the wind had re-energized, driving the windchill into the cellar. For that reason, his stocking cap wasn't cutting it.

When he saw the door opening, Martin uncovered his ears.

A thirtyish woman smiled and said, "It's a holiday. You can't be selling anything."

"We're looking for Cohen Walters," Martin explained.

"Is Cohen expecting you?"

"No. We're police officers and we're conducting an investigation. It's important we speak with him."

She tilted her head to the side and looked at Pete. "Do you have identification? You can't be too careful these days."

Both men produced their badges and IDs.

"What are you investigating?"

Martin wished she'd stop with the questions and invite them in. "It has to do with Colette Hammond."

"Colette?"

In another minute, Martin would have to cover his ears, again. "Yes ma'am."

Perhaps it was telepathy, because she said, "Sorry, I don't know what I was thinking. Come in." She held the door open and stepped back. After closing the door behind the two men, she turned her head and shouted, "Cohen! Someone needs to see you!"

She said it so loud, Martin wished his gloves still covered his ears.

The three stood there for a few minutes before she said, "He probably didn't hear me. Men and football. What a waste of a perfectly good day! Excuse me. I'll get him."

It took a few minutes before a man in his forties with a buzz cut and glasses resting on the tip of his nose came up the steps from the basement. He wore a University of Minnesota jersey he'd outgrown about thirty pounds ago and rumpled jeans.

The woman who'd answered the door followed in close proximity.

"Looking for me? What's up?"

"My name is Peter Culnane. This is my partner, Martin Tierney. Colette Hammond died early this morning. We're conducting an investigation and have some questions for you."

"No shit?" Cohen Walters led them up the stairs and into the living room.

Pete figured it had to be ten degrees warmer here than in the entryway. He appreciated the improvement.

"Have a seat," Cohen said. "What the hell happened to Colette?"

"That's what we're trying to determine," Pete said. "I understand you worked for her."

"Yes, I do all of the book design." Seeing the questioning looks on the faces of the investigators, he added, "That's like the layout for the pages of the print and electronic books, and the cover designs."

Pete took the first turn. “How long have you been at Read Ink Press?”

“Four years. Holy crap, now what will happen?”

“Who had the job before you?”

“A guy with limited talent and even more limited ambition.”

“What’s his name?”

“I’m not sure I ever heard it.” Cohen sighed and shrugged. After several seconds, he said, “If I ever heard it, I can’t remember it. Either Avery Renner or Jennifer Jasper can probably tell you.”

“What does Jasper do at Read Ink?”

“She and Avery are both editors.”

“Was the person who had the job before you fired?”

“According to Colette, no. According to some of the other employees, yes.”

“Who thinks he was fired?”

Cohen rattled off three names. It amounted to everyone but him, Avery, and Colette.

“You didn’t include yourself. Do you think he quit?”

“Well, I never met him. But, I think he quit to keep the firing off his resume.”

“Who gave you that impression?”

“I’m not sure. You know how it is. People talk.”

Hoping to move to more fertile ground, Martin changed the subject. “Did anyone have an axe to grind with Colette?”

“Employees or otherwise?”

“Both.”

“I’m just an employee. I know little about her personal life.”

“But you and your fellow employees talk around the water cooler.”

“Sure.”

“No doubt Ms. Hammond was, at times, the topic of conversation.”

"Some of the staff talked about her boyfriend. I kept my mouth shut."

"What did they say about him?"

"That he's young enough to be her kid. Avery thought Colette experienced an identity crisis when she turned sixty, and it was part of that."

"What do you think?"

"I have no idea."

"In your opinion, did Colette change when she turned sixty?"

"I don't know her well enough to compare before and after."

This was going nowhere, so Pete tried another avenue. "We heard for a while she was in a great deal of pain."

"Yes. In my early days with Read Ink, sometimes when I met with her, her head would sink down until her chin rested on her chest. One time she kept doing it until I told her I had to go. I told her I had an appointment I couldn't miss. I didn't want to waste any more time, watching her fall asleep and wake up, fall asleep and wake up. I mentioned it to Avery. She said it was because of the painkillers Colette took so she could function."

"Was Ms. Hammond still taking the painkillers?"

"I don't know. I do know she stopped falling asleep in our meetings."

Martin moved to the next topic. "Is Read Ink operating in the black?"

"Never heard it wasn't. Colette handled the books. Don't know if she ever shared that type of info with any of the staff."

Striking out when it came to finances, Martin tried another subject. "I understand some of the authors published by Read Ink became irritated with Colette or the company."

"You can please some of the people some of the time, and …. I'm confident you know the rest. It's that way with any organization, isn't it?"

"Are you saying none of the problems were significant?"

"I'm sure the authors categorized them as significant."

"Who are those authors?"

"The only author I know with significant issues is K. C. Fisher."

"Is K. C. still with Read Ink?"

"No. She took her ball and went home."

"Doesn't sound like you sympathized with her."

"Because I didn't."

"Why was she unhappy?"

"It was all about the timing. She claimed we dragged our feet."

"Why did she think that?"

"She didn't get her proofs as quickly as she'd anticipated."

"Did you work directly with K. C.?"

"No, I worked through Colette."

"How long ago did this woman abandon Read Ink?"

"About two months ago."

"Did she find another publisher?"

"I don't know, but I'd be surprised."

"Why is that? Aren't there several small presses in the Twin Cities?"

"Yes, but we're a tight-knit group. The word gets out."

"And an author gets blacklisted?"

"No, no, nothing like that."

Pete changed the subject, asking, "How did your fellow employees feel about Colette?"

"We all know on which side our bread is buttered. None of us would hurt her. None of us wants to be unemployed." He looked anxious.

TWELVE

Back in the car, Martin asked, "Now whose New Year should we interrupt?"

"I'd like to select the person who killed Hammond and ruin their New Year."

"That sounds mighty cold. Is the ambient air temperature chilling your normally warm heart?"

"A distinct possibility. Let's talk to the other editor."

"You think she did it?"

"So far two Read Ink employees are pointing in two directions. Before barking up those trees, I want more information. Jasper is another Read Ink employee, and she knows the name of the employee who left under questionable circumstances. She could help us diversify our search. Diversity is a good thing, don't you agree?"

"I sure do. How else would a debonair hunk like me get partnered with a guy who barks up trees?"

"So true. In fact, I spend all my nonwork hours marveling at my good fortune."

It surprised Pete when he found the second editor home. So far, they were batting a thousand. That never happened. New Year's Day must be a good omen, except for Colette Hammond, that is.

Martin went west on I-694, until he reached University Avenue. Exiting the Interstate, he traveled south on University to

Columbia Heights. During the trip, he asked about Pete and Katie's wedding plans.

"I can't believe how much there is to do. It's my second time, so I'd be happy with a small wedding. You know what I mean? Just family and a few close friends. Since it's her first time, Katie wants more than that. I understand. If we switched places, I might, too. I want it to be everything she's ever dreamt of. I don't want her to look back and wish we'd done it differently."

"Is that likely?"

"No. It's highly unlikely. Still, like I said, I want it to be the wedding of her dreams. Katie's friends already scheduled two showers. They're couples showers. That's a new one on me." Pete shrugged.

"Pete, a nice boy like you is showering with her before the wedding? How many couples will you be showering with, and where will you find a shower large enough to accommodate all of you? Are they holding them in high school gyms?"

"Don't give up your daytime job, Martin."

The second Read Ink editor lived in a working-class neighborhood.

Pete pegged her home as circa the 1950s or '60s. It had a modest porch, canvas awnings and a detached two-car garage. "Too long a commute," Pete said.

"Now I understand the problem. It's impossible to satisfy you. You don't want to move."

Pete bit his lip.

Jennifer Jasper answered the door before Pete's right hand could reach the relative warmth of his overcoat pocket. She appeared close to Colette's age. Despite its length, her short gray hair hung in her eyes. She looked over her glasses at the two men. Like the other Read Ink editor, she wore a holiday sweatshirt. Pete wondered if it indicated a genetic predisposition for book editors.

"Mr. Culnane?" she asked.

"Yes, ma'am, and this is my partner, Martin Tierney. Would you like to see our IDs?"

"Please."

Martin and Pete each removed one glove, dug for the cases, and held them out for the woman.

"Okay," she made a brushing-off motion with her hand. "Come in. I want to know why you are here. Can I get you a hot cup of coffee or tea?"

"Coffee would be great, thanks," Pete said.

"Same here," Martin chimed in.

"In that case, let's talk in the kitchen, okay?"

New appliances constituted the only updating in this room, which must double as Jennifer's home office. A computer sat on a stand and crowded the corner to the left of the kitchen table. By all appearances, the table served as a holding area for file folders, mail, Post-its, pens, paperclips, and anything else needed to stock an office. A variety of containers organized the lot.

One of these containers, a miniature wagon sporting a logo that said "Summit," caught Pete's eye. "I like your radio flyer," he said. "Spent a lot of time playing with one when I was a kid."

"You look too young to remember radio flyers," she remarked patiently.

"But I have an uncle who took meticulous care of his, and I inherited it."

"I got that one from my brother-in-law. He owns an advertising specialty company. Thanks to him, I always have a ready supply of pens, notepads, calculators, flashlights, you name it. Before I make the coffee, let me save this file. I've been editing this manuscript for hours. I don't want to lose track of this version."

Jasper tapped away at the keyboard at lightning speed. As soon as the screen went blank, she looked up and said, "Okay, coffee. Decaf or regular?"

"Makes no difference to me, how about you, Pete?"

"Whatever's most convenient would be great."

"Regular it is. What brings you here today?"

She hadn't heard about Colette, so Pete broke the news.

Jennifer's jaw dropped. "You're kidding. Sorry, of course you're not. That was a stupid thing to say. What happened? Was she in an accident last night? New Year's Eve and early New Year's morning are dangerous times to be on the road. Poor Colette. How is Demetrius dealing with this? They're so close. Poor Demetrius. Oh my gosh, that's right. He got married yesterday." She blushed. "I know. Shut up, Jennifer, so we can tell you."

The apparent lack of communication between Read Ink employees amazed Pete. The company had five employees, plus Colette. Read Ink Press published books. Did they communicate strictly via tomes and ebooks? Did the fact today was New Year's Day explain it?

"Ms. Hammond died of a drug overdose," Pete said.

"Not heroin, I hope," Jennifer said. "It took all the strength she could muster, but she conquered that demon. I was so proud of her. She struggled for months, but she refused to give in."

"Do you know how she got into heroin, Ms. Jasper?" Pete asked.

""Please, call me Jen. Ma'am makes me sound ancient. Heroin use is now so common. For some, the source for prescription painkillers dries up, and heroin is a ready replacement."

"Is that what happened with Ms. Hammond?" Pete asked.

"That's my understanding. I do know she had crippling back pain for years, and nothing seemed to help. Not even surgery."

"A friend must have helped her find an alternative to prescription painkillers," Pete said.

"Sounds reasonable. I don't know how I'd go about finding a source for the stuff and learning how to do it. I have no idea how Colette went about it."

"Could you tell when Colette was using, Jen?" Martin asked.

"The only indication I ever had was when she started nodding off, during an occasional meeting. I would have assumed exhaustion, but a friend told me what it meant."

"Was that friend a Read Ink employee?" Pete asked.

"No."

"Was it one of Colette's friends?" Pete asked.

"Funny you should ask. Yes, it was. Harper Morgan told me one day when she was in the office, and Colette kept doing it. I think Harper knows, because her husband's a pharmacist."

"Did you ever see any of her friends do anything similar?" Martin asked.

"No. Keep in mind, I rarely saw her friends. When I did, it was brief, like when they picked her up for lunch. We didn't socialize."

"Did you ever see any indications that some of the other Read Ink employees might be using heroin or other street drugs?" Martin asked.

"Definitely not."

"How did you ring in the New Year, Jen?" Pete asked.

"I went next door. My neighbor and I have gotten together on New Year's Eve ever since my husband died. We watched the ball drop in Times Square, and at the stroke of midnight we toasted the New Year with a glass of champagne."

"Do you have any children?" Pete asked.

"Yes, two daughters. One is in Chicago, the other's in Denver. I accuse them of abandoning their dear old mother. They just laugh. It isn't all that funny. Maybe I should get a cat, *huh?* I may be forced to retire at this point anyway. This has been my main job for years."

Martin started them down another path. "Tell us about Read Ink Press, Jen."

"We're a very small but growing book publisher. Five employees, plus Colette."

"How long has Read Ink been in business?"

"Seven years."

"And how long have you been there?"

"Going on six years. Colette hired me when her business grew to the point there were too many manuscripts for Avery to handle by herself."

"What's the turnover rate? What I'm asking is, are people who join Read Ink generally in for the long haul?"

"Yes, for the most part. I know of just one exception, Raleigh Zimmerman."

"Did he get a better offer?"

"I wish that was true. He was tormented, until he couldn't take it any longer." Jen frowned.

"By?"

"I hate to disparage someone no longer able to defend themself."

"And that's the person we're here about?"

"Correct."

Pete took another turn. He began with, "What kinds of problems did Ms. Hammond have with Zimmerman?"

"Raleigh Zimmerman was our interior and exterior designer, prior to Cohen. Colette said his layouts could no longer cut the mustard. I always thought there was more to it."

"Why is that?"

"I'm not really sure. Initially, everything seemed fine. I liked his work. Thought he had a special knack. It happened so fast. Everything was fine, but suddenly Colette found it unacceptable."

"Did you agree with Colette?"

"Once things changed, I no longer saw any of his work."

"Prior to that happening, did you observe any deterioration in the quality of his work?"

"None. If I had, I'd have spoken with him. I'd have tried to help."

"Do you think he may have gotten into drugs?"

"No. He didn't drink, didn't smoke. His personality remained the same. He was interested in everyone, but too shy to talk about himself. Besides, like I said, I saw no evidence of a decline in his output, either quality or quantity-wise. Off the record, in my opinion, he was head and shoulders above Cohen, the guy hired as his replacement."

"Did you share that opinion with Colette?"

"You'd better believe it!"

"And?"

"She said I never saw the projects that led to his departure, so I wasn't qualified to have an opinion. I don't understand why she wouldn't let me see the stuff."

"Did anyone other than Colette see it?"

"I don't think so."

"Sounds like you liked Raleigh."

"I did. Very much. He was like the son I never had. He cared more about my well-being than my daughters. Regularly, he asked how I was doing. He took a genuine interest. He noticed my clothes and jewelry, and he complimented me on my selections. He was such a dear."

"Did you stay in touch after he left Read Ink?"

"I tried. It seemed he wanted nothing to do with anyone connected with Read Ink. Can't blame him, even though Colette made up her mind and there was no changing it. It was her company. She neither wanted nor accepted input on some things."

Martin stayed the course. "Was Zimmerman angry about being forced out?"

"As soon as it happened, he withdrew from the rest of the Read Ink staff. He never discussed it with me, but Colette said he threatened her. People do things like that in the heat of the moment. It really doesn't mean anything, you know."

"Did Ms. Hammond tell you what he said? How he threatened her?"

"I heard he said she'd be sorry. Said he'd make sure of it."

"What could he do to make her sorry?"

"I can't imagine how he could hurt her or that he actually would."

"We're trying to determine who had a reason to hurt Colette. Any ideas? Anyone she owed money? Anyone, such as an author or another employee, who had a business or personal beef? A former boyfriend or someone else who might have a reason to get even?"

"As I mentioned, my only connections with her were job-related. I know nothing about her personal life. As far as Read Ink is concerned, I can't believe any of my coworkers would hurt her. I never heard about any significant problems with any of us. We all think we're overworked and underpaid, but killing her wouldn't solve either of those complaints. Excuse me a minute. I'll be right back."

Pete watched her pull three medium-sized plates from a cupboard and a container of muffins from the refrigerator. She opened the container and passed out the plates. "Help yourself," she said. Before sitting back down, she refilled all three coffee mugs. "I'm starving," she said, by way of explanation. "My grandmother would roll over in her grave if I ate in front of you." A smile spread across her face.

"If you've spoken with other Read Ink staff, I'm sure you've already heard that some of our authors had issues with us. I think that's normal for any publishing company. Many authors have no idea what they're getting themselves into. Some expect to have the publishing world handed to them on a silver platter. We're a small press. We do our best, but we're limited by the projected sales. We can't afford to spend tens of thousands of dollars on a book that won't sell a thousand copies—and that's most of them."

Jen took a bite of her muffin and a sip of coffee, then continued, "I can't think of a single one of our authors who would have reason to murder Colette—or any of us. We do practice tough love, but I think we go the extra mile to help each author understand the rationale behind all of our decisions."

"Has Read Ink ever lost an author to another publisher?"

"Well, yes, but it wasn't because we didn't try. I think it was due to a mismatch between that author and Read Ink. The author asked Colette to cancel her contract, and Colette did as requested. I think it was the best thing for her and us."

"Was she angry with Read Ink?"

"I guess, but I can't imagine her being angry enough to kill Colette."

"Did you speak with her about canceling the contract?"

"No. I'm an editor. Colette handled all of that. You know, if that author wanted to kill someone, I'd think it would be me, not Colette."

"Why is that?"

"The author had an unrealistic timeline, and I didn't permit her to dictate my schedule."

Pete moved the discussion back to Ms. Hammond. "Was Colette an understanding and sympathetic person?"

"Yes and no. If she got impatient, she might brush you off."

"Did Ms. Hammond grow impatient with the author who left Read Ink?"

"Yes. Colette took my side."

"What's that author's name?"

"Kara Fisher."

Pete hadn't succeeded in obtaining Fisher's address from Grayson, but got it from Jen.

Fisher had an apartment downtown in Galtier Plaza. That was in the same complex as Demetrius Brewster's condo. It was also very close to Christos.

THIRTEEN

Ready for a change of pace, Martin? How about switching gears and speaking with an author?"

"Well, I'm a little hesitant to move away from publishing before we've covered all aspects. I'm planning to write a bestseller. I guess an author will give me a chance to learn what to look for and what to avoid when selecting a publisher."

"Fiction or nonfiction?"

"Fiction. I'm writing my life story."

"The X-rated version?"

"No. Then it would be nonfiction."

"I'd like to place an order for ten copies."

"That's all?" Martin chuckled.

"If I reach K. C. Fisher, let's stop at her place. Then, returning to your needs and wishes, we'll check out Read Ink's marketing person." In response to the questioning look on Martin's face, Pete added, "Wondering why we aren't concentrating on the people at the reception?"

"Yes and no. I realize the layout person added potentially valuable information about an employee who left Read Ink under questionable circumstances. I also understand Fisher may have had a motive. She wasn't invited to the reception, but you can get to the restroom where the victim likely ODed without going through Christos. Even so …."

"So much about this case is hard to comprehend, Martin. OD at your brother's wedding reception? Doing it just before midnight on New Year's Eve? I realize that would probably be irrelevant for a hardcore addict, but supposedly she'd been clean for months. I'm trying to get to know the victim, both professionally and socially. I'm hoping this case makes more sense when contextualized."

For the first time today, Pete struck out when trying to reach one of the people on his list. The author was home. The marketer wasn't.

Martin took I-694 east to I-35E, then went south and took the Wacouta exit into downtown St. Paul.

Pete wondered if Fisher knew Colette's brother. They both lived in Galtier. One lived in a condo, the other in the apartment tower. Each had its own entry and bank of elevators. Even if they'd shared elevators, in this day and age, they might not even know they're neighbors. The common aversion to conversing in an elevator did nothing to increase the likelihood.

Martin parked on Sibley, alongside Mears Park, and they walked to the entrance just west of Fifth and Sibley.

Pete looked up Fisher's code and entered it on the key pad.

Fisher did her part, and the lock on the secure door to the elevators released.

The two investigators took the elevators up to Fisher's floor and found her apartment. The units were circa 1970s, but the hallways appeared well-maintained and clean. The carpet and light fixtures looked new. The paint looked fresh.

Martin rang the doorbell.

A tall, stately middle-aged woman opened the door several inches and looked out.

Pete saw that the chain kept it from opening further.

"Peter Culnane?"

"Yes ma'am."

"Do you have identification?"

Pete nodded, and he and Martin produced their badges and IDs.

She closed the door, and Pete heard metal scraping metal as she undid the chain.

"You mentioned you wanted to talk to me about Colette's death. What happened? When?" K. C. asked as she stepped aside, permitting their entrance.

"That's what we're attempting to determine," Pete said.

The door opened into an entryway. The living room lay just beyond. Pete saw the Mississippi River out the sizable picture windows. The river reminded him of the case of the homeless man he and Martin worked a few years ago. Thinking about that case reminded him of his friend Doc, a middle-aged homeless man he met during that investigation.

He wondered how Doc was doing. He'd made a dozen or more trips to Reaching Out, the soup kitchen where Doc got some meals. He wanted to check on his friend who had been instrumental in solving that case. Thus far, he'd failed to make a connection and it had been months.

Doc was still around, and he still spent some time at Reaching Out, according to his friends there.

But Pete refused to give up. He'd committed to finding a way to help this man, who seemed so out of place living on the streets.

"Great view," Pete commented to K. C.

"I agree. That's why I selected this unit."

"How do you like living downtown?" Pete asked.

"Love it! Everything I need is within walking distance. I only wish Macy's hadn't closed. Even so, when you live downtown, so much is accessible via the skyways, including my job. During the winter, I can and often do go a week or more without going outside."

"I understand you're a writer," Martin said, stepping up to handle the initial line of questioning. "Is that the job you referred to?"

"That's my second job. I also work for Ramsey County."

"What department?"

"The county attorney's office."

"What do you do there?"

"I'm a paralegal. Do as much if not more research for my writing, as I do for my profession. And I have a third job, too."

"What's that?"

"I'm searching for a publisher." She smirked.

"I thought you had a contract with Read Ink Press to publish your book," Martin lied.

"You're correct. I did. Not anymore. I'm still trying to strike a deal with a couple of other publishers."

"What genre or genres do you write?"

"Historical romances set in the 1800s."

"What happened with Read Ink?"

"I grew tired of the games and broken promises."

"Anyone in particular?"

She locked eyes with Martin. "Yes, the person you're here about. Colette Hammond."

"Can you be more specific about the problems?" Martin asked, after waiting a few seconds to permit Pete to jump in.

"They promised to publish the book last September. They promised advanced reader copies in April or May. Nothing happened in April, May, or September. Believing Colette was a woman of her word, I'd arranged to send advanced copies to several bestselling romance authors. I'd hoped one or several would provide an endorsement blurb. I set up book events. Arranged signings at book stores, that sort of thing. I was furious when I had to cancel everything. For nine months, I'd nurtured and polished the manuscript. I did everything I could think of to create buzz about the book before the release date. Then, the rug was pulled out from under me. Those are only a few of the details. It went on and on ad nauseum. I was furious. I decided to walk."

"I found out that Colette sat on my manuscript for six months before giving it to the editor."

Martin nodded. "I'd want revenge."

"Believe me. I did!"

"What did you do?" Martin asked.

"I cried. I told all my friends. I slammed Read Ink every opportunity I got."

"Including the social media?" Martin asked.

"No, everything but. I didn't want other publishers to slam the door in my face."

"And?" Martin asked.

"I got over it. I had to. It consumed me. I couldn't concentrate on my writing. I couldn't do my job. I found consolation in knowing I was better off not putting my faith in a druggie."

"A druggie?" Pete asked, switching places with Martin.

"Yes. Colette likes to get high."

"On?"

"Heroin."

"You must have a basis for a statement like that."

"I was out to lunch with a friend. Colette happened to be at the same place. My friend said she heard from the friend of a friend that Colette shot up."

"What's the name of the friend who told you?"

"I don't remember."

Pete hoped K. C. told the stories in her books more effectively than this tale. "Someone said that about the woman who could make or break your writing career, and you don't remember her name?"

"I talk to a lot of people."

"You work for the county attorney. I'll bet you know the implications if you lie to us."

"Dory Carlisle. Please don't tell her I gave you her name."

"Does she have a connection with Read Ink?" Thanks to Avery Renner, one of the editors, Pete already had the answer.

"She's one of Colette's authors."

"How do you know her?"

"From Read Ink get-togethers."

"What made her think Colette was into drugs?"

"She's a shining star. Colette wants to stay on her good side. Bond with her. Occasionally, Colette took Dory out to lunch with some of her friends."

"How did you spend New Year's Eve?"

"I was here, ringing in the New Year with the Boston Pops."

"Anyone here with you?"

"No, my husband died two years ago. It was a long haul. He had Alzheimer's."

"Tough road." Pete empathized. Lots of his friends had firsthand knowledge. Thankfully, thus far he'd been spared. "Did you speak with anyone as midnight approached?"

"No, all of my friends attended parties. I just wanted to stay home and stay warm. It was too cold last night. Still is. What difference does it make? Wait a minute! Are you saying Colette was murdered? She must have been. Otherwise, you wouldn't be here, would you? You can't think I had anything to do with it? Someone had to have an even better motive. I can't believe I'm the only author Read Ink hurt. I got over it."

"No one said she was murdered," Pete said.

"Then why are you here?"

"As I said when we arrived, we're investigating her death."

"Are you homicide detectives?"

"Yes, but we handle more than homicides," Pete said. "That's all, at least for now. Thanks for your time."

On their way to the elevators, Pete hit the redial button on his cell calling Sabastian Tracy, Read Ink's marketing person, again.

Fourteen

The gods are smiling down on us," Pete said, after speaking with Tracy. "Could be, because I have yet to break any of my New Year's resolutions."

"That's remarkable! The year's already," Martin glanced at his watch, "almost fifteen hours old. You are a man of resolve. I admire that in you—along with your wild imagination. Wait a minute! You ate the muffin Jasper put in front of you."

"But, it was a bran muffin. I was grateful for the sustenance … and even more grateful it wasn't poppy seed."

Martin chuckled.

"What are your resolutions this year, Martin?"

"I'm going to be patient, even when Michelle's physical problems are exasperating. I'm going to tell her at least once a day how much I love her and how much she means to me. I'll do everything in my power to spend more time with Marty and make sure he understands he means the world to me. Ditto for Olivia, even though I don't think she yet comprehends most of what I say to her. I plan to spend some special time with each of my kids every week. Finally, I'm going to lose some of the extra pounds I'm carrying that bother Michelle much more than me. I figure that's enough to keep me busy all year."

"I'm impressed, Martin. Hope you succeed across the board."

"Okay, I was honest with you. Fess up, Pete. Do you have any New Year's resolutions?"

"Just one. I resolved to do everything in my power to ensure that Katie never regrets saying, 'I do.'"

"That, my friend, is a given." Martin smiled.

"Since Christos is just a few blocks away, let's stop there before continuing your research with the distribution side of publishing. The staff circulated through the dining room all last night. One of them may have seen something. Unfortunately, they left before we arrived. With their help, we might better prioritize our meeting with the guests."

"You didn't say anything about the Read Ink person responsible for distribution. I hope you're not planning to skip that facet of the business. Without it, my bestseller won't make it into the hands of my adoring fans." Martin grinned.

"The impressive thing is your ability to create a fan base without a book."

"My appeal is broad-based."

"As is your imagination."

"One more reason I'm destined to become an award-winning, bestselling author."

Whether a result of the incident last night or the original plan, Christos was closed.

"Well, hell," Pete said.

"I'm the author and you're the poet. No wonder we work so well together. Between the two of us, we have it all."

"To give you the opportunity to fine tune your skills, Martin, from now on you can write up all the reports."

"I'd love to, but your reports are a poetic masterpiece," Martin said as he parked in front of Sabastian Tracy's home.

Located in West St. Paul, it was a beige, stucco, two-story. To the right of the driveway, alongside a middle-aged oak, rested a massive rock. Paul Bunyan, a glacier, or a piece of heavy equipment must have deposited it there. A sign in the front yard warned anyone contemplating helping himself to the contents of the home that a security system stood watch.

The temperature hadn't topped zero all day, but now retreated from the day's high. Under Pete and Martin's feet, the crunch of the hard-packed snow might have tipped off Sabastian to their arrival. He left them outside, freezing, for less than a minute.

Tracy appeared to be closing in on middle age. His argyle sweater and khakis showed off a trim physique. His nose looked like it had been broken a few times. "Come in," he said, and led the two investigators into the living room. On the way, they passed a piano covered from side-to-side with nut crackers.

"Nice collection," Pete said, motioning toward the nutcrackers.

"Thanks. My wife and I have collected them for years. Added the Boy Scout to our collection a few months ago when we were in Europe."

Pete smelled roasting turkey and hoped their arrival didn't delay the family's dinner. He'd try to keep it short.

Martin started the questioning by getting a summary of what it meant to do the marketing for a small press.

Sabastian explained he did things like sending advanced copies to obtain reviews and endorsement blurbs, sent press releases to media outlets, helped authors with their marketing plans, that sort of thing.

"How did you spend New Year's Eve, Sabastian?" Martin asked, progressing to part two.

"I was here with my wife and kids."

"How many kids?"

"Three. Two boys and a girl."

"How old are your kids?"

"My boys are eighteen and thirteen. My daughter is six."

"We spoke with several other Read Ink employees," Martin said.

"Yeah, I've heard. Can't believe Colette is gone. She was murdered, *huh?*"

"What makes you think that?" Pete took up the questioning as they moved into the next phase.

"Why else would you be talking to everyone? Do you think someone with Read Ink did it?"

"Don't know that anyone killed her. That's what we're working to determine. Do you know of anyone who had a reason to hurt her?"

"No."

"How about the Read Ink guy who handled layout before Cohen Walters?"

"I heard rumors. I heard Raleigh said it had nothing to do with his performance."

"What did he give as the reason?"

"Not sure he gave one. Just heard he insisted that the quality of his work wasn't the reason. Heard he produced samples that seemed to support his contention."

"Who told you that?"

"A friend at the *Pioneer Press*."

"How about a name?"

"Look, if I tell you and you talk to her, she may refuse to cooperate in the future. I can't afford to let that happen. Next thing you know, I'd be looking for a job. Publishers are a tight group. The word would spread. I'd be out of luck when it came to any publisher in the Midwest."

"Did that happen to Raleigh?"

"I don't know. Never spoke with him again."

"Newspaper people know all about withholding sources, so tell us her name."

"Can't."

"After seeing the samples provided by Raleigh, did this friend at the *Pioneer Press* agree it had nothing to do with performance?"

"Seemed to."

"How about current Read Ink employees? Did any of them have problems with Colette? You know, problems with her style, her demands, anything like that?"

"There were disagreements, of course. You can't have a brain or use your intellect and agree with all of the thoughts and decisions made by another person. Even so, there is nothing destructive going on within the organization. None of us hate each other. None of us would harm any of the others. Something like that is destructive to an organization, especially a small one like Read Ink. We couldn't function efficiently or even survive if something like that happened. It would tear us apart."

"Did Colette experiment with drugs?" Pete proceeded to the next topic.

"If she did, I never saw any signs of it."

"How often did you see her?"

"Maybe once every week or two."

"But you were part of the grapevine. You heard comments."

"Let me put it this way. If she used drugs, she was too smart to permit anyone at Read Ink to know about it."

"Did she socialize with the staff?"

"I can't speak for the rest of the staff, but she didn't socialize with me. However, I'm very family oriented. Most of the nonwork things I do are with my family."

"Did you tell her that?"

"I don't know. Perhaps during my initial interview."

Pete heard pots and pans clattering in the kitchen. He wondered if Tracy's wife sought to give her husband, or all of them, a hint. "Did Colette like to gamble?" he asked.

"I have no idea. She never offered me a bet of any kind. I don't think she cared enough about sports to bet on games."

"I understand Ms. Hammond's New Year's Eve plans became a major topic of conversation around Read Ink," Pete said.

"If you mean her brother's wedding, of course we all knew about it. Colette spent months arranging things."

The questioning reverted to Martin. "Was anyone from Read Ink invited?"

"I know Colette and Avery were close. Even so, if Colette invited Avery, I didn't hear about it. Avery may not have wanted to hurt our feelings. Like it would." He gazed skyward and shook his head.

"Even if you didn't socialize with Colette, no doubt rumors circulated about her, the company, that sort of thing. For example, did she borrow money to keep Read Ink afloat?"

"I don't know that either. I heard a few snide remarks about the guy she's been seeing. Most of them came from other women. Maybe they were jealous. Who knows? Women can be pretty catty." Tracy shrugged.

"So, what you're telling us is that, to the best of your knowledge, Colette had no enemies. At worst, just some detractors."

"Correct."

"Okay," Pete said, standing up and grabbing the overcoat he'd laid over another chair, "if you think of anything that might help this investigation, please give one of us a call."

He and Martin handed Tracy business cards.

"One last thing," Pete said. "Please wait here with my partner. I have a question for your wife."

Sabastian Tracy's left eyebrow elevated, but he remained silent.

Pete walked to the kitchen.

The countertops and table indicated preparation for the holiday meal constituted a major undertaking.

"We're almost finished. Just a couple more questions," Pete told Sabastian's wife.

"I have my hands full right now." She moved quickly from job to job, completing final preparation. She looked frazzled. "I was afraid everything would either be overcooked or cold."

"Did you and Sabastian celebrate New Year's Eve together?"

"Yes."

"Where?"

"Right here."

"Did you stay up past midnight?"

"Of course."

"Thanks. Enjoy your dinner. Happy New Year."

FIFTEEN

How did you entertain Sabastian while I spoke with his wife?" Pete asked Martin after they reached the unmarked car.

"We talked about kids. Since he has a thirteen-year-old, I asked him about thirteen-year-old boys. Told him I have a twelve-year-old son and wonder what to anticipate when he hits his teens."

"And?" Pete asked.

"He said about the time both of his boys reached their teens, they started flexing their muscles and got smart mouths. His friends told him the eighteen-year-old will rejoin the human race in a few years. He hopes that happens before his daughter reaches her teens. Did his wife corroborate his story? Were they both home last night?"

"Yes."

"Took you a long time to find out. Did she give you dinner?"

"No. Didn't even offer. Can you imagine?"

"One look at you, and she probably concluded food is against your religion. You should have sent me." Martin chuckled.

"The sun is already setting," Pete said. "I love the sixteen hours of daylight in June. Hate the fact the sun sets after eight-and-a-half hours this time of year."

"I wouldn't mind the short days if you went home when the sun set. Unfortunately, that's not the way it works—or the way you work."

"Come on, Martin. I know you're dying to speak with the final Read Ink employee. No doubt you're also chomping at the bit for another perspective on the design aspects of publishing."

"Meaning Raleigh Zimmerman?"

"None other. Let's see if, by some miracle, I reach him."

"Haven't you already exceeded your share of miracles for one day?"

"Several times over."

Martin checked his phone and said, "While you make those calls, I'll call home. Marty texted while we were with Sabastian. He asked me to call ASAP."

During Martin's conversation with his son, he said little and nodded a lot. After he disconnected, Pete took one look at him and said, "Want to talk?"

"Michelle put in another bad day. She isn't feeling up to preparing dinner. Marty offered, but I told him to wait until I got home. He was so relieved I called. Glad I did!"

"I'm so sorry, Martin. Anything I can do?"

Martin shook his head and shrugged.

"Enough, already! I didn't reach Randall in distribution or Zimmerman, the former employee. If I hear from Randall tonight, I may go see him or I may wait until we get together tomorrow. Depends on the time. Meanwhile, drop me off at headquarters, so I can get my car. Then, go home, Martin."

"Are you sure?" Martin knew Pete itched to keep going.

"Positive."

Martin's face brightened several shades.

"By the way, Martin, you already know this, but I'm going to tell you anyway. Marty is a rock-solid kid. He's one in a million. You and Michelle have done a great job with him. If he gets testy during his teen years, send him over. He can camp out with Katie and me for a while."

Martin smiled. "Thanks, Pete. That's how I feel about him, but I could be a tad bit biased."

It was New Year's Day, so Martin had few options. He was glad to find a place open that offered roasted chicken, mashed potatoes, and a couple of salads. At a time like this, he didn't even think about dessert.

He walked in the back door of his home and glanced around, looking for Michelle. Spotting her collapsed in a recliner in the living room, he took the food to the kitchen. Then he went to her side.

She must have heard him approaching, but didn't open her eyes.

Martin bent over and kissed her on the forehead.

Her eyes remained closed. He knew from her breathing, she was awake.

Martin reached down and took her left hand in both of his. "Bad day, *huh?*"

"Yeah."

"Sorry you're going through all of this, Sweetheart. How about if we check out the Mayo Clinic?"

She shrugged.

That simple gesture lightened Martin's spirit. It indicated she might be giving ground on her insistence that she stick with her primary care doctor.

"I don't think your doctor's doing enough," he continued. "How about if I make a few phone calls. A friend of mine went to Mayo. I don't think he had an appointment. I think the system permits you to show up and wait your turn. They work you into the schedule. I'll check. I can get all of your test results. Maybe we can go tomorrow or the next day."

"What about the kids?"

"We'll take them along."

"They'd never survive one or two days of sitting in waiting rooms."

"Marty's good with Olivia. As long as we're nearby, he could take her walking. They must have play areas for kids. We can't be the only ones to find ourselves in this position."

"What about the case you're working?"

"The case be damned. You're more important."

"What will Pete say?"

"Probably that it's about time. He always says family comes first."

Michelle opened her eyes and smiled. "I'm so lucky to have you, Martin."

Martin smiled, reveling in the compliment. "Glad you feel that way, Michelle. It goes both ways, you know."

Failing, again, to reach Randall, Pete changed clothes, got a status report from his mom, then picked up Katie. "Sorry my job got in the way of our spending the day together," he told Katie on the way to his mom and dad's.

"Don't worry. We'll have lots of opportunities." She kissed his cheek. "Now, tell me about your aversion to late-night phone calls."

"*Huh?*"

"Last night, correction, early this morning, you told me it had to wait until you had more time."

"Oh, yeah." Pete took a deep breath. "When I was ten, Dad's mom called around four in the morning. I answered. Grandpa had collapsed. In addition to the time, Grandma's voice told me it was bad. I heard Dad tell Mom to call Grandpa's doctor and the priest. I lay awake the rest of the night, crying and praying."

"Oh, Pete," Katie saw the tear welling up in the corner of his eye.

"They rushed Grandpa into surgery. Dad said Grandpa came through the surgery just fine, but afterward the surgeon couldn't revive him. His organs had shut down. That was the first time I saw Dad cry. Dad idolized Grandpa. So did I."

"Oh, Pete, I'm so sorry." Katie patted his leg.

"A late night or early morning call from family rarely carries happy news. There have been other instances, but none stands out like that one. I remember it like it was yesterday, and when I think about it, I still feel the shock, the upheaval that call triggered."

"Let's change the subject. Tell me about the case that called you away last night, interrupting your plans for a prolonged goodbye."

Pete appreciated Katie's interest in his work. He spent the remainder of the trip telling her some of the facts he could share.

When they arrived at his parents' home, Pete's mother was serving dessert. She stopped long enough to pull the leftovers out of the oven for Pete and Katie.

Again, Pete apologized.

"I don't know why you don't get a job with normal hours," his mother said.

"He likes turning on the strobe lights and sirens," his mother's mother said.

Pete bent down and kissed her. "You know me so well, Grandma."

Sixteen

Friday morning, before Martin removed his overcoat, Pete said, "Still unable to reach Kim Randall or Raleigh Zimmerman, so let's work on Ms. Hammond's friends who attended the reception. Dory Carlisle, the coveted author, works right out the door at the Minnesota Department of Natural Resources. She goes home at three. Let's start with her. Meredith and Lyle Kingston, the friends who drove Odin back to Colette's after the reception, are leaving midmorning. We'll go there next."

Pete had assessed Martin's appearance. He looked for a clue indicating the situation when Martin got home last night. "Before we head out, Martin," he said, "I have a few questions."

"Namely?"

"How was last evening?"

"I was looking for a way to tell you. I have to cut out on Monday. If you want to take me off the case right now, I understand."

"Michelle, *huh?*"

"Yeah. I'm taking her to Rochester. Sorry to be doing this to you, Pete."

"You're doing the right thing. Did you make an appointment?"

"No. I wanted to go today. My connection said Monday is a better idea. That way, we'll already be on a list of people waiting to be seen. I'm concerned about forcing Michelle to sit there for hours. Some days she can manage it. Some days she can't. I'm itching to go right now, but this seems like a better idea. We'll drive to Rochester on Sunday, as soon as I get home and pack up Michelle and the kids. I have a reservation at the Kahler Hotel. By staying there, we can walk across the street and into the clinic."

"What will you do with the kids?"

"I talked to Marty this morning. He's good with Olivia. He's so glad we're doing something more to help his mom, he offered to take care of Olivia before I had a chance to ask. We'll take along some books and some toys. It isn't ideal, but they'll be fine. The timing is poor. Winter break ends on Monday. We'll work around that."

"Martin, I have an idea. How about if I call my grandma and see if she'll watch Marty and Olivia? She's good with kids and, physically, she's up to it. Since Marty will be back in school, she'd probably be willing to stay at your house. That would make the situation less disruptive for your kids. If it's okay with you, I could also stay there. I could go there after work and give Grandma a hand."

"I couldn't ask your grandmother to do that."

"You don't have to. I will." Pete smiled.

"Are you sure?"

"Positive." Pete spent several minutes explaining the situation to his maternal grandmother.

Martin listened, trying not to get his hopes too high.

"Good idea, Grandma. Let me check. I'll call back in a few minutes." Pete smiled and said, "It's a go."

The two men conferred over the advisability of introducing Pete's Grandmother to Martin's kids beforehand. Martin went back and forth a few times, uncertain, then decided it would be best, at least for Olivia.

"Want to discuss it with Michelle?"

"I hate to risk waking her, but I probably should."

Michelle was thrilled. She liked the idea much better than taking the kids along.

Pete called his grandmother and confirmed. "I'll pick you up tonight, if we finish early enough. I'll let you know by seven o'clock if that isn't going to happen."

"Martin, are you sure you should work today? You may want to spend the day with your kids and preparing for your trip."

"The trip is in two-and-a-half days. I've done everything I can for now, including spending some quality time with Marty last night. I need a distraction."

"Okay. Let's go see Carlisle."

"Assuming Carlisle writes novels, not short stories," Martin said, "we'd better get the abridged version or we'll never make it to the Kingston's by midmorning."

"I'll settle for the name of the friend of a friend who knew Hammond used heroin, as long as she throws in the name of the supplier." Pete smiled.

"We could walk to her office," Pete added, buttoning his overcoat.

"You can. I'm taking the car. Do you know how cold it is out there?"

Martin got his way. He drove, and the distance from the parking lot to the office building nearly equaled the distance from headquarters to the building.

Pete asked the receptionist to speak with Dory Carlisle.

While waiting for her, Pete asked Martin, "Did you hear the news? Because of the polar vortex, the thing that's causing the fifty below predicted for Monday, the governor closed schools statewide. He announced it today, so working parents have time to make arrangements for their kids."

"What's a polar vortex?"

"The way I understand it, it's a counterclockwise rotation of a pool of cold, dense air."

"If the air is that cold, wouldn't the pool be frozen?"

"In combination with the jet stream and cold temperatures, it's delivering a special gift, starting Sunday. It's supposed to be something like twenty degrees colder in northern Minnesota and the Twin Cities than in the Arctic Circle. Imagine that."

"I'd rather not, thanks. That means Sunday will be a bad day for travel."

"True. Do you think you should leave for Rochester no later than noon, before the intense cold arrives? If you don't and have car trouble, it could be life-threatening."

"Let me think on that. Here's another consideration. With the schools closed and it being too cold for Marty to go outside, he might be too much for your grandmother. Are you sure she can handle him all day, under those circumstances?"

"Positive. When I was his age, I spent a lot of days with her. She has a hundred tricks up her sleeve for entertaining kids. She used to do scientific experiments with me. Things like creating a tornado in a bottle, and building a smoking volcano. Don't worry, they'll be just fine. By the way, I'm supposed to ask you about Marty's favorite cookies. She wants to bake a batch to bring along on Sunday."

"He loves peanut butter and, of course, the old standby, chocolate chip. Would she consider waiting and making them with Marty? He loves helping Michelle cook. Unfortunately, they haven't done much of that, since Olivia was born."

A slender woman of average height, shoulder-length medium-brown hair, and a warm smile exited the elevator and approached, interrupting Martin.

Pete and Martin identified themselves, and Pete requested a private place where they could talk.

"I don't understand why you want to speak with me. I didn't do anything wrong."

That makes her unique, Pete thought and said, "You know why we're here. This shouldn't take long."

"Fine."

The two investigators followed her into a compact meeting room with an oval table and a dozen high-backed chairs.

Carlisle pulled out a chair and plopped down. "Okay, what do you want to know?"

Pete began with a statement, rather than a question. "You and Colette Hammond were friends."

"Not really."

"Explain," he said.

"She invited me to Demetrius's reception and occasionally included me in gatherings of her friends. Those were strictly strategic moves. She wanted to keep me in the Read Ink family. Neither Colette nor I had any misconceptions of it being anything more than that."

"In the process, you got to know her better than a casual acquaintance or many of her clients."

"A bit, perhaps."

"I understand you have it on good authority that she used heroin," Martin said.

After a prolonged intake of air, Dory said, "I hate to speculate."

"She may have been murdered. If she was, providing that information could help find the murderer."

Dory shrugged.

"We're committed to solving this case," Pete said. "We can do this the easy way or the hard way. The choice is yours."

"What's the hard … Never mind. What do you want to know?"

"How do you know Ms. Hammond used heroin?"

"Kara told you that, didn't she?" Dory's jaw tightened.

"How we found out isn't the issue. The question is, who told you?"

"No one told me. I picked up on it right away in a couple of our meetings. She kept nodding off. It's a sure sign."

"Who confirmed your conclusion?"

"No one. It didn't require anyone else to confirm. It was obvious."

"Just the same, that's quite a rumor to circulate without confirmation. Narcotic painkillers might create the same effect."

"Perhaps, but I got a glimpse of her forearms. I don't believe for a second that she mainlined prescription painkillers."

"What about the friend of a friend who said Ms. Hammond was hooked on drugs?"

"Now I know you got the information from Kara. There was no friend of a friend. I just said that, because I didn't want to go into the details with her."

"I understand you also discovered Ms. Hammond's supplier."

"If Kara told you that, you should hook her up to a lie detector. It's one hundred percent *false*!"

Martin and Pete provided business cards and departed. Reaching the Kingstons before they left home wouldn't be a problem.

SEVENTEEN

Where do the Kingstons live?" Martin asked on the way back to the unmarked car.

"In St. Paul, just east of St. Thomas."

"St. Thomas University?"

"That's the one."

"If we'd planned this and gone there right after we endeared ourselves to the victim's live-in, we could have saved a lot of time."

"True, but I enjoy the spontaneity. It keeps me from getting bored."

"When was the last time you were bored, Pete?"

"I think I was two years old at the time. My parents wouldn't buy me LEGOs. My only toy was a hoop and a stick."

Martin rolled his eyes. "You know, Pete, if you weren't so full of it, a stiff wind would blow you away."

Exiting I-94, the two investigators traveled south on Snelling to Summit Avenue. Some of the oldest mansions in the Twin Cities, including the governor's mansion, found their home on Summit.

The Kingston home, a two-story Victorian, had an enclosed three-season porch. This wasn't one of those seasons. Parking in front of the home was feasible, but a challenge. Plowed snow ventured into the street, making driving incompatible with parking. That didn't dissuade those attempting to navigate the street nor those intent on parking. It also made getting out of the driver's side door a risky business.

Martin waited impatiently for an opening in the traffic before opening the door and venturing out. He hoped the door would be operable and free from dents and scrapes when he returned.

Lyle Kingston answered the door and led them through the porch and into the living room. A Christmas tree crowded one corner, and opened gifts flowed from the base.

Lyle appeared to be in his early seventies. A gene for balding gave him an island of brown hair in the front of his head. Prominent ears drew attention away from a pockmarked face.

Pete smelled ham and said, "I hope we're not interrupting breakfast."

"Not even close. After hearing from Avery, we're anxious to talk to you. Avery said Colette died yesterday … of an overdose?"

Pete nodded. "We can save time by splitting up. I'll speak with your wife, and you can meet with Martin."

"Whatever you think. I'll get Meredith."

Kingston returned, followed by his wife. A holiday headband pulled Meredith's hair back tight against her scalp. She looked sixtyish and like she met regularly with a personal trainer. She wore a long-sleeved shirt and a vest displaying a wreath on one side and a decorated tree on the other.

Pete greeted her, saying, "I'd like to express my condolences on the loss of your friend."

Husband and wife nodded. "It's shocking," Meredith said. "It's the last thing I anticipated when we left for Demetrius's reception."

"I told Lyle we can wrap this up in half the time if my partner and I each speak with one of you."

"Okay. How do you want to do this?"

They settled on Pete meeting with Meredith in the living room, and Martin moving to the den with Lyle.

Pete began, asking, “Did you spend much time with Colette on New Year’s Eve?”

“A fair amount. She sat at the head table. We sat nearby. She stopped and chatted each time she passed, and she sat with us for a while.”

“What time?”

“I didn’t notice. Fairly late. Maybe eleven?”

Trying to narrow the time frame, Pete asked, “Was it close to the time she began having a problem?”

“Not long, before, I guess.”

“I understand Ms. Hammond went to the restroom with a friend, shortly before midnight. I’m trying to determine which friend, in hopes of obtaining information about her physical condition at that time. Were you that friend?”

“No.” The answer sounded more like a question.

“Any idea who it might have been?”

“No.” This time Meredith sounded more certain.

“Could you see the restrooms from your table?”

“Only if I walked around to the other side.”

“Who sat at your table and faced the restrooms?”

“Mattie and Wyatt.” In response to the look on Pete’s face, she added, “The Underwoods.”

“How long have you and Colette been friends?”

“Going on twenty years. She’s like a sister.”

“Who were Colette’s closest friends?”

“Esther Lancaster, Mattie Underwood, Beverly Atwater, Rhina Dalton, and me.”

“Were you all at the reception?”

“All but Esther.”

“Was she invited?”

“Some of our friends said yes, others no.”

"If she wasn't invited, any idea why?"

"Schedule conflict? Who knows?"

"I understand Colette had problems with prescription painkillers."

"Yes. It was horrible! It started with Oxycodone for her back pain and got totally out of control."

"How so?"

"I'm sure you've heard it all before. The supply of Oxycodone dried up. She had to find something else."

"What did she find?"

"Heroin."

"And?"

"She became addicted and couldn't get off the stuff until Lyle and I interceded. We convinced her to go into rehab."

"When?"

"Last February. She made it her birthday present to me." Meredith sighed.

"What happened with her company while she was there?"

"Avery, one of her editors, kept things on track."

"Where did Collette get the heroin?"

Meredith did a hands-up shrug. "She refused to talk about it. At first, I thought she feared I'd report him to the police, and she'd lose her source. She was right, of course."

"Were any of her friends using?"

"None of the friends we have in common."

"In other words, you always knew when Ms. Hammond was using?"

"Well, no."

"Who are the friends you have in common?"

"Rhina Dalton, Esther Lancaster, Beverly Atwater, Mattie Underwood, and Harper Morgan."

"When did Ms. Hammond start using again?"

"She didn't. Well, she didn't prior to the night before last, that is. She seemed fine when she sat with us."

"When did you become aware Ms. Hammond had a problem?"

"When Demetrius yelled for coffee. I wondered who had a problem, and I went and looked."

"Did you think the problem was heroin-related?"

"No, I thought it was the alcohol."

"Any idea what could have caused Ms. Hammond to start using again?"

"No. If she was going to, I thought it would have happened last May, when she turned sixty. That birthday threw her for a loop."

"How so?"

"The day she turned sixty was *not* a happy one. She felt she was on a fast track to a nursing home. Her fortieth birthday brought denial. The fiftieth prompted a facelift. The sixtieth took her over the edge and led to a bout of depression. To compensate, she did insane things like hooking up with Grayson. Believe me, under normal circumstances that would *not* have happened. She needed to feel alive. She needed to feel desirable."

"Did you tell her how you felt about him?"

"No way. I refused to let him come between Colette and me."

"Did she get counseling for the depression?"

"If so, I'm sure she'd have told me. So no. I think she eventually got used to the idea and began coping. I think the fact she planned to dump Grayson served as a good indication."

"Was Grayson aware of her plans?"

"I don't think so. I saw no indication of it at Demetrius's reception."

"Was Colette ever married?"

"Yes. Gilbert died about nine years ago. Cancer. Well, Colette said it was cancer. Someone, and I don't remember who, said he contracted HIV while fighting the cancer and actually died of AIDS. If AIDS was the official cause of death, maybe Colette said cancer to protect Gilbert's reputation. The stigma attached to AIDS back then was far worse than now."

"Gilbert's death almost destroyed Colette. She withdrew. She cut herself off from her friends. Read Ink Press proved to be a blessing. It forced her to get out and get involved. I think Read Ink became her tribute to Gilbert. He was a voracious reader."

"After Gilbert's death, did Collette have a serious relationship with anyone besides Grayson?"

"Yes, a wonderful guy named Fred Staples. Fred's job took him to Seattle. He asked Colette to go with him. Thanks to Read Ink, she couldn't. If she had, I'm certain sixty would have been less traumatic, and she'd still be here." Meredith swiped away a tear.

"When did Fred ask her to go with him?"

"About two years ago. She had a long dry spell after Fred."

"Did Ms. Hammond have financial problems?"

"Her business drained her bank accounts. She barely eked out a living. I think her expectations far exceeded the reality."

"If it was a losing proposition, why didn't she walk away or sell the company?"

"I asked her that more than once. Her refusal to make a rational decision is why I think it became a tribute to Gilbert. Sometimes the heart gets in the way of rational decision making."

"Where did she get the money to start the company?"

"She used savings and some of the money she inherited from her parents' estate."

"Did she ever ask to borrow money?"

"No. She would never do that. She knows Lyle and I couldn't afford a loan."

"Did she borrow money from other friends?"

"If so, she never told me."

"Knowing you couldn't help, would she?"

"I don't know."

"Can you think of anyone who might want to hurt Colette?"

"Frankly, no."

Meanwhile, Lyle told Martin that Colette stopped at their table late in the evening. The best he could estimate was between eleven and midnight. He said she was alone at the time. The next time he saw her, she was on the floor.

"You're aware of her use of heroin?" Martin asked.

"Yes. Meredith recruited my help in getting her off the stuff. Is that what killed her?"

"Who was her supplier?"

"Some of the other husbands and I speculated it was Bart Lancaster."

"Why is that?"

"Because Esther used the stuff for a time? It was just speculation. I don't think we had a good reason."

"What was Colette's financial status? Did she owe anyone?"

"All I know is she asked me for a loan."

"Why did she need the money?"

"For her company. My guess is, too many expenses and too little income."

"How long ago?"

"About a month. The amount of money they must have pumped into Demetrius's reception blew me away. It bothered me that she wanted to borrow money and could spend a sum like that. I'd have been seriously irritated if I'd loaned her the money."

"Why would she fund even a portion of her brother's wedding?"

"I'm only in the bleachers, far from the action, but I thought they had a peculiar relationship."

"How so?"

"I just got the feeling she was more of a mother than a sister to him."

"How much did she want to borrow?"

"Twenty-five grand."

"Did Meredith want to loan the money to Ms. Hammond?"

"Colette made me promise not to tell Meredith she asked. She didn't want to risk hurting their friendship. Her asking wouldn't have done that, but my loaning Colette the money would have destroyed my relationship with Meredith. All three of our kids graduated from Ivy League schools. After the last one graduated, I heard the best move is to complete general education courses at a community college. Doing that doesn't reduce a kid's chances of getting into a top university, and the only thing that matters is the name of the school on the diploma. Wish I'd known that before I sunk a fortune into tuition. "Lyle winced and shook his head.

"Did Ms. Hammond find another source for the money she needed?"

"I have no idea."

"Are you sure she needed the money for her company, not for the reception?"

"I got the impression she wanted it for her company. It's possible she planned to spend some or all of it on the reception."

EIGHTEEN

Approaching the driver's-side door of the unmarked car, Martin checked for dents and scrapes. There wasn't a mark on the car. That saved him the headache of completing all the reports any damage necessitated. He smiled.

After settling back in the car, Pete and Martin compared notes. Hearing about Bart, Pete made a note to check with the Narcotics Unit and the Criminal Justice Information Services Division of the FBI for his name.

"I hope you and Katie communicate better than those two. You know, if we keep splitting up the couples, we might find time for lunch."

"Such an optimist. Didn't I tell you, Michelle is paying me ten dollars for every pound I starve off you?" Pete grinned.

Martin rolled his eyes.

GPS helped Martin wind his way to the home of Harper and Donovan Morgan, two of the friends who attended the reception. The street on which they lived ended a short distance past their house, but tell-tale signs announced plans to extend the road and erect more houses. If not for the commute and a price certain to exceed his means, Pete would love to get his hands on a house like the one where the Morgans lived. Field stone bases supported the wood pillars of the mission-style house, the porch, and an arch above the front door. Sage green siding covered the remaining exterior.

Harper Morgan answered the door. She looked at least a decade younger than Meredith. Her straight, strawberry-blond hair hung behind her ears and past her shoulders. Big blue eyes and ultra-white teeth welcomed the two detectives.

"Avery called last night," she said, glancing at their badges and IDs. "She told me about your visit. Was it alcohol poisoning? Was Colette murdered? Donovan and I went to Regions last night. Couldn't believe she died. Demetrius was inconsolable. Sorry, I'm rambling. Come in. Follow me."

Martin and Pete followed Harper through the foyer, past an office and into the living room. On the way, Pete changed his mind about wanting a house like this. He and Katie would need a lot more furniture if they lived here.

Handling the first series of questions, Pete began with, "We are trying to determine whether Colette's death was murder or suicide. Had she been depressed?"

"When she turned sixty, she went into a tailspin. She told me she couldn't concentrate. Couldn't get her work done. Didn't want to do anything but sleep. That lasted several months. Somehow, she worked her way through it. I think alcohol played a large part. It made me nervous when I saw her drinking so much last night. I worried that she'd reverted to that time, was again depressed."

"Did you spend much time with her last night?"

"Five minutes here, ten minutes there. She was spread pretty thin."

"When you did see her, did she seem depressed?"

"Anything but."

"I understand Colette also had a problem with drugs," Pete continued on this path.

"I wouldn't have known, if it wasn't for Meredith. Not sure how she knew Colette used heroin. A few times, when Colette and I were talking on the phone, she sounded a little weird. Could have been alcohol, but she didn't sound like she did when she was drinking. After talking to Meredith, I decided it had to be the heroin."

Stepping up to the plate, Martin asked, "What's your take on Grayson?"

"After she turned sixty, Colette went a little wild. That's when she hooked up with him. Lately, she's appeared ready to move beyond all that. For the last few months, she's been more like herself. She's been happier, more carefree."

"Was her relationship with Grayson doomed?"

"When people drift apart, things change. Everything from the way they look at each other, to how close they stand, to dropping the use of pet names. I saw all those things."

"Did it go both ways? Did Grayson, too, display those symptoms?"

"No. If anything, he was more obsequious."

"Because he knew what was happening?"

"I don't think so. It sounds nasty, but I don't think he's that bright. I think he went merrily along, thinking he had the world by the tail."

The questioning reverted to Pete, and he asked, "Was that the case on New Year's Eve?"

"He was grumpy that night, but it probably had nothing to do with his relationship with Colette. She treated him nicer that night than she did the last few times I saw them."

"How often did you see them?"

"Every two or three weeks."

"For the past few months, has he been with her each time you got together?"

"Only when it's couples. Lots of times we girls get together."

"When did the girls last get together?"

"A week before the reception. She wanted to bounce a few ideas off us."

"Would Colette tell the group if she was afraid of anyone or anything?"

"Several times she mentioned an author who became furious with her over a book her company was supposed to publish. The woman got released from the contract, and now the book may never get published. It was all the author's fault, but Colette said the author didn't see it that way. Failure of any type bothered Colette. She liked to be in control, but lost control of that project. She found that highly disconcerting."

"Did she mention the woman's name?" Pete asked.

"Yes, Kara something. I don't remember the last name."

"Anyone else?"

Harper closed her eyes and scrunched up her face. After a significant pause, she looked at Pete and said, "Nothing comes to mind."

"Did she owe anyone money?"

"I know she was trying to borrow some money. We couldn't help her. Could have, had she asked a few months earlier. By the time she asked, all of our liquid assets were tied up in the down payment and closing costs for this place."

"Why did she need money?"

"She said she was cash poor after several books were printed. She said it was very temporary—that she was waiting for the money the book warehouses owed Read Ink."

"So she only needed money for her business?"

"Yes. I think her personal finances are fine."

"But she didn't have the money to loan the company?"

"Guess not." Harper shrugged.

"Did Colette gamble?"

"I don't think so. If she did, I never heard about it—from her or any of our friends."

Martin jumped on that opening and picked up with the social aspects, starting by asking Harper to list Colette's best friends.

Harper repeated the list provided by Meredith, again including Esther Lancaster.

"I understand Esther Lancaster wasn't invited to the wedding reception. Did that surprise you?" Martin continued.

"Esther told me Colette invited her, but she decided not to go. Try as I might, she wouldn't tell me why. I know something was bothering her, but she refused to discuss it. I offered to meet with the two of them and serve as an intermediary of sorts. Esther would have none of that. My impression is that Colette, too, was baffled by Esther's change of heart. She said Esther had become standoffish. Said it made no sense, but she refused to lose any sleep over it."

"Besides you and your husband, and Demetrius and his bride, did anyone go from Christos to Regions?"

"Yes, the Daltons and the Atwaters. Mattie and Wyatt Underwood would have gone, but she had a migraine. No one in our circle of friends would willingly abandon Colette at a time like that."

"Was Colette close to any of the other people at the wedding? Did she socialize with any of them?"

"She told me that aside from our group and the employees and the author she invited, she had no desire to spend New Year's Eve with any of the guests."

"What was the cause of death for Colette's husband?"

"Cancer. It was a long and tough battle."

"What kind of relationship did she have with her deceased husband?"

"She idolized him."

"How about a relationship gone wrong, after Gilbert's death?"

"You gentlemen don't leave a stone unturned, do you?" Harper smiled.

"Not if we can help it." Martin shook his head.

"Aside from Grayson, the only other relationship I knew about after Gilbert ended when the guy was transferred."

"Transferred to?"

"The Pacific northwest, I believe."

"That was the only reason the relationship ended?"

"I think so."

"How long ago did it end?"

"A year or so ago. Awhile before she began seeing Grayson."

"Did she stay in touch with that guy?"

"Yes. He's been calling her a lot lately."

"Did Colette mention seeing that guy again?"

"Not to me."

"Was there any type of connection between Colette's husband, Gilbert, and her publishing company?" Pete asked.

"No. He died a year or two before she even had the idea for the company."

Pete and Martin thanked Harper for her time and handed her their business cards.

"If you think of anything else," Pete said, "please contact one of us."

"Count on it. I want you to find out who did this. I know it wasn't Colette. She had so many plans. There was still so much she wanted to accomplish."

NINETEEN

Get out your publishing notebook," Pete told Martin. "Kim Randall, the distribution person for Read Ink, lives in Bryn Mawr. He's next."

Martin headed west on I-694, went south on I-35W, then west on I-394 to the Penn Avenue exit to this Minneapolis neighborhood. The homes in Bryn Mawr, dating back to the twenties and thirties, displayed signs of meticulous maintenance. Randall inhabited a tan, two-story stucco with dark-brown trim.

The two investigators ascended the four steps to the porch. The open porch did nothing to guard against the biting cold.

Martin rang the doorbell and returned the gloved hand to the place both hands frequently resided these days—covering his ears.

A woman answered who looked like she'd partied much of the last few days.

"We're looking for Kim," Pete said. The name could go either way. When he called to make sure Kim would be home, he learned this time it was a man.

The woman motioned them in.

Pete calculated the whole first floor of this home could fit in the living room of the last one.

Just inside the front door, a stairway led to the second story. Area rugs protected or hid the condition of the hardwood floors. The clean and well-maintained furniture had been around a while. The exception was a leather recliner.

Despite the woman's instructions to have a seat anywhere, the two investigators remained standing, waiting for Colette's distribution person.

Kim Randall entered the living room through the adjoining formal dining room. He was wispy with thin flyaway hair and a scraggly beard. He wore baggy sweats and carried a large mug of something.

"Can I get you some coffee?" he asked, holding out the mug.

"Please," Pete said. Thanks to the draft that blew across his feet, the living room didn't feel appreciably warmer than the deep freeze in which they'd resided for almost a week. He hoped holding a warm mug of coffee would warm his hands and radiate out from there.

"Honey?" Kim said.

"Yes, I'll get the coffee," she sighed. "Would you like some, too?" she asked Martin.

"Yes, please."

Martin introduced the two of them, then began the questioning. "Is Read Ink closed for the day?"

"No, I'm working from home."

"Do you often do that?"

"No. Colette didn't like it. Special circumstances today."

"Oh?"

"Yes, I talked to Sabastian. I know all about Colette."

"What did Sabastian tell you?"

"That someone murdered Colette."

"Interesting," Martin said. "Who told him that?"

"He said you did."

"Guess we didn't make ourselves clear. We don't yet know whether she was murdered."

"Oh? I guess either Sabastian or I must have misunderstood," Kim sputtered.

The woman returned with two mugs of coffee and gave them to Martin and Pete.

"How was your working relationship with Colette?" Martin continued the questioning for the time being.

"Fine."

"Any issues?"

"None."

"How long have you been with the company?"

"I was hired shortly after Colette created Read Ink."

"Ever thought about spreading your wings?"

"Things aren't all that rosy in the publishing business. The options are limited. I'm in trouble now if Read Ink falls apart."

"Did anyone in the company have a grudge against Colette? A bone to pick?"

"Just one person. Got so bad she almost quit, but she got over it a long time ago. Everything is fine, now."

"So it was short-lived."

"Anything but." Kim snorted.

"Who is that person?"

"Avery Renner."

"What was the issue?"

"Got me."

"I think you know more than you're saying."

"You think wrong."

"Did you side with Avery?"

Kim paused, then said, "Colette was an okay boss. She had her own ideas and standards, and they dictated how she ran Read Ink. If you conformed, everything was copacetic."

"Avery didn't conform?"

"I think she did."

"Did you ever associate with Colette outside of work?" Martin wondered if Pete had fallen asleep with his eyes open.

"Do you mean like did we have a thing going?" Kim's eyebrows flew up.

"No, I mean did you ever go out to lunch or dinner together. I mean it on a completely platonic basis. I'm just trying to determine how well you knew her."

"I saw her only at work. I talked to her only about work. I don't know anything about her personal life."

"How did you spend New Year's Eve?"

"My wife and I went to my sister's home."

"Where does she live?"

"St. Louis Park."

"What's her name, address, and phone number?"

"You're actually going to verify it?"

"Do we need to?"

Kim shrugged and provided the information.

Both investigators took notes.

"What time did you get home?"

"Around one a.m."

"I understand you knew all about Colette's plans for New Year's Eve."

"Yeah, everybody heard all about it. Avery wanted all of us to know she was invited. She likes us to understand that she is part of the inner circle—and the rest of us aren't part of any circle. Like I care." He seethed.

"Tell us about the employee who was either fired or forced out."

"I don't know anything about that."

"You said you've been there almost since day one. I'm talking about the only employee who left the company. You were there at the time. What happened?"

"Raleigh is the only person who left Read Ink. I know he left of his own volition."

"He got a better offer?"

"No."

"He decided to change his career path?"

"No."

"I understand you and Raleigh are friends."

Kim's expression said, busted. "Yeah. So?"

"After he left Read Ink, how long did it take him to find another job?"

"I don't know." Kim looked at the floor and scratched his ear.

Pete took the reins. "But you're friends. I'm sure you have an idea how long he was unemployed."

"It was awhile. He didn't line up another job before he left. The publishing community is a tight group. Read Ink belongs to MBA. The members talk. Raleigh figured Colette said things that didn't help his job search."

"Yet he left Read Ink of his own volition?"

"Yes." Kim's tone broadcast his irritation.

"What's MBA?" Martin moved back into the driver's seat.

"Midwest Book Association."

"Is Raleigh currently working for a publisher?"

"No."

"What is he doing?"

"Don't know. He moves around a fair amount."

Martin glanced at Pete.

Pete nodded surreptitiously.

Both investigators thanked Kim for his time and gave him a business card in case he changed his mind and decided to help.

"Do you think he already spoke with Raleigh?" Pete asked Martin as they returned to the car.

"My guess is he's on the phone with him right now. The real question is, what is he hiding and why?"

TWENTY

Confident Raleigh would know what to expect even if he lived within ten seconds of their current location, Pete and Martin stayed with the original plan. That placed another of Colette's friends, Beverly Atwater, next on the list.

The Atwaters lived in a coveted location, along Minnehaha Creek in south Minneapolis.

Even though Cedar Avenue provided a direct route, Pete told Martin to drive to Park Avenue. "We aren't far from a restaurant I know you'll like. Katie told me about it."

Martin's jaw dropped. "Are you feeling okay? Is your brain frozen? Should I head to the closest hospital?"

"No, head for Twenty-Sixth and Park. The name of the restaurant is Fika. It's located in the American Swedish Institute. The food is Nordic, and you'll love it."

"I love that you're thinking about food."

While waiting for their food, Martin checked on Michelle and his kids. Marty answered and said his mom wasn't moving much, but took an interest in his and Olivia's activities. At least that was better than yesterday.

Pete attempted to reach the Christos employee who saw Collette go to the ladies room just before midnight with another woman. Again, he failed to make contact and resorted to calling Michael Pennock, the manager. Failing there, he called Christos and hung up as the canned message greeted him.

Pete was right. Martin raved about the open-faced sandwich he ordered.

Turned out, the Atwaters could see Lake Nokomis from their front door. They lived in a two-story, cottage-style house. Tan brick accentuated the white stucco exterior.

Martin parked in front, and Pete held his breath while he and Martin ascended the steps to the front door. That kept the frigid air out of his lungs. Did nothing, however, to protect his hands or ears. Pete decided he needed a pair of choppers. His dress gloves couldn't cut it.

When she answered the door, Beverly's rosy cheeks gave the impression she'd either run a marathon or just come inside. She ushered them into the living room. Lamps furnished much of the light on this cloudy day. A lit fireplace gave a cozy feel to the room.

"My husband had to leave. Our daughter's car won't start, and she has to work today. I hope he'll be back before you leave." Beverly shrugged.

Not what he'd hoped to hear, but a common problem these days, Pete knew. If you had AAA, the wait for a jump currently lasted hours.

Pete began the questioning.

Beverly provided the same list of six close friends as Meredith and Harper, including Esther.

Pete asked why Esther wasn't invited to the wedding reception.

Beverly said Colette told her Esther was mad at her, and Colette didn't want to give Esther the satisfaction of slamming the door in her face. "When I asked if that meant she and Esther were no longer friends, Colette insisted everything would be back on track by Valentine's Day."

"Why Valentine's Day? What's the significance?" Pete asked.

"Got me." Beverly gave a hands-up shrug. "Could be because at the time it was a few months away? You know, time heals all …."

"Did Colette know why Esther was mad at her?" Pete asked.

"I don't think so. I don't think she was just refusing to share the information. It's curious that both of them were so hush hush about it."

Beverly said she spent yesterday and this morning talking to her and Colette's friends. They'd all decided, pure and simple, it was murder. Then she busied herself trying to determine "who done it." She didn't think Colette had any enemies, save the Read Ink author who demanded to be released from her contract and the man she'd fired.

"I know the employee situation was more than a performance issue," Beverly said. "Can't imagine why she was so secretive about it. Wondered if she was afraid of being sued and having all her friends hauled into court. Couldn't risk us having to testify under oath. That's the only thing that makes sense. I know I, for one, love her dearly, but would never have perjured myself."

"Obviously, you've spent time thinking about it. What charges could the ex-employee have brought against her?"

"I have no idea."

"But you knew her well, and there's no longer the chance she'll be sued. What's your best guess?" Pete asked.

"Colette was pretty closed-minded. Problem is, she was tight-lipped about the whole situation. I know nothing about the man. Maybe it got out that he was walking out on his wife and kids. Maybe he was hiding after a hit-and-run accident. Maybe he beat his wife. Maybe he was gay. The possibilities are endless."

"In your opinion, could each of those situations lead to a termination?"

"Knowing Colette, definitely."

Martin wondered about a woman who lived with a guy young enough to be her son and addicted to heroin being closed-minded. Apparently that applied to the lives of others, not Colette's own life.

"Are the members of your group generally closed-minded?"

"No, only Esther, and she seems to be coming around."

Martin moved the discussion to heroin. "The use of heroin has reached epidemic proportions," he said. "We're not here to bust anyone. That isn't even our department. Our only mission is to get to the bottom of what happened with Ms. Hammond. Do you know where she got her heroin?"

"She never discussed those things with me. She knew both Meredith and I were adamantly against it."

"How about Esther, Harper, and Mattie?"

"I don't think they know, either, but I can't be positive. Colette admitted she was using, only because Meredith and I confronted her. Otherwise, I doubt she would have."

"Her death may be attributable to what was used to cut her heroin. Fentanyl has resulted in numerous accidental overdoses. If that is why she died, don't you want us to catch the supplier of her drugs?"

Beverly bit her lip and shook her head. "Sorry, I can't help. If I was a user I could be more helpful, but I wasn't and never will be."

"Any idea who would know?" Martin asked.

"Sorry, none. Like I said, she didn't share that information with me."

Beverly didn't think Colette had financial concerns or owed money to anyone. She doubted Colette contributed to the cost of the wedding. She didn't know if Colette had a life insurance policy. To the best of her knowledge, Colette and Demetrius had a close and loving relationship, and he'd never think of hurting her. "You should have seen him at Regions. He was a wreck even before she died. Her death about did him in. That's true of all of us. So far, this is the worst New Year ever!"

The two investigators went through the drill with their business cards and left in search of a different perspective. Hoping to uncover one.

Twenty-One

Next, you get another opportunity to research publishing, Martin. Since you're pushing to save gas by eliminating as much back-and-forth as possible, we'll check out Raleigh Zimmerman, the ex-employee of Read Ink."

"And it doesn't hurt that so far he has the best motive. We could wrap this up by lunchtime."

Martin took I-94 east, then Lexington Avenue north to reach the Zimmerman home.

On the way, Pete continued attempting to reach the Christos waitress and manager, and also Colette Hammond's friends, Esther Lancaster and Mattie Underwood. Batting zero, he talked about the weather. Minnesotans coveted the bragging rights they believed they'd earned by withstanding Minnesota winters. "I heard this morning that Twin City temperatures for December qualified as the twenty-seventh coldest in recorded history. I'm surprised they ranked that low. It was the seventh coldest on record in St. Cloud, and the second coldest in Bemidji."

"Glad we don't live and work in *Brrr*midji. I'd have to get regular transfusions of antifreeze."

"Have you heard the seven-day forecast, Martin? We may set records for the lowest high temperature and the lowest low temperature. They're predicting highs in the twenties below zero, and wind chills as cold as fifty below for Monday."

Raleigh Zimmerman lived a few blocks off Lake Como, in the Como neighborhood of St. Paul.

When Pete saw his house, he wished there was a for sale sign in the front yard. At least on the exterior, this two-story Cape Cod style home qualified as his dream home. "This makes for two houses in a row I'd love to own," he told Martin. "Do you think that's significant?"

"Ask me when we leave."

Martin was unusually quiet this morning. *Understandable*, Pete thought. His partner had a lot on his mind.

A woman with an auburn mane that flowed past her shoulders answered the door. Makeup accentuated large brown eyes and prominent cheekbones.

"I called this morning," Pete said. "We're here to speak with Raleigh."

"That's what you're doing. I didn't say anything then. I changed my name to Roni. I'm transgender."

"I admire your courage. It can't be easy," Pete said and introduced himself and Martin.

Roni asked to see Martin's and Pete's IDs, then said, "I was just reading about it. Kim called and told me. As soon as I hung up, I went online and read the *Pioneer Press* article. I don't understand how I can help. I haven't seen her in years."

Pete took the lead. "We have a few questions, primarily about you and Read Ink," he said.

Roni Zimmerman invited them in, and led them to the living room. It could have passed as a showroom for IKEA-style furniture. Both investigators avoided the curved chairs with ottomans and sat on the couch.

"Okay, what do you want to know?"

Martin's jaw almost dropped when Pete kicked it off with, "How did you spend New Year's Eve?"

"Do you think I killed Colette?" Roni emphasized the "I."

"Just answer the question." Pete said.

"I was with friends."

"Where were you and your friends?"

"At a friend's house."

"The friend's name and address?" Pete asked, as he pulled out his pen and notepad. He wrote as Zimmerman shared the information.

After a brief pause, Martin stepped up. "What time did you get there?"

"Eight o'clock."

"What time did you get home?"

"Ten o'clock the next morning." Roni smiled. "I wasn't in any condition to drive before then."

"Glad you exercised good judgment," Martin said.

Pete decided to launch into the Read Ink questions and began with, "I understand you left Read Ink under unfortunate circumstances."

Roni's eyes went wide and she gasped, "Who told you that? Kim?"

"A few of your fellow employees. What happened?"

"I'm sure you've already heard."

"We want to hear your take. After all, who knows the story better than you?"

"Well, you see, I've been on a journey for a long time, trying to figure out how being transgender fit into my life. After many, many years, I finally decided to live full-time presenting female. I decided I'd also change my body to be the woman I truly am—the person I believe I was meant to be. I was tired of walking around, trapped in a man's body, while identifying with women. I don't expect you to understand. Most people don't. Many of my friends, now former friends, don't." Roni sighed and shook her head.

"I'd presented only as a male at work. I went to great lengths to keep my transgender secret from my coworkers and Colette."

Moving her gaze to the hands clenched in her lap, she inhaled deeply, paused several seconds, then exhaled and continued. "When I decided to go through the change, I knew I had to tell Colette. I thought I owed it to her. After several sleepless nights and cancelled meetings, I found the courage to go through with it. I set up a meeting with Colette at the end of the day on a Friday. I thought that would give her the weekend to process the information. I hoped by the following Monday she'd be able to accept my news. The day came, and I met with her. I shared my plans and the schedule I'd arranged with my doctors. I didn't expect an endorsement. I only hoped and prayed for acceptance. She was very formal. Said she knew it wouldn't be easy and wished me the best. Obviously, she knew she couldn't get rid of me, because of what I was doing in my personal life. I told her I planned to begin taking the hormones in six weeks. Everything was fine for a few weeks. Equipped with my schedule, she knew she had plenty of time."

Perhaps hoping to catch Pete's reaction, Roni shifted her attention from her hands to his face. "Two weeks and a weekend after that meeting, Colette called me into her office. She said my recent work was not acceptable or creative enough. From then on, no matter what I did, she found fault with it. Some of the layouts were as good as or better than others she'd approved. When I showed her examples, she only found fault. She said finally that continuing to accept my work threatened the company's survival and, as much as it pained her, she had to let me go. That was so bogus, especially in light of the timing. Don't you agree?" She shifted her gaze to Martin.

"Based on what you've said, you could have built a case against Colette and Read Ink. Why didn't you?" Martin asked.

"It was a very emotional time for me. My transition was my priority. Every penny I could save funded that. I had neither the money nor the energy to take on Read Ink Press at the same time."

"How long ago did that happen?"

"Four years ago."

"I understand you've had trouble finding another job."

"In my field? Yes. I spent months on unemployment, searching for a job." Roni's face reddened. "When the unemployment ran out, I settled for a variety of jobs. I've done everything from waitressing to grocery store checkout to walking dogs."

"That had to infuriate you," Martin said.

"Of course it did. For a while, I hated Colette. But that's a lot of wasted energy. If I was going to get even, I'd have done it while I still had the energy that hate engenders. These days, I concentrate on finding happiness in knowing the bastards can only get me down if I permit it."

"Do you know of anyone at Read Ink with a reason to hurt Colette?" Martin asked.

"No. While I was there, she seemed fine with everyone else. Besides, it's been too long. The only Read Ink person I know anymore is Kim. He knows what I've been through and he's promised that everything I tell him stays between the two of us."

"Why don't you want the others to know? They might be able to help."

"If they wanted to help, they should have done so when I was unjustly fired. That's when I needed them. Now it's too late. I've put that life and all of them, except Kim, behind me."

"Does Kim keep you posted on the developments at Read Ink?" Martin asked.

"Not until today, when he called to tell me about Colette. He knows I don't like to talk about the place. He understands it's a sore subject for me."

"Does Kim hate Colette because of what she did to you?" Pete asked.

"Definitely!" Roni nodded vigorously.

"Kim told you about the wedding reception at Christos?" Pete asked.

Quickly diverting her attention back to her hands, Roni said, "I didn't know about it until today."

"What are you trying to hide?" Pete asked.

"Nothing." Her attention remained fixated on her hands.

"You know and I know that isn't true. I don't yet know why you're lying, but I will find out. Telling me the truth now will keep you out of the middle of this. Trust me, that's not where you want to find yourself."

"There must have been something in the newspaper."

Standing and handing her a business card, Pete said, "If you want to make your life easier, here's how you can reach me … *any time*."

Back in the car, Martin said, "Wow, he makes a beautiful woman."

"I agree, but I doubt she finds much consolation in that, now that life is such a hassle."

"I'm surprised she thinks it's worth it."

"Obviously the alternative wasn't worth it. She's gone through hell and, unfortunately, it isn't likely to get better in the near term."

"Especially if she's guilty of murder," said Martin.

TWENTY-TWO

Rhina and Gabe Dalton, two more of the victim's inner circle of friends, now stood at the head of the line.

Martin drove from St. Paul's Como neighborhood on the north side of I-94 to their Crocus Hill neighborhood on the south side.

Meanwhile, Pete resumed efforts to reach the less cooperative people on their list. He thought he'd struck pay dirt when Elizabeth Frost, the waitress from Christos, answered. His optimism faded when she explained she was in Eau Claire with her grandparents. She didn't plan to return to St. Paul until ten forty-five tomorrow morning—just in time for work. "Michael gave me permission to arrive at the eleventh hour, so I could maximize my time with Grandma and Grandpa. You see, my grandpa is dying." That did it. Pete settled for ten fifteen tomorrow morning.

Efforts to reach Esther Lancaster and Mattie Underwood were even less productive.

Pete looked up from his notes as Martin parked in front of the Dalton home. Was mansion more fitting? Pete's residence envy took a rest.

The Dalton's two-story Victorian stood nestled in a yard filled with massive trees. It sported a sizable addition on back. Taupe wood siding with white trim highlighted porches and bay windows on both stories. Pete figured it would take a full year's wages to replace all the windows in this place.

Once again, the two investigators wasted no time in reaching the front door. Thankfully, the enclosed porch provided a modicum of warmth while they waited for someone to answer the door.

The woman who obliged stood just short of Pete's armpits. Her holiday earrings looked like they might outweigh her.

She greeted them with, "Peter Culnane?"

"And my partner, Martin Tierney."

"Come in, before you turn to ice."

She led them to the living room and ushered them into chairs that matched the home's exterior. "Coffee?"

Both men nodded, and both checked out the interior while she busied herself with that.

When she returned the coffee mugs became a source of warmth as much as a beverage.

"I can't believe the news about Colette," she said as she eased onto the davenport. "Poor Demetrius. I hope this doesn't cause his marriage to start out on the wrong foot. That's the last thing he needs."

"Why is that?" Pete asked.

"He's a lost soul. Colette always said he needed a keeper. She thought Shelby was incapable of fulfilling that role."

Martin reverted to the line of questioning they'd used thus far, hoping for at least a few additional details. He started by asking her to list Colette's closest friends, and the people who accompanied her to the hospital. Rhina's answers provided a mirror image of the information already gathered. The exception came with her remarks about Esther's absence from the reception. Per Rhina, Esther was invited and subsequently uninvited. Upon further questioning, she said Esther told her Colette was a loser and she never wanted to see her again. Rhina attempted to find out why Esther felt that way but failed to get any details.

"Is your husband here?" Martin asked. "If so, I'd like to meet with him while Pete speaks with you. That'll save some time."

When Rhina returned with her husband, Martin and Gabe moved to another room. Martin hoped the privacy would loosen Gabe's tongue, especially if he'd drawn the same conclusion about Bart Lancaster. A little substantiation would be helpful.

Pete continued with Rhina. "I understand you helped Colette find relief when her supply of Oxycodone evaporated," he said, opening what he hoped to be a more fruitful line of questioning.

"Who told you that?" The decibel rating of Rhina's voice more than doubled.

"Pull up your sleeves. Let me see your forearms," Pete said.

"Do you have a search warrant?"

"Not yet. But if you force us to get one, we'll be looking at a lot more than your arms."

"I tried it a few times. I never became addicted the way Colette did. And I never had a supplier. Colette always took care of that." Rhina pulled her sleeves up to her elbows. By all indications, she told the truth about a limited history.

Pete continued this line of questioning. "Some of your and Colette's closest friends knew you were using, didn't they?"

"I think you're wrong. I know they didn't hear it from me, and I don't believe Colette would tattle."

"Where did Colette get the stuff?"

"I have no idea. I asked, but she wouldn't say. It may have been her way of keeping me from getting hooked. I wouldn't be surprised if that was why."

"Were any of your and Colette's other friends using?"

"I don't think so, but I can't be positive. After all, they didn't know about me. Even so, I'd be shocked if Meredith or Harper did. They were adamantly against it and vocal in their opposition."

"Where were you seated at the reception?"

"On the far left side of the head table."

Pete knew that meant they were almost as far as possible from the ladies room. "Did you face the head table?" he continued.

"No, and that irritated me. Guess I shouldn't have let it. It's only reasonable that Demetrius's friends would face the head table, isn't it." That was a statement, not a question.

"Did you have many opportunities to speak with Colette that night?"

"Quite a few. She was good about mingling."

"I understand the two of you went to the ladies room just before midnight."

"No, you've got that wrong. Colette stopped by our table and asked me at one point if I wanted to go with her. I said no. I drank very little that night, because I almost had to undress to use the facilities. I went to the bathroom before I put on my dress, and planned to wait until I got home to go again. Would have succeeded, too, had Gabe and I not gone to the hospital. That, of course, doesn't mean I'm sorry we did. I wanted to be there, in case there was anything we could do. As it turned out, we didn't have the opportunity to do anything for her. I still can't believe she's gone. I heard it was a heroin overdose. I can't believe it. She told me she'd never touch the stuff again. Not in a million years."

"How long ago was that?"

"Less than a month."

"Did you see her head toward the ladies room a little before midnight?" Pete asked.

"No. Is that when it happened?"

"That's what we're trying to determine. Have you spoken with Esther Lancaster since it happened?"

"No. We talked early on New Year's Eve. She and Bart were on their way to their son's home, somewhere in Iowa. I can never remember the name of the town. It's a little south and east of

Albert Lea. I know cellphone service is spotty there. I've tried several times to reach her, and I know for sure Meredith and Harper tried. I'd be surprised if she wasn't home sometime Monday afternoon or evening."

"Did she say anything about going there before that conversation?"

"No, but things were a bit strained between Esther and the rest of us, due to the wedding. I don't blame her. I'd do the exact same thing, only I wouldn't have called to say I was doing fine. That's the difference between Esther and me. I'm more spiteful."

Pete followed with questions about Colette having enemies. Once again, the only people mentioned were the problem author and the former employee. Rhina had nothing to add in either instance.

Martin returned as Pete stood and thanked Rhina for her time.

TWENTY-THREE

Out of the wind and in the comparative warmth of the car, Martin shared the news, or lack thereof, from Gabe. "He said he hasn't a clue about Colette's supplier. Doesn't think she shared that with anyone. Mentioned Demetrius trying to buy the information from him. And that's the highlight of our conversation." Martin rolled his eyes.

Pete listened to the voicemail message received while he spoke with Rhina Dalton. After finishing he said, "Okay, Martin, if one of Colette's friends played a part in her overdosing, it seems unlikely they'd go to the hospital. We've spoken with all her friends who accompanied her to Regions. We've spoken to all her current and former employees, and the only Christos employee we know of who might help won't be available until tomorrow morning."

"Are you suggesting we hang it up for the day? If so, you sure took the long way to get there. I could have been home by now." Martin grinned.

"On our way to headquarters, let's work out the plan for bringing my grandmother over to meet your kids. Is that still the game plan?"

"It is in my book."

"Great. It's just past five. What arrival time is best for you, Michelle, and the kids?"

Martin conferred with Michelle, and they decided on seven o'clock.

Pete offered to take his grandmother out for dinner, but she insisted on fixing dinner for the two of them. "That will provide extra time when I can have you all to myself," she explained.

Pete smiled. He would take all of that time he could get. Their bond grew closer as the years passed, and they never lacked things to say and do together. If only there were more hours in a day.

Pete's grandma was dressed to the nines when he arrived, and the smells of homemade rolls and meatloaf rushed out to meet him as she opened the door.

"Perfect timing!" she announced.

"Knowing you, it would have been whether I arrived thirty minutes ago or an hour from now." He kissed her and followed up with a protracted hug.

He finished setting the table while she dished up their dinner.

After they said grace, Pete mentioned the Union Depot. "When I walked in early New Year's morning, I couldn't help thinking about our trip to the reopening, Grandma."

"Yes? I often think about that. Pete, you are such a dear! Your willingness to take time to do things with me means a lot. You make my life so much fuller. I can never thank you enough."

"And what would my life be without you? That day at the depot, you told me about going there to meet Grandpa's train when he returned from World War II. I love that story. Please, tell me again. I can't hear it often enough." Pete pulled out his phone. "In fact, how about if I record you telling it. How about doing it right now?"

"I'd feel more comfortable telling you over the phone than telling your phone."

"Just look at me. Pretend it isn't here. You're doing it for posterity. One day, I'll play it for my kids … and their kids."

"If you get a move on, I can tell your kids myself." She chuckled.

"They, too, will want to hear it again and again, year after year."

"If I tell the story now, my dinner will get cold. Let's finish eating and move to the living room."

Pete accepted her recommendation. After dinner, while she combed her hair and freshened her makeup, he set up his phone to record her narrative. She sat in her favorite chair, a platform rocker, and began with, "I'll do my best, Pete. Hope you're not disappointed."

"Not a chance. You know you looked perfect before, don't you, Grandma?"

"For you, perhaps. Not for posterity. Do you want the abridged version or are you going to use this to put your kids to sleep?"

"I want the whole story, and I'm confident they'll hang onto every word the first time and the forty-first time. Everything is ready. Start whenever you're ready, Grandma."

She crossed her ankles, clasped her hands in her lap, took a deep breath, and began. "I remember it like it was yesterday. Jack sent a letter from Antwerp, Belgium, saying he was scheduled to sail from Antwerp on October 28, 1945, and should arrive in New York City nine days later. After he landed, he sent a telegram, saying he'd board a train home and should be at the Union Depot at one twenty-five in the afternoon on November 10th. He warned me his schedule was dependent on weather conditions, and he'd do his best to notify me in advance of any changes."

"When I read that, I started jumping around like a crazy woman. I hadn't seen him in two-and-one-half years. It felt like an eternity, even though I knew he was doing what he had to do. Just like you are now, *huh*, Pete?"

"I had my heart set on meeting his train, whenever he arrived. I realized that could be a problem. In those days, I was a regular Rosie the Riveter. I worked on the assembly line at the Ford

Plant in Highland Park. I was a nervous wreck when I asked my supervisor to take off one or two days. I told him I didn't know which it would be, because the schedule was too uncertain. I said I had to meet my fiancé's train and explained he was returning from the war. Fortunately, in those days, everyone stood behind our veterans. I got the days off." She smiled, remembering that success.

"I didn't hear another word from Jack, prior to his scheduled arrival. I didn't think there was any chance of an early arrival. Did worry about unanticipated delays. The night before he was due in, I washed and ironed his favorite dress. I polished my high heels, and manicured my nails." She glanced down at her nails. "That night, I bathed, and washed, and set my hair. In those days, we didn't have curling irons or blow dryers. Women slept in curlers. Some of the curlers were so hard, it felt like you slept on a pillow made of soup cans. I barely slept, and it wasn't because of the curlers." She chuckled.

"I got up at seven thirty. Ordinarily I'd have been at work by then. I went downstairs for breakfast. Tried to be quiet, but Mother heard me and came down. She knew how excited I was. She also knew I was a bundle of nerves. We sat and talked for almost two hours. Then I read the newspaper before going upstairs to get dressed. I spent almost an hour on my makeup and hair. I wanted everything to be perfect for Jack. As I mentioned, I hadn't seen him in two years, six months, and two days." She counted the numbers, one by one on her fingers.

"When I was all primped up, I put on my coat, hat, and muff. I went out the front door. Made it down the steps and went maybe another twenty feet before I turned around and went back inside. I'd realized my high heels wouldn't do. Not that day. There was just enough fresh snow to rule it out. If I managed to stay on my feet, my feet would be frozen before your grandpa arrived." She shook her head and shrugged.

"If Jack told me once, he told me a hundred times that I was just the right height for kissing when I wore heels." She blushed. "As much as I hated to disappoint Jack, I put on my galoshes and resumed my trip to the Union Depot."

"I arrived a little before noon. Almost ninety minutes before Jack's scheduled arrival, I wasn't taking any chances. I was going to be there when his train pulled in. Period. I went straight to the platform."

"As you know, Pete, the depot was considered a tactical location during the Second World War. For that reason, they blacked out the skylights in the concourse leading to the platforms. The intent was to conceal the building in the event of enemy air raids. Thankfully, the mainland was never bombed."

"There were already lots of people on the platform. I hoped most would meet an earlier train and leave before Jack arrived. I was lucky that proved to be the case. As people left, I edged my way to the far end of the platform. I hoped Jack had a window seat on my side of the train. I wanted him to see me the minute his train pulled into the depot." Pete's grandma nodded as she explained her tactics.

"A few minutes after one, I heard Jack's dad calling my name. He was Jack's and your height, Pete, so he towered over most of the crowd. Otherwise, he'd never have seen me. He waved to me to join him, his wife, and Jack's two sisters. I already knew that wasn't possible. The crowd kept me from making it back to them. Even so, not wanting to upset Jack's mother, I made a few attempts. Those efforts brought some angry looks and nasty remarks. I was glad. It meant I had to stay where I was, and that was exactly where I wanted to be." She smiled broadly.

"At one twenty-eight, I heard it. I heard a train whistle in the distance. Turned out, I didn't need to worry whether Jack would have a window seat. All of the windows were open, despite the fact we're talking November. The smiling faces of soldiers filled each one. All wanted a glimpse of their loved ones."

"Suddenly, I saw Jack. I don't know if I was more nervous or more excited."

"Jack was in the middle of the train. Somehow, he plowed his way back through all of the men on that train. He was the third person off the car that stopped right in front of me. It turned out, I didn't need my heels to be the best height for kissing. Jack swooped me up and gave me a long hug. He interrupted it only long enough to kiss me." She smiled broadly.

"My nerves calmed. My excitement didn't."

"Jack continued holding and kissing me as the crowd thinned. He didn't put me down until his mother arrived and asked when it was her turn."

"'Sorry, sweetheart. I'll make it up to you later,' Jack whispered in my ear as he put me back on my feet."

"For days, I felt like I was floating on a cloud. I had to keep pinching myself. What if this was only a dream? To my relief, turned out it wasn't. The end." She threw her hands up and grinned.

TWENTY-FOUR

As Pete approached Martin and Michelle's house, he saw the colored lights along the roofline and the lit Christmas tree in the picture window. He smiled. They'd accomplished those things for the kids, despite Michelle's illness.

Marty answered the door. "Uncle Pete!" he threw his arms around Pete. "Dad told me. I'll go running with you, and we can build robots with Mindstorms."

"Sounds like a plan." Pete held up a hand, and Marty gave him a high five.

"Marty, this is my grandma. She's the best."

"So glad to meet you, Marty. I've heard a lot about you. Pete thinks you're the best, too. Looks like soon you'll be as tall as Pete, if not taller."

Marty beamed.

One down, one to go, Pete thought.

"Follow me. Mom, Dad, and Olivia are in the living room."

Martin had decided to stay put on the couch, giving Marty a chance to fly solo while making an initial assessment. The look on his son's face told him this arrangement would be the next best thing to having Michelle and him at home. He felt relieved.

Pete's grandma made a beeline to the baby sitting on a blanket and waving a stuffed dog with one hand. A terrier lay protectively at her feet. "What a beautiful little girl! You have your dad's eyes and your mom's smile, don't you?" She sat down on the floor, facing the baby. "Do you have two puppies?

A little one you can hold, and a big one who will soon play with you."

She reached over and let the dog sniff her hand.

The terrier licked her hand and wagged his tail.

She scratched behind his ears and said, "What's your name?"

"That's Benji," Martin said. "He thinks he's her guard dog. Right, Marty?"

"Yeah. He used to be my dog, but that's okay. I can take care of myself."

"You've proven that," Martin said, wishing circumstances didn't force his son to grow up so quickly.

"Look at Olivia," Michelle said, pointing at her daughter. "She's reaching for you, Jackie."

"Do you mind if I hold her?"

"Not a bit."

Beaming, Pete's grandmother lifted Olivia. "You're light as a feather, sweet girl. I love holding babies. Could do it all day long. Do you want her to sit on the floor a certain percentage of the time to avoid spoiling her?"

"No, do whatever you're comfortable with. I see she'll be just fine. Thanks so much for doing this. Pete is a blessing. He's so patient and understanding."

"I'll second that," Jackie nodded.

"Is it okay if I ask a couple of questions?" Marty asked.

"Of course. Have at it, buddy," Martin said.

"Pete's grandma, will you help make school lunches and bake cookies?"

"Before I answer your questions, let's come up with a better name for me. Would you like to call me Jackie or Mrs. Schmitt?"

"Or you could call her Grandma Jackie. That's what I call her when both of my grandmother's are together."

"I like that. What kinds of cookies do you make, Grandma Jackie?"

"Do you have a favorite?"

"Chocolate chip!"

"He's a traditionalist," Michelle said.

"What do you like in your school lunch?"

"A peanut butter and jelly sandwich, chips, and cookies."

"I can handle that, and I'm open to suggestions. We'll fine tune as we go along. Okay?"

"Sure!"

"Let me show you around, Jackie."

"Do you want me to do that, Sweetheart?"

"Thanks, Martin. I'll be fine."

Martin took Olivia, and Jackie followed Michelle into the kitchen.

During the tour, Michelle said, "I'm thrilled with the way the kids have taken to you. Unfortunately, my parents winter in Florida and won't travel north in January. Martin's parents are in California and have the same take on Minnesota winters. Marty's bowled over by you, and it's rare for Olivia to be so quickly drawn to a stranger. I'll post our cellphone numbers on the fridge, in case you have any questions, and Marty will be a big help … as long as you keep him supplied with cookies."

"Glad you mentioned that. Shall I place any demands or restrictions on his eating?"

"He loves meat and potatoes and shies away from cooked vegetables. A gentle push in that area won't hurt, but there's no need to go further than that. And if he doesn't eat anything but meat, potatoes, and cookies while we're gone, that's fine. A break from routine won't hurt anything."

Jackie got a list of Marty's favorite main dishes. Once she knew the locations of the things she'd need, Pete drove her home.

Marty fought the disruption to the Mindstorms project they'd begun, until Pete said, "To be continued."

En route, Pete said, “I’ll pick you up as soon as I can get away from work Sunday evening. Plan on between six and eight. I hope it’s closer to six. Is that okay?”

“Whatever you manage will be perfect.”

“Okay. On the way to Martin and Michelle’s, we’ll pick up groceries. Make a list of the things you think you’ll need. Plan for four days, but don’t worry. I’ll pick up whatever else you need as we go.”

“Is this your dry run, Pete? Is it like adjusting to a dog before having a baby?”

“I think it’s more like adjusting to a baby before having a baby,” he laughed. “The thing is, I don’t need to adjust to the idea. I’m ready! Bring them on!”

Twenty-Five

Martin wore a broad smile when he walked into Pete's office on Saturday morning. "It's like Michelle just had the weight of the world lifted from her shoulders," he told Pete. "She was up and fixing breakfast by the time I got out of the shower. Marty talked about Grandma Jackie until he went to bed, then woke up talking about her."

Pete knew his grandmother had won the hearts of everyone in Martin's family. He loved it when others appreciated this very special woman.

"Once again, I struck out with Esther Lancaster, the friend or ex-friend who missed the reception," he told Martin. "It'll be dark by five. If I can't reach her by then, let's drive by her house and see if any lights are on. She may have timers, but she may also be ignoring the phone."

"Or maybe, like she told Rhina Dalton, she's in a dead zone in Iowa."

"Ready for some good news, Martin?"

"Better news than finding a babysitting team for my kids?"

"Well, no. But I finally reached Mattie Underwood, the friend who faced the ladies room at Christos. She's expecting us."

"Why didn't you tell me the minute I walked in?"

"I thought it only fair you have a chance to warm up before I drag you back out in the cold."

"I warmed up, but my car cooled down. The Underwoods live in Arden Hills, correct?"

"Do you spend nights memorizing the names on our list and their addresses?"

"No. I have a friend in Arden Hills. His first name is Matthew. The location stuck with me. The car should be almost warm by the time we reach Arden Hills. Give or take a few miles."

Martin took I-35E north to I-694, headed west to I-35W, went north to the Highway 96 exit, then turned east to Lexington Avenue. On the way, he and Pete talked about the trip to Rochester. "Glad you're coming tomorrow night. We're planning to leave at five in the morning. That way, we'll say goodbye to the kids Sunday night and avoid a potentially tearful departure. We'll have time to check into the Kahler Hotel and be at the clinic by the time it opens. I've completed all the preliminaries I can from here. We'll do the rest when we arrive. I'm so glad we're going to the Mayo Clinic, Pete. If anyone can figure it out, it's them. But you know, Pete, I'm also afraid of learning the answer. What if it's terminal? There are nights I can't sleep. I lie there worrying about Michelle."

"Do you pray, Martin?"

"Not enough."

"Join the club. Prayer might help, both with Michelle's health and when it comes to coping with her problems."

"Do you believe that prayers can change what lies ahead, the course of history, Pete?"

"Yes."

"Really? I'd like to believe it, but I just don't know."

"I believe in miracles, Martin. I believe that prayers can obtain intercessions for our loved ones. I believe they can change the future. Remember Nick Rice? He should have died when that kid hit him with that car. Not only did he live, he's back running on all cylinders. I call that a miracle. I know a lot of people prayed for him. I believe that made a difference. If you aren't praying for Michelle, you may want to start, but keep in mind, this is my belief system. One size does not fit all."

"I should also be praying for Marty. He's totally stressed over the situation. He was more relaxed while you and your grandmother were there than I've seen him in months."

"Do you know what Grandma Jackie does, Martin? Unless there is a special need, such as an illness, she places the people she prays for in groups. She does that, because 'the Lord knows better than I who is in the greatest need.' She asks the prayers be divvied up according to the needs of which she is aware and unaware. Leave it to her to put a whole new spin on prayer."

"And leave it to you to spend the whole trip discussing a topic I could never in my wildest dreams anticipate."

TWENTY-SIX

The Underwoods' two-story house had an attached three-car garage that dwarfed the first story of living space. The tan brick first story supported a beige vinyl second story. The only tree in the front yard appeared to be on the neighboring lot. By way of contrast, judging from what you could see growing above the house and between this one and those alongside, the backyard imitated a forest.

"Since the Underwoods didn't go from the reception to Regions, how about if we question them separately, Martin?"

"Sure. I'll take Wyatt and follow up on Lyle's speculation."

Wyatt answered the door. He glanced at their IDs and said, "We've been expecting you. Mattie will be right down." The front door opened into the living room, and Wyatt signaled for them to have a seat.

"Unbelievable news about Colette. Mattie's still in shock. Had I not had a migraine, we'd have gone to Regions. Mattie's feeling guilty about not going. She refused to leave the party before midnight. I wasn't happy about that. The last thing I needed was to hear noise makers and people shouting 'Happy New Year.' Do you know what it's like to have a migraine? All I wanted was darkness and utter silence. It would have been better if we'd left when I wanted to. Then Mattie's final memories of Colette would be pleasant. The two of you look cold. Can I get you some coffee? Mattie kept it warm, just in case. On days like this, holding it is even better than drinking it."

My sentiments exactly, Pete thought as he gripped the mug Wyatt handed him in both hands. He noticed Martin did the same.

When Mattie arrived, Pete said, "We can save your time and ours by splitting up. Ms. Underwood, where shall we meet?"

"Wyatt and your partner can stay here. You and I will go into the kitchen."

Pete followed her. She looked like she might weigh one hundred pounds, but only if she had a five-pound weight in each hand. Her dark-brown hair was too uniform in color to be natural, but complemented her complexion.

"Before you say a word," she said, "I want you to know that Colette loved Demetrius far too much to pull something like this at his wedding."

"In that case, what do you think happened?"

"All of my friends are saying someone else must have injected her, and she had to be too drunk to know what was happening."

"Who would do that to her?"

"I think it was the author who put her through hell. That's the only person I can think of."

"What did that author have to gain?"

"Revenge."

"Was that author at the reception?"

"No, but you can get at the restrooms without going through Christos. I understand you think it happened in the restroom."

"Probably, but not necessarily. Could you see the ladies room from your seat at the reception?"

"I faced in the direction of the restrooms, but my attention wasn't focused there. There were, fortunately, more interesting things to observe."

"Other things may have been more interesting, but this is critical. Did you see Colette head for or enter the ladies room sometime after eleven thirty and before midnight?"

"No. The only person I remember doing that is Avery, one of her editors."

"Did you see Avery return to the reception?"

"No. Guess I was distracted, perhaps by Colette when she collapsed."

"Can you give me an approximate time when Avery entered the ladies room?"

"Wyatt started bugging me about leaving the party. I looked at my watch, and it was eleven forty. Had he not asked, I wouldn't have checked my watch. I saw Avery sometime after that, but I can't be sure how long after."

"Did you see anyone enter the ladies room either shortly before Avery or after her and before Colette collapsed?"

"I don't think so, but I can't be positive. Had I known it would be important, I'd have paid more attention and taken notes." Mattie threw up her hands and shrugged. "There are so many cameras these days. Don't they have camera surveillance of the restroom hallway?"

"If they did, I wouldn't be here. Where did Colette get her heroin?"

"I have no idea. Never asked. I wasn't looking for a supplier."

"Tell me about Esther Lancaster."

"Esther's in Iowa at her son's house."

"Did Harper tell you that?"

"No, Rhina did."

"Have any of your other friends talked to Esther since December 30th?"

"I've spoken to everyone in our circle. Only Rhina has spoken with her. That's how Rhina found out. About Iowa."

"Why wasn't Esther invited?"

"She was, then they had a big falling out in early December or thereabouts. I heard because of that Colette uninvited her. I asked Esther, but she refused to talk about it. Whatever it was, she was fuming."

"Could Esther kill Colette?"

Mattie tapped her lips with an index finger and considered this. After a pregnant pause, she said, "No, that would never happen. Not Esther. Her husband? Maybe." She shook her head. "Not Esther."

"Did Esther ever use heroin?"

"I don't think so, but I was shocked to learn that Colette had."

"Do you remember what Avery was wearing at Christos?"

"Sure do. It was an exquisite, red sequined dress. Gorgeous! I'd love to get one for myself."

Pete thanked Mattie and asked her to remain there while he checked on her husband and Martin.

Martin stood as soon as Pete walked in. "Ready when you are," he said.

Walking down the driveway, over the crunching sound of snow, Martin said, "Did she confess?"

"No. But she told me who did it."

"Really? I'll go home and pack."

"She told me who she saw enter the ladies room a bit before midnight. Did her husband give you a name?"

"No. He said watching who went to and from a ladies room had to rank up there with watching hair turn gray. He said the only person he saw head that way was his wife. Who did she see?"

"Avery Renner."

"For real? Did Hammond go with her? Did they come out together?"

"No and no."

"Her husband believes Meredith was Colette's supplier, and that Meredith got her hooked. He said the spouses speculated that's why Meredith worked so hard to get Colette to quit using. She felt guilty."

"So Mattie had no idea, but her husband and the other spouses figured it out? Maybe the women aren't willing to rat on one another."

"No surprise there."

Pete told Martin about Ms. Underwood's take on Esther and her husband.

"In other words, we need to start doubling back."

"Yes, and the top candidates on that list are the disgruntled author, Avery Renner, and Meredith Kingston. Toss in Roni Zimmerman, and Esther's husband for good measure. Let's see what I can arrange, before our meeting with Elizabeth Frost, the Christos waitress."

"The problem with Frost is, she can't remember the woman she saw going to the restroom with Ms. Hammond."

"I'm hoping to jog her memory."

Twenty-Seven

Avery Renner answered Pete's call. Esther Lancaster did not.

Martin took I-35W south from Arden Hills, and they worked their way toward Read Ink's offices.

"You know how Marty loves to research our locations. He discovered Read Ink is located in the Minneapolis Grain Exchange. It looked for a while like I wouldn't have a chance to share his findings. Are you interested?"

"I know it's an historic old building, and they used to do trading here. What did Marty find?"

"It was built in 1888. Originally they called it the Chamber of Commerce Building. The Minneapolis Grain Exchange has been in operation for more than one hundred years."

"Better kick it up a notch or two, Martin. It's right there." Pete pointed out the windshield.

"Here's the part I find most interesting. On December 19, 2008, the Minneapolis Grain Exchange stopped operations of the open outcry trading floor, but continued daily operations for electronic trading."

"What would I do without you and Marty?"

"Without Marty, you'd be far less educated. Without me, you'd spend your life sitting in the parking lot at headquarters, wondering who was going to drive."

Martin parked a block from the ten-story brick building located at Fourth Street and Fourth Avenue South, in the middle of a bustling downtown Minneapolis. Today was Saturday. It reduced the volume, but didn't eliminate the traffic.

The downtown buildings created a wind tunnel.

Walking the short distance, both Martin and Pete pulled up the collars of their overcoats, seeking a bit more protection.

Standing in the lobby, waiting for an elevator, Martin said, "How does Read Ink afford a location like this?"

"I was wondering the same thing."

Reaching the third floor, the two investigators discovered Read Ink occupied a compact space. A glass door with glass panels on either side displayed the company name and logo. An area probably designed as a reception area served as an office. To avoid presenting a totally wrong picture to visitors, plants, trees, a few comfortable looking chairs, and a coffee table with magazines also occupied this space. Unlike the majority of trees in the Twin Cities, these had leaves. The wonders of controlled temperatures.

The desk sat unoccupied, but a bell announced their arrival.

Avery appeared immediately. "Come on back. We'll meet in my office."

Martin and Pete followed her down a short hall that lay beyond the reception area. Large mahogany doors loomed on both sides. Pete checked out the only office they passed. He figured it had to be Colette's. A large mahogany desk, a leather couch and matching chairs, and a meeting table displaying a dozen or so books filled this ostentatious, wood-paneled office.

"This is my space," Avery said, walking through the second door on the left.

It looked humble, comparatively speaking.

"Staying the course?" Pete said. "I admire your tenacity."

Avery shrugged. "This author slaved away for two years, putting all the energy he could muster into this novel. It's scheduled for a February release. Until I know Read Ink is folding, I'll continue doing my part. Obviously, you two are also tenacious. Making any headway?"

Pete nodded.

"Good. What do you need from me?" She smiled.

"Where did Colette get her heroin?" Pete asked.

"You're asking the wrong person."

"Let me see your forearms."

"I edit a lot of crime fiction. I know you can't make me do that without a search warrant."

"Should we get one?"

"This is insane! I don't use illegal drugs. Never have, not even in the sixties when everyone was getting high on something."

"In that case, you won't mind pulling up your sleeves."

Avery yanked her sleeves up, glaring at Pete.

If looks could kill ..., Pete and Martin both thought.

Her forearms displayed no sign of needle tracks.

Martin took the next topic. "What did you wear to Demetrius's reception?"

"A green formal."

"Can you be more specific?"

"It is floor-length, with long, clingy sleeves and sequins."

"Are you certain?"

"Of course I am! I spent days shopping before I found that dress. What do you think I wore, a Santa costume?"

"One of the people with whom we spoke raved about your red, sequined dress."

"Perhaps he suffers from red-green colorblindness."

"Did you or a friend take any pictures of you at the reception?"

"Demetrius had a photographer there for a short time. She may have some. Wait a minute. One of Demetrius's friends wore a red, sequined formal. I don't think she looks at all like me, but a couple of people asked if I'd had to change my dress. Are you talking about her?"

"What's her name?"

"I have no idea. You know how it is, you're introduced to five people, and by the time you've heard the fifth name, you can't remember any of the names."

Yes, Martin knew.

Pete tried another subject. "Colette treasured your friendship so much that you became a member of her inner circle. How did you spend your time together?"

"Apparently I gave you the wrong impression the last time we met. Colette considered me a friend, in part because of our working relationship. Colette had an inner circle of friends, but I never made the cut."

"Yet that was the perception from the outside looking in."

"Kim Randall, right? He's such a twit. From his vantage point, the woman who cleans these offices looks like a member of the inner circle. Compared to him, I guess she is." Avery smiled.

"We heard you went to the ladies room with Colette on New Year's Eve," Martin decided to revisit this topic.

"Didn't we talk about that the last time I saw you?"

Martin flipped through his notepad, passed the applicable page, and asked, "What time were you in there?"

"As I already told you, I went to the ladies room one time. That was at approximately eleven o'clock. Colette was not there at the time. I have a lot to accomplish today. Are you about finished?"

"Almost," Pete said and asked, "Was Colette suicidal?"

"I told you she got depressed about turning sixty. I don't think it was anywhere near that bad. However, my degree is in English, not psychology."

"We spoke with Raleigh," Pete continued, "His perspective on his departure from Read Ink is radically different from yours."

"Sour grapes."

"By the sound of things, he had grounds for a lawsuit and a reason to be angry with Colette."

"That may be his story. It wasn't Colette's."

"You knew him for at least a few years. Is he capable of murder?"

"I haven't spoken to him since he walked out the door for the last time. You saw him recently. You tell me."

"Did he threaten her, either to her face or to someone else?"

"I'm probably the last person he'd tell."

"Who would he tell?" Pete asked.

"Kim Randall? His family? I don't know." Avery shrugged.

"Did you see him at Christos on New Year's Eve?" Pete asked.

"No. It goes without saying, he wasn't invited."

Pete thought about revisiting the subject of K. C. Fisher but, convinced the answers would resemble those they'd already gotten regarding Raleigh Zimmerman, decided to pass.

He and Martin departed, and Avery resumed her efforts.

TWENTY-EIGHT

Failing to reach Demetrius, Pete left a message requesting the name of the photographer at his reception. Approaching the Mississippi River on their way back to St. Paul, he said, "We have almost an hour. Could spend that time in a coffee shop, but I'll feel like a traitor to Michelle if I allow you to be exposed to pastries. Instead, let's drive by the Lancaster home. It's on East River Road. I want to see if it looks occupied. See if the steps were shoveled after it snowed early New Year's morning. See if the drapes are closed."

"And if it looks occupied?"

"I'll know the fact Esther isn't answering her cellphone has nothing to do with poor reception. We'll return after our meeting at Christos."

Martin exited I-94 at Cretin Vandalia and followed Cretin to Marshall. Then he went right, back toward the Mississippi.

Reaching the front door of the Lancaster home required conquering twenty-one steps if you attacked it from the street. Martin counted them. The steps had been shoveled.

The house was a two-story Tudor that qualified as another McMansion. Courtesy of the hill on which it perched, the house offered a spectacular view of the Mississippi River.

Martin parked alongside the curb so he and Pete could gather the desired information. "Either the Lancasters are home or they're pros at faking it," he said.

"I agree. We probably have enough time to speak with them, assuming they answer the door. I'm going to try to delay the meeting with Ms. Frost, just in case. That way, we'll save a return trip."

Elizabeth Frost loved the idea of delaying their meeting. It gave her extra time to get ready for work and decreased the chances she'd have to twiddle her thumbs between their meeting and the time she had to be at work.

Pete led the way. A quarter of the way up the steps to the Lancaster home, his feet slid out from under him, but he saved the day by grabbing the railing. Had he failed to connect, he'd likely have found himself back at street level.

Observing that, Martin said, "Thanks for the heads up." He grasped the railing before beginning his ascent.

Esther Lancaster answered the door after Pete pounded on it a third time, shouting, "Police. We want to speak to you!"

Sounds emanating from the home indicated at least one person currently inhabited the place. That and the failed attempts to reach them by phone made Pete more demonstrative.

Esther stood about five seven and, as one of Pete's cousins described it, was fluffy. Mascara, blush, and red lipstick announced her readiness to face the day.

"Police? I don't understand. What do you want with us?"

Pete nodded and produced his ID without being asked.

"Can you hold it a little closer?" she smiled. "I can't see it at that distance."

When satisfied, she said, "Come in. Did you come down the alley? I hope so. The stairs are treacherous."

The two investigators could attest to that.

The home's interior lived up to the standards set by the exterior. The foyer had a tile floor and a narrow table, complete with a silk flower arrangement. A pottery fountain occupied a narrow wall. The Victorian-style furniture in the great room stood in carefully organized groupings. The walls held a variety of paintings that couldn't be purchased at any starving artist sale. A log fire burned in the fireplace, and Pete felt its heat as he entered the room.

Esther laid claim to a couch.

The two detectives took the chairs in closest proximity.

Pete began by asking if her husband was home.

"He won't be home until noon or a little later. Had a crisis at the office. It forced us to return earlier than planned. Is he the reason you're here?"

"We want to speak with both of you. Maybe he'll return earlier than expected."

"Never happen. If anything, he won't stroll in until the cocktail hour. Now, what could you possibly want with me? I have no moving violations and no unpaid parking tickets."

Pete moved to the questions that brought them here. "Who are your closest friends?"

Esther repeated the six names they'd heard so often they could recite them in their sleep or so it seemed.

"When's the last time you spoke with any of them?"

"New Year's Eve. I spoke with Rhina on my way to my son's house. He lives in Iowa. We returned late last night. I've been too busy unpacking and doing laundry to call anyone. You know how that goes … or at least your wife does."

"Do you have an online subscription to the *Pioneer Press*?"

"No, I do email and Google searches. I have friends who spend hours each day on the Internet. Personally, I think it's a waste of time."

"Did you hear about Colette Hammond?"

"What about her?"

"She died early New Year's morning."

"Oh my God! I should never have let the trip to my son's keep me from attending the reception. He asked last summer if we'd ring in the New Year with him and his family. Even so, we could have done that next year. I missed my last opportunity to be with her. Poor Colette. Poor Demetrius! Colette was such a wonderful person. What happened?"

"The cause of death is a heroin overdose."

"Suicide? I thought she was over the depression. I tried to get her to seek help. I told her there was nothing wrong with getting some Valium. I told her she wouldn't believe how many women our age rely on a little pick-me-up."

The change in topic provided a good opportunity for Martin to take over. "What did she say about that?" he asked.

"She said she couldn't take the stuff and do her job. She said she needed that fine edge to stay profitable."

"Was Read Ink profitable?"

"I'm sure it was. She gave it her all."

"Did she ever ask to borrow money from you?" Martin stuck with it.

"No. Why would she?"

"I imagine you were upset Colette didn't invite you to her New Year's party."

"Who told you that? She invited me. Like I said, I had a prior commitment."

Martin changed the subject. "Have you ever been to Christos in Union Depot?"

"Yes. Several times with Colette and some of our friends."

"So you're familiar with the layout and the accessibility to the ladies room from other parts of the depot."

"Yes. Why?" Esther looked questioningly at Martin, then Pete.

Pete decided to move the questioning to a delicate topic. "I understand you and Colette often got high together."

Esther stiffened and pulled her arms and legs in close. "Who told you that? Colette and I never got high together! I never get high. I think you have to be crazy to use illegal drugs."

Pete knew a lie when he saw and heard one.

"You rely on prescription drugs?"

"I only use drugs my doctors recommend I take."

"Do you have a prescription for a narcotic pain reliever?"

"Yes, I have rheumatoid arthritis."

Pete knew some people ground down schedule II controlled substances, such as Oxycodone and Percocet, dissolved the granules in water and injected the mixture intravenously. "Ever inject it?" he asked.

"How would I do that? My pills come in tablet form."

Martin moved to the next line of questioning. "It's possible Colette's death was suicide and possible it wasn't. Do you know anyone who might want to hurt her?"

Esther stretched out her legs and said, "Colette was such a good person. I didn't think she had any enemies. If I had to come up with someone, the first person who comes to mind is Grayson. I think Colette was ready to dump him. He's such a leech. I was glad she'd started wising up."

"Anyone else?"

"Well, there's the author who gave her such headaches. There's also her brother, Demetrius. I know money can be a motive. That could have been a motive for him. I don't know his financial status, but he may be in dire straits. Why else would she pay for the reception?"

Pete heard a door closing oh so carefully in the back of the house and said, "Sounds like your husband wrapped things up faster than anticipated. We'd like to speak with him."

Esther stiffened again. "You must have heard our cats. They can be rambunctious. Please excuse me. I drank too much coffee this morning. I'll be back in just a minute." She stood and hurried toward the back of the house.

Pete heard hushed tones, coming from the direction of the kitchen.

It took a good five minutes before Esther returned.

"Sorry. I had to stop and get water for the cats. The dry air from the furnace running all the time dehydrates them. Poor things."

"Can I use your facilities?" Pete asked. He wanted to check out the kitchen and what lay past it.

"Yes. Please use the one upstairs. The one down here is such a mess. I'd be embarrassed to have you see it."

"Don't worry. I'm a bachelor. It can't possibly look worse than mine."

Martin had been in Pete's bathroom. It looked the way his own did right after he or Michelle finished cleaning it.

"But, but …" Esther stammered.

Before she could voice a convincing protest, Pete was out of his chair and on his way to the kitchen.

She started getting up, but sighed and dropped back down.

Once out of Esther's line of sight, Pete proceeded cautiously, hand resting on his Smith and Wesson. He took in everything as he made his way through the kitchen and toward the bathroom in the back hall. He looked for anything suspicious. He looked for signs of cats and their water and food dishes. He saw nothing. What compelled Esther to lie about her husband? He knew no cat made the sound he'd heard.

On his way to the bathroom, he scanned the backyard. He saw the garage. The overhead door was closed. Lacking a search warrant, he walked into the bathroom. Then he made his way slowly back to the living room, while double checking his previous work.

"I apologize for the mess," Esther squirmed.

"No problem. While I was gone, did you think of anyone else who might want to hurt Colette?"

"No. In fact, I think it's a stretch to think either of the people I mentioned would hurt her. It must be suicide. I feel guilty I didn't see the signs."

"Were there signs?" Pete asked.

"Well, actually there were, now that I think about it. She's been withdrawn, irritable, lacking an appetite, and always looked exhausted. I never put it together. I feel guilty for not recognizing it and stepping in to help."

That description of Colette stood in stark contrast with the descriptions gathered thus far. Pete wondered if Esther suffered from depression or looked up the symptoms in case it came in handy.

He said, "I understand the two of you haven't been on speaking terms for more than a month. How long ago did you notice those things?"

"What reason could there be for us not to be speaking? That's crazy. We're best friends."

Pete and Martin exchanged a glance. Esther was the only one who knew why they weren't speaking. Their close friends claimed not even Colette knew the reason.

"Please call when your husband returns," Pete said, as he and Martin handed Esther their business cards. "We have just a few questions for him. It won't take long."

As they approached the stairway to the street and the unmarked car, Pete said, "Martin, if you respected your elders, you'd offer to drive around to the alley and pick me up there."

"And spoil the fun? No way!"

TWENTY-NINE

Thanks to the snow that began falling while they spoke with Esther, the stairs proved even more slippery on the way back to the car.

After his experience ascending the steps, Pete undertook the return trip cautiously. He'd descended just three steps, and nearly lost his footing as many times. Rather than staying the course, he decided to take advantage of his long legs. Maintaining a firm grip on the railing with his right hand, he stepped over it with his left leg. Before transferring any weight to that foot, he dug a foothold with his heel. Then gripping the railing with his left hand, he repeated the process with his right leg. He looked back and saw Martin watching, smiling and shaking his head.

Due to current temperatures, Pete walked across the top of the snow, rather than sinking in. He maintained his grip on the railing and dug each heel into the snow, before transferring weight from one foot to the next. At one point, he considered sliding down on his butt. Deciding against it, he continued the laborious process and eventually reached the street. Turning, he saw Martin mimicking his process.

"Hope the sand trucks are out," Martin said when he reached Pete's side. "If not, the roads will be skating rinks."

Unfortunately, the trucks weren't yet out on Marshall. Car tires appeared to slide almost as much as they rotated as the two investigators made their way to Cretin Avenue and I-94. The light on Marshall and Cretin changed as they approached the intersection.

Martin shifted into second, then third, allowing the engine to slow the car and permitting him to keep his foot off the brake.

The person ahead of them, driving a Honda Accord, didn't realize how slippery the roads were, never learned that trick or forgot about it. When she stepped on the brakes, her car went into a spin. She struck a Taurus on her right, sending that car, too, into a spin. Then continuing in a forward and circular motion, she took out a Mustang entering the intersection from Cretin Avenue.

That bump pushed the Mustang far enough to slide it into the Volvo on its right. The Volvo slid sideways until the curb stopped it. Thankfully, the slippery roads diminished the force of the impact in all instances.

Martin flipped on the strobe lights and emergency flashers, attempting to warn everyone behind them, while Pete called it in.

Concern for the people in the four cars involved in the accident propelled the two investigators. They threw open their doors, looked for any looming threats to their safety, then maximized the likelihood of remaining on their feet by skating to the cars involved in the pile up.

Meanwhile, cars approaching the scene managed to stop without adding to the mess. Not all traveled a straight line while accomplishing that, but all succeeded in staying in their own lane and avoided tagging another vehicle.

Martin hurried to the Accord—the car that initiated the pile up. On the way, he did his best to assess the status of the people in the other vehicles. The driver of the Accord appeared in greatest need. The young woman's seat belt kept her erect, but appeared to be the only thing doing that. Martin spent several minutes talking to her and reassuring her that help would arrive momentarily.

Pete skated toward the Taurus—the car sideswiped by the Accord. As he approached, the driver lowered his window and said, "We're fine. The guy in the Mustang looks like he needs help."

That's where Pete was headed. He, too, was concerned by the appearance of the Mustang's driver, whose head rested on the steering wheel.

Reaching the crumpled driver's side door, Pete tapped on the window. He felt relieved when the driver looked up and at him.

"Are you okay? How do you feel?"

"Groggy. I think I'm going to throw up. This is my brand new car." The corners of his mouth sank and his lower lip quivered.

"Stay put …"

Sirens traveling toward them via Marshall drowned out the remainder of Pete's words.

Simultaneously, Pete heard the sound of spinning tires coming from the Volvo. He knew what that meant. Gaining traction, the Volvo moved through the intersection, leaving the scene.

Pete noted the license plate number and that a stocking cap and enormous sunglasses hid his view of the driver. A St. Paul squad reached the intersection and turned north on Cretin in pursuit.

Within minutes, another squad and two ambulances arrived. Paramedics and EMTs piled out of the ambulances and scattered to the three remaining vehicles.

Both Pete and Martin described the accident to the cops. After insuring there was nothing else they could do, Martin took advantage of an assist from a uniformed officer to move into the westbound lanes and get past the scene. Then he went north on Cretin to the freeway.

Reaching I-94, they saw MnDOT crews plowing and doing everything possible to keep the roads passable. Cars on the shoulder and in the median indicated drivers failed to heed the travel advisories, as well as the diminished effectiveness of the salt, sand, and brine applied by MnDOT at these temperatures.

THIRTY

Thanks to the slippery steps and roads, Pete and Martin were running nearly forty minutes late for their meeting with Elizabeth Frost. Pete called her cell to report their new expected time of arrival.

"I know exactly what you mean," Elizabeth said. "It's stop and go for me. I already called Michael and told him I'll be late. I'll speak with you whenever you arrive. Michael said that was fine. He is such a dear."

As soon as Pete hung up, Martin said, "What did I miss? Why did you tell Esther Lancaster you needed to use her restroom? I wouldn't have thought anything of it had you not said your bathroom is a pit. That will be the day." Martin shook his head.

"Lyle Kingston and Mattie Underwood gave us reasons to corner Bart."

"Right. Lyle thought Bart may have supplied Colette with heroin. Mattie could envision Bart killing her."

"Yes, and Esther seemed set on keeping us from speaking to him. Hated to miss him if he was home. Hoped to 'accidentally' run into him on my way to the bathroom."

Martin drove into the Union Depot ramp and looked for a parking space close to the elevators.

"Okay Martin, Ms. Frost said she'll sit near the maître d' table. She has shoulder-length, medium-brown hair and is wearing a red headband with a large red bow. That should narrow the field. Christos lunch buffet opens soon. Are you hungry?"

"Can you remember the last time I wasn't? I wonder if that's her, Pete." Martin pointed to a woman walking toward the elevators.

"Could be. I see her face, but that's no help. Don't know what she looks like. The hood on her jacket isn't helping. It could be hiding a headband and bow."

"The hood may not be helping you. I'm confident it's keeping her from freezing."

"Fair enough. Let's try to catch her."

To expedite things, Martin pulled into the first available parking spot. It took little effort. Either most folks remained home today or parked elsewhere.

As he shifted into park, the deafening *boom boom* of two gunshots rang out. The concrete structure magnified the reverberating sound. Both investigators knew the shots originated nearby and to their left.

Before Pete and Martin could get out of the car to search for the shooter and target, they heard an engine turn over and race, then squealing tires. A car on their left lurched from its parking spot and hurried toward the exit.

Out of the corner of his eye, Pete saw the woman they'd wanted to catch sink to the concrete. The red spot near her left shoulder heightened his concern. Grabbing the door handle, he said, "I'll check on her, Martin. Call it in and follow the Escalade."

"Go! Catch them!" the woman shouted as Pete exited the car. She waved him off. Back on her feet, she ducked behind a pillar. "Please, catch them."

Martin activated the lights and siren. As soon as Pete was back in the car, he threw it into reverse and raced after the fleeing Escalade.

Pete keyed the radio and requested an ambulance and backup. He felt torn between staying with the woman and chasing the shooter. Her request and the fact she'd gotten back on her feet decided it for him. Even so, he had mixed emotions.

The Escalade exceeded the posted limits. Even so, its speed indicated either the driver's fear of greater speed in this enclosed space or the absence of fear of a pursuer.

Pete took the loudspeaker and announced in a measured voice, "Police. Pull over. Get out of your car, hands in the air! Do what I say and you won't get hurt."

Martin took advantage of the plethora of open parking spaces. He edged up toward the driver's side of the SUV.

Another shot rang out. Martin heard the *boom*, followed by the tearing of metal and fabric.

"Dammit!" Pete muttered instantaneously with the sound.

"Where did they hit us?" Martin asked, slowing down.

Pete not only heard the gunshot. He felt it. The searing pain in his right arm left no doubt whether the bullet hit their car. He couldn't let that deter them. They had to catch the crazy in the Escalade who shot that woman. A shot of adrenaline helped distract him.

"Went through my door, Martin. Let's catch them."

"Are you okay?"

"I'm fine." Pete removed his Smith and Wesson from the holster. A shot of searing pain radiated from his shoulder. He felt the wet, warm sensation in the area spread. The warmth dissipated quickly, replaced by a cold, wet sensation. He barely noticed. The chase took precedence. Keying the mike he held in his left hand, he repeated the demand to the people in the Escalade.

The driver sped up and fired twice more at the unmarked car. Both shots connected with cement and ricocheted harmlessly off a few other surfaces.

Martin knew what to do. He accelerated.

Pete wouldn't be deterred. He and Martin focused on catching the Escalade. The growing patch of blood on Pete's overcoat failed to alarm him.

Concentrating on the driving and due to the obstructed view he had of his partner, Martin remained oblivious to Pete's injury.

Pete ignored the burst of pain he experienced while reaching for the button to lower his window. Before he would shoot, he looked for dangers of collateral damage. He saw none. He aimed for the left rear tire of the Escalade. He squeezed the trigger.

Pain engulfed Pete as the kickback sent blood oozing down his arm to his elbow. To avoid crying out, he bit his lip so hard it bled. Using his tongue, he instantaneously eliminated any sign of that damage.

Not losing sight of the mission, he said, "One down," as he watched the left side of the Escalade sink a few inches. "If you move just a bit to the right, I'll be in a better position to get the right rear, too."

Martin strained to understand. The deafening blare of the siren made it almost impossible. The echo off all this concrete didn't help.

Pete got the picture and motioned with his left hand. His right still gripped his Smith and Wesson.

While Martin maneuvered the car, Pete repeated the command ordering the driver of the Escalade to pull over.

The response? More gunshots.

Apparently that response distracted the driver. Missing the exit, he or she was forced to make another tour of the ramp.

Seeing that, Pete smiled. He preferred this contained chase. Repeating the steps preceding the last time he fired, he shot out the other rear tire. That drew a volley of gunfire from the Escalade. Thankfully, not one bullet entered the passenger compartment of the unmarked car.

Bracing his right arm against his abdomen, Pete leaned toward Martin. "Backup should be here any second," he yelled. "Pull further left. I'll aim for the front, driver's side tire."

Cupping a hand around his right ear, Martin indicated he didn't understand.

Using his left hand, Pete signaled the desired move.

Martin vigorously shook his head. He shut off the siren long enough to say, "Too dangerous. You'd be a sitting target."

Focused almost solely on one thing, Pete missed the unintended pun. "Stay back far enough, so I'm not," he said. "The driver has the gun. If we're back a ways, he can't drive and turn far enough to shoot me."

It made sense. Martin reactivated the siren then did as Pete, his commanding officer, instructed. Even so, Martin knew he'd find little consolation in that if Pete died due to this.

Turned out, Martin didn't have an opportunity to comply. Before he could, he saw the flashing lights of one, then two patrol cars in his rearview mirror.

Apparently the driver of the Escalade also saw them. He slammed on the brakes. The car rocked to a stop. The driver and passenger side doors flew open.

For the fifth time in half as many minutes, Pete ordered them to get out of the car with their hands in the air.

Martin and Pete opened their doors.

Pete waited until Martin's progress in getting out made it difficult for his partner to see him. He knew he couldn't hide his bullet wound from Martin much longer. But every minute moved them closer to apprehending the shooters. The shooters he still refused to pass off to anyone. Again holding his right arm tight to his abdomen, he reached across and opened his door with his left hand. His right arm hurt like a son of a gun. He'd limit the use and hopefully, minimize the pain and blood loss. The hospital could wait.

He had to apprehend the people in the Escalade, then check on the woman shot by the driver or the passenger. By all indications, the driver brandished the only gun. Was the woman okay? Was it Elizabeth Frost? If so, what did she have to do with the people in the Escalade? No one, other than he and Martin, knew about their planned meeting. If the woman was Frost, did it have something to do with this case? How could it? Did the woman Frost saw going to the ladies room with Hammond fear Frost would identify her? If so, how did they know when and where to find her? Pete needed to have answers to all those questions.

Getting out of an SUV without the use of your hands is a challenge. A gymnast might execute this move in seconds. Thanks to strong abdominal muscles, Pete would require an extra second or two. It would take Martin a minute or more. Thus far, the age group of the Escalade passengers remained in question. The speed at which they followed Pete's instructions indicated advanced age, sedentary lives, or both. Eventually, they wriggled their way out.

Pete and Martin observed this, standing behind their opened doors and using them as shields. Penetrable shields, Pete knew. His right arm offered painful proof of their inadequacy. Even so, under the circumstances, it was a matter of best available.

Both investigators wondered if anyone besides the two people standing in front of them occupied the Escalade. It seemed unlikely, but how many lost lives could be attributed to unlikely occurrences?

The people who'd exited the Escalade wore bulky, knee-length down jackets. The raised hoods hid much of their faces. They appeared to be a man and a woman, but the only hint of gender came from their heights and shoulder versus hip dimensions. Heaven knew that was no guarantee.

As Pete and Martin assessed the situation, four uniformed officers ran up and joined them, weapons drawn.

One of the two on Pete's side of the car said, "Okay if we … Commander, you're bleeding. We'll take it from here? You need medical attention."

Pete didn't require a reminder. It felt like his upper arm was on fire. For now, even with assistance from these officers, it couldn't take precedence. "I need to check on the woman back by the elevators," he said. "They shot her, setting this whole thing in motion. Hate to leave this to you, but anxious to know if she's okay."

"We have enough uniforms to handle this situation and three more just like it, sir!" With a gun in his right hand, saluting wasn't feasible. "We'll get them cuffed, so there's no danger of more gunfire. It'll only take a minute."

"Keep them here until we return, Sergeant. I want to get a look at their faces. I want to know what this is about."

Thirty-One

While watching the officers advance on the former occupants of the Escalade, Pete shifted his weight from foot to foot. This would have kept his blood circulating, but the adrenaline surge he still experienced already accomplished that.

He knew each of these officers. He'd met their spouses and kids. The kids still needed their mothers and fathers. All four of these officers put their lives on the line every time they put on their uniforms. Hours and hours of training helped. It didn't guarantee a safe outcome. The only way to do that? Shoot the two people. Pete knew all four of these officers valued life. He knew they wouldn't consider doing something like that. No one meriting the honor of wearing this uniform would.

Uncertainty loomed. Its weight felt stifling.

Pete wondered if it also weighed down the two people in down jackets. Had to, didn't it? If only he and his fellow officers knew what those people thought and felt right now. It would lift some of this tremendous weight. It would also reduce the wave of adrenaline that coursed through his veins. Intentionally or unintentionally, those two would dictate the outcome.

Pete also felt the weight of his guilt. He should be up there, participating. He shouldn't be back here, observing. The knowledge his right arm made that a stupid move provided no relief and little consolation.

Time stood still as the uniforms advanced. Pete's mind raced. He thought about the people who'd shot at Martin and him.

The reason was obvious. The looming question? Why did they shoot at the woman?

He grabbed his right shoulder, hoping applying pressure would diminish the pain. It didn't. He thought about putting his left hand under his right arm. The right one already occupied his left armpit. The result? Negligible warmth, but warmth nonetheless. The only other warmth he experienced came from the flow of fresh blood that accompanied each movement of his right arm. That warmth passed quickly. Pete wondered why his blood hadn't yet coagulated enough to stop this confounded bleeding.

One of the people from the Escalade said, "I'm freezing. I have to put my hands in my pockets."

"You have to keep your hands right where they are," the sergeant ordered.

"You don't understand."

"Keep your hands in the air!"

Pete prayed the person would do as instructed. The pockets might be empty. They might not. They might hold a gun.

The approaching officers had guns drawn. That was protocol. Shots were fired. Pete knew the time required to react to the appearance of a gun pretty well guaranteed the wounding or death of the officer.

He knew about auditory exclusion and optical affinity. These phenomena often occur in life-threatening situations. Both can distort the perceptions of anyone in a high-stress situation. One through auditory shutdown. The other through an increased ability to see things in the distance and a blurring or hiding of things happening nearby. Both can result in misperceptions.

Pete feared for the lives of the officers. He also feared for the lives of the two civilians. At the moment, each might perceive the other as having the advantage.

The civilian who'd spoken started hopping from foot to foot.

That raised Pete's anxiety level. He figured the four uniformed officers and Martin reacted similarly. Pete continued a version of the same action, striving to warm up. Observing someone they feared doing it felt different. Did it indicate an impending defensive move?

Thankfully, the civilians stood on both sides of the Escalade. That made any private, verbal communication impossible.

Fanning out, the advancing officers hastened to close the distance, approaching from three sides. While the two on the outer edges of this semicircle kept their guns trained on the people from the Escalade, the two in the center holstered theirs. They needed both hands. Working quickly, each of these officers reached up and grabbed a wrist of one of the down-clad people. Yanking that arm down and behind the person's back, they fought layers of clothing to snap on the handcuff. Achieving that for one wrist, each repeated the process for the second. Eventually, both people were handcuffed, hands behind their backs.

During this process, the larger of the two, the driver, grunted as the officer yanked his or her arms behind their back. The other remained silent.

The two officers with guns drawn advanced cautiously from the driver's and passenger sides of the Escalade. One job remained. While approaching, they looked through the tinted windows for any sign of an additional passenger. Someone with a gun could be crouched there. The tinted windows complicated their efforts. Using their free hand, each officer grabbed a door handle and struggled to open the door. Both had the gun in their dominant hand, making this awkward. Throwing the back doors open, they double checked their work. "Clear," both announced.

Exhaling a cloud of steam, Pete realized he'd been holding his breath. "Let's check on that woman, Martin," he said.

Pete holstered his gun. Using his left hand, he pinned his right arm to his abdomen. One or both of those acts sent a new burst of warmth gushing down his right arm. Otherwise ignoring it, he grimaced and sprinted toward the elevators and the woman.

That move placed Martin on Pete's right side. Martin saw the right sleeve of Pete's overcoat and felt a burst of anger and fear. Anger that Pete lied to him. Scared because Pete had obviously lost a lot of blood. How was the man still standing and moving that fast? Martin ran after Pete. Despite Pete's condition, the distance between them grew.

Just before he reached the woman, Pete saw the crew lift the gurney into the ambulance. "How is she?" he asked.

"Doesn't look too bad. Hey, what about you?" the paramedic asked, seeing Pete's right sleeve. "Let me take a look at it. We need to stop that bleeding."

"It's nothing. Take care of her. I'll get it checked out, shortly."

"I'm not leaving before I put a tourniquet around it. Unbutton your overcoat, so I can get a look."

"Seriously, I'll be to Regions in a few minutes."

"At this rate, you might not be conscious in a few minutes."

Pete decided to stop wasting time arguing. Using his left hand, he unbuttoned his overcoat.

Martin arrived, panting, as the paramedic folded back the overcoat and got a better idea of the location where the bullet did the damage.

Moving to Pete's right and in close, Martin got a better look. "Are you crazy?" he yelled. "Is a bleed out your goal? Wondering how it feels? Look at your sleeve. It's drenched in blood all the way to the elbow! You said you were fine."

"And I am. It's just a surface wound. They always bleed like crazy."

"I'm going to put a tourniquet over your suit coat," the paramedic interrupted. "It'll stem the bleeding. It will also immobilize your right arm. Let it! If you don't, this isn't going to help."

Completing that task, the paramedic took a couple of warm blankets from the ambulance and wrapped them around Pete. "You need to stay warm. This will help, but not enough and not for long. Keep them around you until you get to the hospital."

Turning to Martin, the paramedic added, "Get him to Regions, *now*. Do you *understand*?"

"I need to ask her a question," Pete indicated the woman in the ambulance. "It'll just take a second."

"Make it quick. Or if you ride along, you can ask her several questions."

"One will suffice for now."

The paramedic opened the rear door.

Pete leaned in and asked, "Ma'am are you Elizabeth Frost?"

She nodded. "I'm supposed to meet someone. Would you please go to Christos and look for two men? They should be the only two there, if you do it right away." Looking at the paramedic, she asked. "Where are you taking me?"

"Regions."

Looking back at Pete, she added "Please tell them they can find me at Regions."

"You already told them, Elizabeth. I'm Peter Culnane."

"Pete, do you want me to get the car and pick you up here?" Martin asked.

"About as much as I want to check out the water temperature of the Mississippi by diving in," Pete said on his way to the car. The words were barely out before he realized that could be the best way to stop the bleeding and the throbbing in his arm.

"Where are you going? Get in the car!" Martin yelled as Pete continued past the unmarked car and toward the Escalade.

"In a minute," Pete said over his shoulder.

THIRTY-TWO

Martin sped along Sibley, slowing slightly to take a left on 10th Street. He accelerated, then moved his foot from the gas pedal to the brake to take a right onto Jackson. Pete's silence alarmed him. His driving had exposed Pete's side of the car to gunfire. Martin sped through the yellow light on 11th Street and glanced both ways before running the red light on 12th Street. A second later he turned right at the emergency entrance to Regions. Concluding a driving exposition that would have made Michelle shudder, he pulled up to the emergency department door.

He looked over at Pete.

Pete's eyes remained shut. His face looked gray. "I'll be right back," he said, opening the car door.

Martin's jaw dropped when Pete opened his eyes and said, "No need. I'll walk."

"Like hell! Sit tight. I'll be right back."

Martin slammed the door and ran through the sliding glass doors to the registration desk.

"I'm a police officer," he gasped. "My partner was shot. He's still in the car. I need help! He's lost a lot of blood!"

The receptionist reacted as Martin had hoped. Two men wearing scrubs and jackets, and guiding a gurney arrived instantly. The receptionist said, "This officer's …"

"Follow me," Martin interrupted. "My partner was shot. He needs help *now*!" Without waiting for a response, Martin turned and ran back to the car.

The men hurried to keep up.

Pete sat in the unmarked, eyes closed, head tilted back.

Martin opened the passenger door slowly. Discovering it didn't support Pete's weight, he threw it open. "Pete, we've got a gurney. We'll get you out."

Pete didn't respond in any detectable manner.

"Back up. We'll handle it."

Somehow the men in scrubs maneuvered Pete out of the car and onto the gurney in a few swift moves.

When they did this, Martin noticed the blankets the paramedic wrapped around Pete while they were still in the ramp. The one he could see was bloody.

As soon as the scrubs-clad men had Pete strapped in place, they moved with lightening speed to get him inside and settled into a room.

This time, Martin ran to keep up. He wasn't sure the place they took Pete qualified as a room. The only thing separating it from the next bed was floor to ceiling curtains.

A nurse arrived immediately and obtained Pete's medical history.

Pete answered all the questions, eyes closed.

Martin knew he could have provided the information had Pete been unconscious. There was nothing to tell. His partner was amazingly healthy.

The nurse was still working on Pete's medical history when the doctor arrived.

The doctor interrupted, introducing herself and saying, "I understand you took a bullet in the right upper arm. Are you right-handed?"

Pete nodded.

"I have everything I need for now," the nurse said.

"I'll help you sit and remove everything waist up, so I can get a look," the doctor told Pete.

Pete sat up before the doctor had a chance to help.

Martin was floored at the amount of blood he saw.

After asking the nurse to get some warm blankets, the doctor instructed Pete to do his best to keep his right arm tight to his chest. She carefully removed the clothing separating her from the wound, providing a running commentary as she worked. "I'm looking for the source of the bleed. Okay, I see the problem. You have a venous bleed. That means a vein was severed. You're either very lucky or unlucky. A centimeter to the right, the bullet might have ripped your clothes, but not touched you. A centimeter to the left, it would have hit the humerus, that is, the upper arm bone. Had that happened, you'd be on your way to surgery."

Pete lay silently, eyes closed. His only response was a wince as she examined the bullet wound. He was far luckier than the doctor realized, he thought. The bullet went through his door as he twisted to his right and leaned forward a bit to pull his notepad out of the right rear pocket of his trousers. That move, in combination with his long legs, possibly protected areas far more vulnerable than his humerus. A miracle? Possibly. He was also grateful for the shooter's limited skills.

Martin watched, dreading and anxious to see the damage. He didn't have a good angle, but it looked like the bullet took a chunk out of Pete's upper arm several inches below his shoulder.

The doctor continued her monologue. "I'm going to tie off that vein."

She hadn't completed that before a lab tech appeared.

"Do a trauma panel and blood type," the doctor said.

Martin cringed when the tech used Pete's left arm and filled vials with his partner's already short supply of blood.

As soon as the doctor and lab tech completed their work, a nurse wrapped two warm blankets around Pete.

Pete smiled and, for the first time in hours, relaxed a bit. He welcomed the warmth.

Martin saw the smile and exhaled a long, slow breath. "Will he be okay?" he asked the doctor.

She nodded. "Surprised he hasn't gone into hypovolemic shock due to the blood loss. Even so, he should show a marked improvement after the transfusions. We'll keep him here in a red room for the transfusions. Then I'll admit him."

Pete's eyes shot open. That last remark got his attention. He remained silent, deciding he'd do so until after the transfusion.

Martin observed that too. He knew exactly what it meant. He was confident the doctor was in for a fight when she attempted to admit Pete. If that didn't happen, Pete must be at death's doorstep.

If the doctor caught Pete's reaction or understood, she let it pass. "I'll be back shortly," she said. "As soon as we get the test results, we'll begin the transfusion. Meanwhile, nurse, let's start an IV and administer lactated ringers solution."

Martin thought about going to check on Elizabeth Frost, but decided to stay put. It bothered him that, despite the blankets and room temperature, Pete's color remained unchanged.

Before Martin could reconsider the decision about Ms. Frost, the doctor returned.

"I have your blood type. You're common in that respect. It's A positive. Nurse, transfuse two units of packed red cells."

Martin couldn't watch the nurse follow those instructions. Instead, he concentrated on Pete's face. He saw nothing. No reaction. No indication of pain. No impatience. Nothing at all.

While the nurse inserted the IV, the doctor told Pete, "There shouldn't be any permanent damage. Keep your arm in the sling for at least five days. That means five, *not* three. Get an okay from your primary care doctor before you stop using the sling. Otherwise, you could extend the recovery time. Are we clear on that?"

Pete nodded.

Looking at Martin, she said, "I hope you'll remind him, should he decide to ignore my instructions."

"I will, for what it's worth," Martin shrugged.

"How long will the transfusion and this IV take?" Pete asked.

"Four hours, give or take," the doctor said. Looking at Martin, she asked, "Will you stay?"

Martin shook his head. "I have a few things I need to accomplish." He bent over Pete and said, "I'll be back in three hours. I'm going to headquarters to get some answers from our friends in the Escalade, get a replacement for my unmarked car, and work on reports. If you finish, before I return, call, okay?"

Not bothering to open his eyes, Pete nodded.

Thirty-Three

Beginning to end, the time in the emergency department took a bit more than five hours. It was four thirty when the doctor instructed the nurse to take Pete to the room she'd arranged for him.

By then Pete looked and acted more like himself.

That took a load off Martin.

"I appreciate all everyone here did for me," Pete said. "I'd like to follow your instructions, but I must leave *now*. I have a case to solve. People are depending on me. I'm fine. I can't afford to lie around at a time like this."

"I'd like to admit you, claiming you haven't the capacity to make an informed decision," the doctor said, shaking a finger at Pete.

Martin gulped, knowing what attempting that would accomplish. "I advise against …" he began.

"I know," the doctor interrupted, throwing her hands up in the air. "Much as I'd like to, I won't take it on. Listen carefully, Mr. Culnane. If you walk out that door, you're doing it against medical advice. Am I making myself perfectly clear? Do you understand what that means? Imagine how Commander Lincoln will react when he hears about it."

Pete nodded. "May I take these blankets if I promise to launder and return them? It's a bit chilly outside to go topless. Otherwise, where are my shirt, suit coat, and overcoat?"

"If you wait until tomorrow, your friend can bring some clean clothes."

"Again, I don't want to seem ungrateful. I'll sleep better at home." *Also less likely to pick up an infection there*, Pete thought.

Attempting to assist the doctor, Martin said, "Commander Lincoln said he'd better not see you again today, Pete."

Pete shrugged. Not exactly what he'd hoped to hear. "Home it is," he said, admitting only to himself he'd welcome an opportunity to recuperate overnight before jumping back into this investigation.

"As long as you understand you're leaving against medical advice."

"Got it. Do I need to sign something to that effect?"

The doctor shook her head and waved him off. "If you experience any problems tonight, I want you right back here. If necessary, call an ambulance. Understand?"

"Sure do."

Pete almost got his way with a second item. Before leaving Regions, he insisted on finding and talking to Elizabeth Frost.

"In that garb, Pete? You'll freak her out."

"She withstood a gunshot wound. She can handle this."

Martin hoped Pete would limit it to a social visit and save the questioning for later. He got his way.

When they found her, Elizabeth Frost lay sound asleep.

Martin warmed up the car, then returned for Pete and accompanied him from a warm building to a chilly car.

"Are you going to call Katie, Pete?"

"Eventually. I'll drag my feet while I warm up and unwind. Katie and my family worry more about me these days. I hate to fuel the fire."

Martin thought of a comeback, but decided this wasn't the time.

"Could Michelle cope if you got shot and remained a cop, Martin?"

"She knows I'm in for the long haul."

"Tell me, Martin, when you saw the blood on my overcoat, did you think, even for a minute, about quitting?"

"All I thought about was getting you to a hospital. Other than that, I think this is partially my fault. Had I handled things differently, they may not have gotten off a shot at you."

"You're right. We should have sat there and watched them drive away. We wouldn't have been doing our jobs, but we would have protected ourselves. I know neither of us is that kind of cop. If you were, I'd have to find a different partner. I'm home. Let's continue this later. Just one more thing, Martin. I refuse to think about you being killed. I couldn't forgive myself, even if there was no way for me to prevent it."

"You'd never let that happen, Pete. But there could come a time when circumstances are beyond your control …"

"I don't want to talk about it."

"Me neither, I'll walk you in."

"That's not necessary."

"Yes, it is."

Martin helped Pete change into sweats and fixed him something to eat. "Call me when you get up, okay? I want to know how you're doing."

"Sure."

"I mean it. Tell me you will."

"I'll call when I've been up long enough to do an assessment."

On the heels of that assurance, Martin returned to headquarters.

After the events of today, he wondered if, by some miracle, he might recruit the right help and wrap up this case before he and Michelle left for Rochester. If so, he could leave town with a clear conscience.

THIRTY-FOUR

Pete loved Martin like a brother, but was glad when he left. He felt exhausted.

He thought about calling Katie. The media was right there in the middle of things at the Union Depot parking ramp before he and Martin escaped. He had his attention focused elsewhere. With modern equipment, you no longer knew what they filmed. He should call Katie in case his face made the evening news. Actually he should call his grandmother, his mother, and Katie. They all watched the news on TV. He had to be proactive and assure all of them that he was fine. He just needed to relax a minute, first.

He sat in the recliner a minute—and fell asleep. He awoke with a start when the phone rang. Without thinking, without remembering, still in a fog, he reached for it with his right hand. That sent a burning pain through his arm. Wide awake, he answered on the third ring.

"Pete, are you okay?" His grandmother sounded panicky.

"I'm just fine, Grandma."

"Are you sure? You wouldn't lie to your grandmother, would you?"

"No, Grandma, I'm smarter than that." Pete glanced at the clock. Ten after five. The sun set thirty minutes ago. The only light in his living room came from the street lamp out front.

"If you were fine, you wouldn't be home. When working a case, you're never home this early."

"Did you watch the news? Is that why you called?" Pete wanted to know what, if anything, was said on the newscast. Knowing that would arm him for his conversations with Katie and his mother.

"Yes. They said a police officer was shot. They didn't give your name, but I recognized you, of course. Tell me what happened, Pete."

He knew only the complete and accurate story would do. He concluded with, "The bullet only grazed my upper arm. No significant damage. Martin took me to the hospital." Stretching the truth a bit, he added, "They cleaned me up and sent me home. I'll be back at work tomorrow."

"I would love to ask you to get a job selling suits at Penney's, but I know you love your job, Pete."

"I do, Grandma. This was a fluke. There's no need to worry about me. Seriously." Pete knew from her voice that she was rattled. He wondered what that meant when it came to his mother. She'd always been less enamored with his career choice. "I'm going to see you tomorrow. You'll see for yourself that I'm just fine."

"I can't wait to go to Martin's. It will be such fun. And Pete, you hold a special place in my heart."

What she didn't say, but Pete heard anyway was, and I don't know what I'd do without you.

"I feel the same about you, Grandma." He meant that in all respects.

One down, Pete thought. Better call before they hear anything—head them off at the pass.

He didn't have the opportunity. As he thought that, the phone rang again. The caller ID said it was his mother.

"Pete, what happened? Are you okay?"

"Yeah, Mom. I'm fine. What did you hear?"

"I heard a police officer was shot and saw footage of you with blood on your overcoat. I don't know what else was said. I grabbed the phone and called."

"Regions put a Band-Aid on it and sent me home. That's all there is to it."

"Pete, you need to rethink your job. You're getting married. You want kids. Those kids deserve to have a father. Don't you agree?"

"I agree with the kids part, Mom, but not with your feelings about my job. When my time is up, it's up. A UPS deliveryman died of a gunshot in an incident where not one police officer was even injured. Very few of my fellow officers are ever injured, much less killed. I'm not quitting, Mom."

There was a long silence on the other end of the line.

"I love you, Mom. Gotta go. I have another call."

And it couldn't have come at a better time, he thought. This time it was Katie. *Three for three*. He worried what this one would bring. He thought it would more closely resemble the conversation with his grandmother than the one with his mother. He hoped he was right.

"Hi, Katie."

"Some people will go to great lengths to get their face in front of a camera, Pete. Didn't realize you're one of them."

"What can I say?"

"Just that you're fine."

"I am fine, Katie. It's nothing."

"I'm relieved. I'm on my way to the car. I'll be there in ten minutes."

"Katie, seriously, there's no need."

"Not for you, perhaps. Please, Pete, I need to see and touch your face. Channel four scared me out of ten years."

"I'm fine, but it would be nice to see you," Pete admitted.

Katie let herself in. She found Pete in the living room in his recliner. Before saying a word, she carefully examined his face. The strain of the afternoon was written in the lines on his forehead.

"Satisfied?" he asked, smiling at her.

"Yes! Is there a way for me to hug you without causing excruciating pain?"

"It's excruciatingly painful any time you hug or kiss me." Pete smiled. "You can limit the damage by steering clear of my right side."

Katie drew a line down the center of Pete's chest and promised not to cross it. She gave him a long, tender hug, without venturing into the forbidden area. Then she kissed him on the cheek.

"Thanks for letting me come over. I feel so much better. Dare I ask how the case is coming along?"

"Made a lot of progress today."

"Enough progress to make someone nervous? Someone who just happened to have a gun handy?"

"Perceptive. Apparently so. Haven't yet had a chance to talk to them."

"I'm hoping to learn enough to become your next partner, once Martin is promoted to chief."

"Martin will be happy to hear your high opinion of him. Katie, you've already gotten the job as my next partner, just not in the police department."

"Oh, yeah. True." She chuckled. "The interview process was excruciating. Thought I might be passed over for another applicant."

"There weren't any other applicants, Katie."

"Oh? Guess the proposal wasn't the victory I'd allowed myself to believe."

"Guess not."

"However, I continue discovering the prize is even better than I'd suspected."

"You're a silver-tongued devil, Katie."

"And proud of it." Katie laughed. "You're not putting me on when you say you're fine, are you, Pete? I value your honesty."

"I have to wear this sling for five days or so. That and the fact the doctor said I can't ski for two weeks are the worst parts. The good news is I now have a battle scar. I can walk around in sleeveless shirts, or no shirt, and show it off."

"Did anyone ever tell you that you're crazy?"

"More people that you'd like to know."

Pete and Katie moved to the couch.

Katie sat on his left side.

Pete fell asleep propped up against her.

She dozed off and on, mostly off, and spent much of the night thinking.

THIRTY-FIVE

Sitting there, alongside the love of her life, Katie worried. Despite Pete's assurances, she worried. She found it impossible not to. The current anti-cop sentiments angered her. *Walk a mile in his shoes*, she thought. Work day and night to find answers for a grieving family. She'd spend the rest of her life worrying about this guy. It was inevitable. And she wouldn't trade him for a thousand guys with mundane lives.

She'd felt attracted to Pete the first time she met him—when she was the victim of a hit-and-run. He came riding in on his trusty steed, assured her he'd find the person who did it, and fulfilled his promise. He was patient, understanding, and kind. He listened to what she said and cared how she felt. It didn't hurt that he was gorgeous. Tall, slender, muscular, with the most beautiful brown eyes and head of thick brown hair.

Back then, she'd struggled to mask her feelings. For all she knew, he was married, but didn't wear a ring. He'd concluded the investigation, and that was the end of it. She didn't see him again. That didn't stop her from thinking about him.

One day, she heard a deep voice that sounded so much like him. She'd spun around, hoping to have a chance to say "hi." She'd felt so deflated when he wasn't back there.

Her life changed dramatically eighteen months ago when they crossed paths in the skyway. Well, their paths didn't exactly cross. She smiled. As was her habit, she'd spent her lunch hour logging her daily walk in the St. Paul skyways. It proved to be a red-letter day. She remembered every detail. Relished every detail.

Hearing a familiar voice call her name, a voice that sounded like Pete's, she'd stopped dead in the skyway. When she did, the guy behind her plowed into her and sent her flying. Somehow Pete caught her before she landed on the floor.

Her heart had raced, and it wasn't due to the near collision with the floor. She couldn't think about it without smiling. Pete had lifted her to her feet then clutched her arms just a second or two longer than necessary—long enough to make her swoon.

She'd done everything in her power to mask that. She'd still thought the attraction went one way only. She didn't want to embarrass herself.

The first hint that he might be attracted to her came a minute after he walked away. She was standing there, still smiling, when he stopped and looked back at her.

Not hearing from him, she'd decided her optimism was unfounded. She'd stopped hoping and waiting. She'd given up on him.

Then one day, he'd called. She'd never forget it. She felt ecstatic. She couldn't believe it.

On their first date, he'd invited her and his homeless friend, Doc, to his home and fixed dinner. They'd celebrated solving the case of a murdered homeless man. She'd instantly felt comfortable with Pete. She felt like she'd known him forever. He was so straightforward, so unassuming. So real.

Over the past eighteen months, she'd gotten to know him. The bonds had strengthened. She'd thought he loved her. He even talked about having kids, but it took a year for him to pop the question. He waited long enough for her to doubt he ever would. At one point, she wondered if he might ask her to move in with him, then decided he was too old fashioned to do that. Turned out she was right.

Did she wish he wasn't a cop? Yes and no. She was convinced that Pete was who he was in part because he was a cop. She didn't think you could separate the man from the job. They were one and the same. She loved hearing the stories. She loved the way each case energized Pete.

She understood that. She, too, was an adrenaline junkie. Pete discovered that the first time they skied together. Both her speed and the way she attacked the hill gave it away.

Did she wish Pete had regular hours? What wife or girlfriend didn't? It wasn't going to happen until he reached mandatory retirement. Would she ask him to switch careers? Never!

Pete always had a project going, even though his job typically prolonged the completion. She knew he'd find a hundred ways to fill the hours after retirement. He loved to run and to ski. He'd never transition into a couch potato. She wondered if he'd become a private investigator. They'd never discussed their post PD lives. That seemed so distant. She, for one, was wrapped up in the here and now—more specifically, the wedding plans part of it.

She'd hesitated to mention a formal wedding. Pete had been through all of that already. His first wife died when her car was struck by a drunk driver. Pete rarely consumed alcohol. That, at least in part, was the reason.

She was thrilled when Pete mentioned the need to get the planning underway for the wedding. She knew he'd gladly forego the formalities and mentioned it because he believed that's what she wanted. That was typical. He was so selfless.

She was thirty-two when she and Pete began dating. She'd dated a lot over the last fifteen years. A few times, she'd even fallen in love—at least she thought it was love at the time. In retrospect, it was infatuation. It lacked the depth of her relationship with Pete.

When Pete proposed, she'd said "yes" without giving it a thought. It was what she wanted—what she dared not hope for.

She hadn't wondered or worried if it was the right decision. She was head over heels. He was a rare prize. She was so lucky. She was so glad for the hit-and-run that led to their meeting. She wondered if it was fate.

Why was Pete working that case? Why did they meet, by accident, in the skyway? She hadn't a clue. She was eternally grateful.

She smiled at Pete and fell asleep.

At five in the morning, she woke up, stood carefully to avoid rousing Pete, gathered her things, and drove home. She thought about staying, but decided Pete would have enough to deal with when he woke up and didn't need any distraction. Another man might need her help. Not Pete. Definitely not Pete.

Thirty-Six

Pete didn't run on Sunday morning. He thought about it. Hated to break his pattern. The throbbing in his arm decided it. He figured keeping it pulled in tight while he ran was a bad idea. Tomorrow, he hoped.

His unmarked car sat in the lot at headquarters. This morning he'd drive his own car. First, he called Martin, said he felt fine and would see Martin at headquarters.

Martin protested.

Pete repeated he'd see him at headquarters.

"Don't forget the Oxycodone they gave you. At this rate, you're definitely going to need it."

Pete appreciated the reminder. He grabbed both the Tylenol and Oxycodone and headed out.

Despite the time saved by skipping his run, he arrived at headquarters close to the usual time. It took time to put antiseptic and a new bandage on his arm. It took even longer to button his shirt, and tie his tie before slipping it over his head and adjusting the knot. He congratulated himself when he succeeded in pulling his feet in and up close enough to tie his shoes with his arm still resting in the sling.

Heck, the contortionist he saw climb into a sixteen-inch cube with a basketball on a YouTube video had nothing on him. Okay, fine. This didn't quite compete with that. He smiled. Combined, all those things took almost as much energy as a four-mile run.

Too bad Martin wasn't here to observe him following at least one of the doctor's instructions to a T, he thought. He had to. Couldn't let this slow him down for long. Had a case to solve. Had to talk to Elizabeth Frost and the people in the Escalade.

He railed at the thought of walking into headquarters wearing the sling, but decided to bite the bullet. Thinking of it that way made him laugh out loud.

"Is that your badge of honor, Commander?" one investigator quipped when he arrived.

"No, it's his Halloween costume, only he's two months late. Still hasn't mastered the calendar on his cell," another announced.

"Go easy on him. He has a booboo."

"I heard the only thing affected was his overcoat. Is that why you're wearing the jacket you bought at the Goodwill thrift store, Pete?"

Pete smiled and kept his mouth shut. Any comeback would only encourage them.

He called Regions Hospital and checked on Elizabeth Frost. He hoped she could shed some light on yesterday's events in the ramp.

He got an answer to the first question. Yes, they could visit her.

As he hung up, Martin greeted him with, "Glad you decided to sleep in this morning. How do you feel?"

"Been better, been worse. What did you do yesterday after you dropped me off? Did you go right home?" Pete felt confident he knew the answer, but asked anyway.

"No, I came here just long enough to learn the Lancasters, our friends in the Escalade, lawyered up, and there's no match for Bart's fingerprints in the Criminal Justice Information Services."

"Yeah? I heard. I'd hoped for a few breaks. Elizabeth Frost is up to visitors. Let's see if she saw their faces and recognized them. Maybe she knows why they shot her."

"And maybe she'll tell us the woman is the woman who went into the ladies room with Colette Hammond. That way, we can wrap up both cases before noon."

On their way out of headquarters, Pete recruited two investigators to canvas the Lancaster neighborhood. Before questioning them, he wanted to know if anyone saw them after noon on New Year's Eve. If no one did, it didn't mean they'd gone to Iowa. It might only mean they'd bothered to create an alibi.

THIRTY-SEVEN

Elizabeth Frost looked wide awake when the two investigators arrived. She looked up from the St. Paul *Pioneer Press* and said, "You're Pete Culnane, aren't you? I was a little foggy when you introduced yourself yesterday, but your picture is in the paper. I didn't notice all the blood on your sleeve yesterday. I hope you're okay."

"I just had a surface wound. I'm doing great. I'm wearing this," he pointed at the sling, "to get sympathy."

That'll be the day, Martin thought.

"Thanks for being there, Mr. Culnane. You saved my life! You, too," she said, looking at Martin.

Or perhaps we're the reason someone shot at you, Pete thought. "This is my partner, Martin Tierney. How about you, Elizabeth? How are you feeling?"

"Much better than yesterday. They took me right into surgery and removed the bullet. I saw the surgeon after I came out from under the anesthesia. He said the bullet didn't do any serious damage, but I won't be able to work for a while. I won't be able to lift anything, much less carry trays of food." She frowned.

"My nurse got me a newspaper. It says the people who did it were in a Cadillac Escalade. I don't know anyone who drives an Escalade. My friends all have cars like Nissan Versas, Ford Fiestas, Kia Rios, cars in that price range."

"Did you see them when they drove up? Get even a glimpse?" Pete asked.

"No. I saw the car parked there. It surprised me that they shut the engine off and stayed in the car. It was so cold. I guess that's why they had their hoods up. The hoods made it impossible to see them."

Pete could attest to that.

Pete changed to the topic of New Year's Eve at Christos. "We understand you know Colette Hammond."

"Yes. She's a regular. Guess I should say she was, huh? She was always very nice. Never complained and a great tipper."

"You saw her go into the ladies room shortly before midnight?"

"Yes. Ordinarily, I wouldn't have noticed or remembered. Only did, because the timing surprised me."

"What time was it?"

"Can't really say. I only know it was getting close to midnight. So many people were ordering champagne, preparing for midnight."

"But they probably started doing that ten, fifteen, even twenty minutes, before midnight. Does that sound reasonable?"

"Totally. No one wanted to risk not being ready."

Martin took a turn. "When you saw her, was Colette alone?"

"No. Like I told the police that night, there was someone with her."

"Were they together or just going to the ladies room about the same time?"

"It looked like they were together. They were chatting."

"Can you describe the second woman?" Martin asked, hoping she'd had a revelation since early New Year's morning.

Elizabeth frowned and shook her head. "I can't help there. Like I told the police that night, I only recognized Colette, because I knew her so well. We were so busy that night. My mind was on filling orders and keeping the guests satisfied."

Seeking any detail that might narrow the field, Pete asked. "Does anything stand out about the other woman?"

"Well, one thing both stands out and doesn't stand out. She had her coat on. It doesn't really stand out, because she wasn't the only guest wearing a coat. Some women are chilly at temperatures that have the wait staff sweating up a storm. I guess it's because we never stop moving."

Not willing to let this go quite yet, Pete continued his search. "Do you remember if her coat was buttoned or open?"

Again, Elizabeth frowned and shook her head.

"Did the color of the coat stand out?"

"No. Sorry."

"Was it down?"

"I don't remember much about it, but I would remember if it was down. The reception was formal. Despite the weather, women came in dressier coats. No down."

"Then you assumed she was one of the guests? You didn't think she'd come from another location in the depot?"

"I definitely thought that. I'm not sure why. Perhaps because she wore heels, not boots, I noticed that when she turned to say something to Colette and stepped on my foot."

"Was she your height?"

"She must have been several inches shorter than me. Her shoes had four-and-three-quarter-inch stiletto heels. I excused myself. She looked at me, then walked away."

"Do you remember her eye color?"

"No. It was a fleeting glance. I didn't really look at her. I hurried off to deliver the drinks and take another order. I honestly don't know why I thought she was at the party. I just did. I'm sorry. I wish I could be more helpful."

"You were mighty specific about the height of her heels," Pete said.

"That's because, as she walked away, I saw the red soles of her shoes and recognized them. They were Christian Louboutin's Kate pumps. I saw that shoe one day at the Mall of America. I was walking through Nordstrom's, and it jumped right out of the display and into my hand. Okay, that's an exaggeration. It was gorgeous. I knew I had to have those shoes, until I looked at the price tag. Six-hundred-seventy-five dollars. Can you imagine? I put it down oh-so-carefully. Didn't want to risk damaging it."

"Please, give us as many details as you can about those shoes."

"I recall all the details. They're black patent leather. As I mentioned, the soles are red, there is also a red line on the top of the shoe, bordering the sole, and another on the heel. It's a very bright red. Jumps right out at you. Do I sound like an ad?" She smiled.

"Thankfully, yes," Pete said, doing his best to take notes with his left hand. Grateful Martin was doing likewise.

"Just a minute," Elizabeth said. "I'll bet I can find them on the Nordstrom's website." She picked up her phone. Her fingers danced across the face of it for a minute or so before she smiled and said, "Here they are." She held the phone out to Pete.

Pete saw the shoes on the page matched Elizabeth's description.

Handing the phone back, he asked her to text him the image of the shoe.

Exiting Regions Hospital, Pete said, "Let's not talk to the Lancasters quite yet. I'd like to wait and see if the people canvassing their neighborhood come up with anything."

Martin nodded. The response was difficult to see. He had his shoulders raised in a futile attempt to guard against a modicum of the cold air.

"Thought we could take a coffee break."

Martin's eyes went wide. This was a first. While immersed in an investigation, they missed as many meals as they ate.

Pete's idea of a coffee break would be Martin's next surprise.

THIRTY-EIGHT

As Arctic cold descended on the Twin Cities, Pete worried that his friend Doc might not have a place to stay when it arrived. What could he do to help? Time was running out.

"I'll give you directions to this new place. I'm sure you'll love it," Pete told Martin.

They drove through downtown St. Paul to Seventh Street and went west. As they neared the Assumption Church, Pete said, "Start looking for a parking place."

"Where are we going?"

"Reaching Out. At least some people should still be there from breakfast. They're staying open, so people don't have to wait outside and freeze between meals. I'm hoping to find Doc. I want to know his plans for Monday, Tuesday, and Wednesday. Since he has an aversion to sleeping in a shelter, I want to make sure he has the bases covered."

"What if he doesn't?"

"When I heard the forecast, I started working to find the best solution. The timing is horrible. If this Arctic front had moved in last week or next week, it would be far easier. Here's the situation. I hope to provide a place for Doc to sleep, while this front is driving temperatures into the hazardous range."

Martin bit his lip, convinced he knew what this meant to him and his family.

"I understand if you're unwilling to have Doc stay at your house, especially while you and Michelle are gone. If I hadn't met him, I'm sure I'd feel that way, too, Martin. You have no connection to Doc. This is my cause. It isn't fair to dump it in your lap. I won't do that. The problem is, it will still affect our plans."

Martin's heart sank.

"If Doc is willing," Pete continued, "I'll take him to my house. I'll spend some time helping Grandma with your kids. Then I'll go home. I know both you and Grandma planned on me spending the night at your house. I wouldn't hesitate to stick with that plan and let Doc stay at my house. The problem is, I don't think it would be fair to Doc. It would be so cold, no pun intended. If I did that he'd probably leave and spend the night outside. I couldn't live with that."

"You can't save the world, Pete."

"I'm not nearly that altruistic. I'm not talking about turning my home into a homeless shelter. I'm just trying to take care of one guy."

Martin rubbed the back of his neck and thought. "I trust you, and I trust your judgment. I'll tell you what. I'll discuss this with Michelle."

"Like I said, Martin, this is my cause."

"I'll talk to Michelle."

Martin found a parking place, and Pete asked, "Do you want to come with me or wait here?"

Staying meant an opportunity to work on his matrix, his case tracking device—the device that seemed little more than a time drain in this case. If he waited in the car, he'd have to leave it running. That would use gasoline. Gasoline didn't combust as efficiently at these temperatures. Marty's mission to save the polar bears made an impression on Martin. "I'll come with," he said.

Walking the two blocks, Martin wondered how a homeless person slept outdoors in these temperatures. Despite his gloves lined with Thinsulate, the brainchild of 3M, his fingers were frozen. He looked over at Pete.

Aside from the fact that he had his jacket clenched beneath his chin, Pete looked comfortable. His rapid gait indicated nothing. Pete always walked fast enough to make it difficult for Martin to keep up. Today, Martin was happy he had to jog. It meant less time out here.

Martin followed Pete through the double doors and to the right.

Pete walked in front of the serving counter and scanned the room.

Doc wasn't there.

Pete sighed. He didn't give up. He saw a guy who made a practice of eating with Doc a couple of years ago. In fact, this guy, Stew, was the person who showed him the ropes and introduced him to Doc.

Back then, in an effort to appear homeless, Pete always changed before going to Reaching Out. He wore jeans and a T-shirt. The manager told him the way the patrons dressed ran the gamut. Even so, he'd stuck with the jeans.

Doc was the only person from Reaching Out, aside from the manager who, to the best of Pete's knowledge, ever learned he was a cop. Doc may have told the others. He doubted it.

He realized his dress slacks and shoes were a radical departure from the way he looked the last time he was here. *Forget it*, he told himself. Tell them you got a job.

Stew glanced up from a magazine as Pete approached. Seeing Pete, he stood, walked to him, and extended a hand. Noticing Pete's empty right sleeve and the bulge in the front of Pete's jacket, he withdrew his hand and said, "That darned ice give you a problem?"

"Me and pretty much everyone."

"For sure. Can't even count how many times I been on my backside this year." Stew chuckled.

Pete knew from Stew's slurring he hadn't yet gotten his teeth fixed. "Stew, this is a friend of mine. His name is Martin." Pete motioned to Martin to join them.

"Hi Martin. Met yer friend here, how long ago was that?"

"More than a year ago." Pete smiled.

"That long, *huh*? I lose track." Stew scratched his chin.

"You're not the only one." Pete nodded.

"I don't remember your name," Stew told Pete.

"Pete."

"Yeah, that's right." Stew smiled with recollection.

"Are you staying warm these days, Stew?" Pete asked.

"Mostly."

"How about Doc? Do you still eat with Doc?"

"Sometimes. Not always."

"When was the last time you saw him?"

"Yesterday. Thought he'd be here for breakfast. I was wrong. Maybe lunch. So glad they changed the rules, at least for now, and let us stay inside. Put in some rough days before this happened."

"Will you be here another ten or fifteen minutes?" Pete asked.

"Yeah, for sure."

"Good. I'll stop back before I leave." Pete wanted to cover his bases. If he couldn't find anyone in the office, he'd find a surreptitious way to word the note he'd leave for Doc. It would be easier to give it to someone in the office, but ….

Stew watched Pete and Martin walk back toward the entrance, then turn right to take the hallway to the manager's office. That turn made the two men invisible to Stew. Pete was glad about that. He didn't know how Stew would interpret his meeting with the management. Could be innocuous. If not, could build a wall between them.

On the way, Pete worked to recall the manager's name, assuming the same person held the job. His mind raced through the letters of the alphabet.

Martin interrupted the process. "I'll wait outside the office. While you're meeting with this person, I want to make a phone call."

Stepping to the door, Pete saw the man he'd met while working with Doc sitting at the desk. Ray! The man's name was Ray.

"Ray," Pete said, extending his left hand. "Tough business these days, *huh*?"

"You have no idea. Even so, not as tough as yours. Read about your injury. Hope it isn't serious."

"Thanks. It's insignificant. This won't last long." Pete pointed to his empty left sleeve.

"What brings you back here? I remember you're a police officer. Sorry, for the life of me, I can't remember your name."

"Understandable. You only saw me a few times, and it's been years. My name is Pete, and I want to request a favor. It's really important to me, and I hope you can find a way to accomplish this. You know who Doc is, right? Remember, he was attacked after leaving here a couple of years ago?"

Ray looked a little vague, so Pete continued, "A guy ran back and reported it. You ran out to help him and called 911."

"Oh yeah. He wound up in the hospital for a few days. I remember."

"I want to get in touch with Doc. Unless you have a better idea, the best way I can think of is to ask you to get a note to him. I realize it's asking a lot, but it's important."

"That may mean a bit more monitoring of the dining room. You found the guy who killed one of our regulars. If it's important to you, I'm willing."

"If I want Doc to call me, could he use your phone? I don't know how difficult it will be for him to get access to another."

"We don't usually permit it. If we did, everyone would be asking. Since you're asking, yes."

"Great." Pete unzipped his jacket, and pulled out his notepad and pen. He thought long and hard before putting pen to paper. He had to find a way to get Doc to do as he wanted. He knew Doc was as likely, or more likely, to toss the note and ignore his request. Pete brought a hand up over his mouth and blew out a long breath. Then he positioned the notepad, so he could write with his right hand despite the impediment.

Finishing, he folded the note in half and handed it to Ray. "Thanks! Can't begin to tell you how much I appreciate this."

Pete pulled out his wallet and removed five twenties. "Please use this however most needed, Ray."

"That reminds me," Ray said. "You sent a hefty check to cover the cost of your meals and everyone else's when you last spent time with us. I know you received an acknowledgment in the mail. Glad for this opportunity to thank you in person. Every dollar helps, especially this time of year, and especially this year."

"No offense, Ray, but I wish places like this were unnecessary."

"That makes two of us, Pete."

Pete did as he'd promised. He returned to the dining room, and he and Martin said goodbye to Stew. Pete added, "Take care of yourself and stay warm."

"Yeah, don't stay away so long next time, Pete. Want me to say 'hi' to Doc for you?"

"For sure. Please tell him I hope to see him the next time I stop in."

As soon as he and Pete crossed the street, Martin said, "I called Michelle. Told her you have a friend who happens to be homeless. She said, 'Oh my God! Do you know the forecast? Do you know how quickly people will get frostbitten?' I told her you kept me informed. It surprised me she knew. I didn't think she bothered to keep up these days. What good news, *huh*?"

"It's great to know she isn't as out of it as you'd feared." Pete wanted to ask what Michelle said about Doc visiting, but didn't want to hurry Martin past this moment of celebration.

"Michelle said, 'Are we getting a package deal, Pete, his friend, and his grandmother all for the price of one?' and laughed. I can't remember the last time I heard her laugh. She sounded like the woman who stole my heart and hasn't yet given it back."

Martin beamed. "I told her I didn't know how it would play out. I said I hated to do anything that would concern or upset her."

"She said with all that's been happening, the least she could do was abide by my wishes. She did worry how Marty would react. I said, 'I'm sure Marty will be thrilled to be in the center of one of Pete's adventures.'"

"She laughed again and agreed. Two laughs in two minutes. She must be cured. We can forget about Rochester."

"Martin …."

"Just kidding. But it could be a positive sign."

THIRTY-NINE

Back in the relative warmth of the unmarked car, Pete checked his phone. It had vibrated while he was with Ray. He found a message from the investigators checking out the Lancasters' neighbors.

He listened to the message, then called the investigator.

While canvassing, they found few people home. Most of them claimed to be unaware of the comings and goings of the Lancasters. One thought they left before New Year's Eve and returned yesterday.

"I'm afraid you or Commander Lincoln will hear from the other one who said they were gone."

"What happened?"

"A woman answered the door at the house on the south side of the Lancasters'. When I opened my mouth to ask about the Lancasters, she cut me off, saying she refused to speak with solicitors. I told her I was a police officer. She asked for proof. I produced it, and she started hassling me about bothering people in a neighborhood like hers. She said it wasn't the inner city."

"I told her to answer my questions or else."

"'Or else what?' she demanded."

"I said I'd haul her in and let her think about it. She blew up. 'Don't you know who I am?' she shouted, waving an index finger in front of my face. I told her, 'No, I don't know who you are.'"

"'I'm Charlotte Preston,' she said, obviously thinking that was all the explanation required."

Pete rolled his eyes and shook his head, glad they weren't using Facetime. He knew Judge Preston. He knew exactly how she'd react.

"When her name failed to register, she said, 'I'm a Ramsey County judge. You've appeared in my courtroom.' I was so embarrassed. Still am. I said, 'Sorry, your honor. I didn't recognize you.'"

"Commander, she looks a lot different in makeup and judicial robes than in sweats and a headband."

"Relax, Joe. It could happen to anyone."

"No, Commander. I'm certain you could never get your foot that far in your mouth."

"Further yet, Joe. Have and no doubt will again."

"Thanks for trying to help. Anyway, Commander, I told her I still had some questions. She threw up her hands and acted like I was asking for her first born. When I finally had an opportunity to ask, she said the Lancasters left on or before December thirtieth and returned yesterday morning. Said they spent the time in Iowa, celebrating a belated Christmas with their son and his family. Also said they carried out a large box filled with wrapped gifts. The thing is, I think she was lying. She overreacted to my wanting to ask a few questions, paused a bit too long before telling me the Lancasters weren't home during the time in question, and stared at their house instead of looking at me when answering that question. I'd already alienated myself, so I didn't press, Commander. Hope I didn't let you down."

FORTY

Pete and Martin discussed possible reasons for Judge Preston to lie to the investigator. All they could do was speculate, so Pete changed the subject. "I'm torn," he said. "Next, we can backtrack, looking for anyone who recognizes the shoes identified by Elizabeth Frost or interview the Lancasters. What do you think?"

"You can take the photo of the shoe around tomorrow. I'd like to participate in the interviews of the Lancasters. I want to know what the hell shooting Elizabeth Frost is about."

Since the Lancasters had lawyered up, Pete called the Ramsey County jail to say they'd be there in about an hour to pick up Bart and Esther for questioning.

Driving to headquarters, Martin asked if Pete had spoken with Katie last night.

"Yes. She called before I could call her. Wanted to know if I was home, then came right over."

"Was she upset?"

"If she was, she did a good job of hiding it. My mother, on the other hand, didn't bother to hide it."

"Did you call your mother or did she call you?"

"She called. Saw me on TV."

"I worried that might happen when the media arrived at the ramp."

"Yeah. Thanks to scanners, the media knows each time we sneeze."

"Actually, I wouldn't care if they photographed my sneezes. Now that you've gotten your face on TV and in the newspapers, Pete, you can retire. You've achieved your number-one goal."

"That was a goal, but not the top one. The most important one is to do the driving some day."

"If not for that sling, I'd punch you in the arm."

"I feared as much. That's why I wear it. The doctor said it isn't really necessary."

"So what did Katie say?"

"She talked around it. I read the concern in her eyes. Does Michelle worry about you?"

"Yes, but she accepts the fact this is what makes me happy."

"Katie, too, realizes it makes me happy."

"Have you ever thought about getting out, Pete?"

"Once in a while, when a case really gets to me."

"Hate to say it, but I'm thinking whatever is wrong with Michelle may force me to get out."

"Why, Martin?"

"If it's really serious, she may need to have me working regular hours, something she can depend on. I also worry I need to be a better father to Marty and Olivia. I may need to be more involved in their lives."

"Martin, I've seen Marty's face when you arrive home. He lights up. He understands you have limited control over your schedule and appreciates your efforts to be there for him. I also think he's proud of what you do. Sure, eight-to-five would be nice, but it's also important that you're happy in your job. If you settled for something you didn't like or, heaven forbid, hated, Michelle, Marty, and even little Olivia would sense your dissatisfaction. It's a lot harder to settle for something you don't like after having a job you love."

"I know, but I also wonder if there isn't something that can be more scheduled and still make me happy."

"Why did you become a cop, Martin?"

"I always wanted to be an architect. Before I reached my teens, I spent hours drawing unique buildings—most or all of which probably qualified as infeasible. When Mom took me to the library, I loved to find books with photographs of architectural marvels. I studied those photos and designed my own architectural marvels. My dad always encouraged me, telling me I could be the next Frank Lloyd Wright. By the time I was ten, I knew all about Frank Lloyd Wright. I had a book that showed all of the houses he designed."

Pete saw that telling the story energized Martin.

"When I was a freshman in college, reality hit me right between the eyes. All architecture majors had to complete two semesters of physics. I wanted to become an architect. Thought I had to be an architect. I had trouble with that class. I found a tutor and joined a study group. I got a D on the first test. That just strengthened my resolve. I spent more time studying physics than all of my other classes combined. It didn't matter. I got a D on the next test. A D won't fly in a required course. I was devastated." Martin shook his head.

"I could have persisted, repeating that class every semester. That would have changed my four-year degree into a five-and-one-half-year program. I was paying half of my tuition. I couldn't have managed it, and I certainly couldn't expect Dad to. I faced the fact I couldn't be an architect." Martin shrugged. "I changed my major."

It appeared that reliving those days was still painful. Pete knew Martin. He knew neither of them accepted failure.

"My folks knew I was depressed," Martin continued. "Dad, God love him, told me I had a world full of options. He said what happened in physics indicated I wasn't meant to be an architect. He stated all the platitudes. I bought it. I'd always liked numbers. Somehow, I drifted into accounting. I was a junior when 9/11 occurred." Martin sighed.

"I told my dad, 'Maybe I can't be an architect. Maybe I can't create buildings. I can become a cop and help take down the guys who destroy them.' I switched majors, and the rest is history. How about you, Pete?"

"I thought you knew all about it. You seem to know everything else about me." Pete smiled. "As you know, my dad worked for Cargill. When I was growing up, it seemed like he spent all of his time traveling. For that reason, my uncle Stan took me under his wing. Stan spent a lot of time with me. He took me to Twins games and North Star games. That, of course, was before the North Stars moved to Texas and became the Dallas Stars. He played catch with me, and he coached me on my fastball. Back then, I had a pretty good arm and planned to be a professional baseball player. I had visions of pitching for the Twins, with my family in the stands, rooting me on. I spent hours throwing a baseball at a pitch back, working on accuracy." Pete smiled.

"Anyway, Uncle Stan was a cop. He had so many great stories. Those stories had me sitting on the edge of my seat. I could never hear enough about it. I always begged for more. Stan was my hero. I grew up wanting to be just like him. I wanted a life as exciting as his. I wanted to help and look out for other people. So, here I am." Pete shrugged.

"Is Stan still alive? You never mention seeing him."

"He's very much alive. He lives in Florida. He grew tired of Minnesota winters. I know he follows the weather up here. He has to be delighted to be down south this year. You'll have a chance to meet him. He and Aunt Sheila are coming for the wedding."

"I'd like to meet the man who planted this thorn in my career path." Martin laughed. "Has this life lived up to your expectations, Pete?"

"Yes and no, but mostly yes. The life is radically different from what it was when Stan was a cop. Public perceptions couldn't be much different. Even so, I don't think I could walk away from it and be anywhere near as content and as happy. This job is not an attribute. It's me. Plain and simple. I love the challenge of taking a detail, a tidbit of information, and constructing a complete picture of what happened. I like the thrill of the chase, and I love the adrenaline high when we solve a case. I may be an adrenaline junkie."

"Yeah, I know what you mean. The hours sometime suck, but how do you go about finding something to replace a job like this?"

"I don't know, Martin. Hope I'm not forced to find out before I reach mandatory retirement. Perfect timing," Pete said, as Martin pulled into headquarters.

FORTY-ONE

The two investigators walked next door and escorted Bart Lancaster from the Ramsey County jail to headquarters. After taking him to an interview room, the wait for Bart's attorney commenced.

As soon as the attorney arrived, Pete stated the date and location. Then he Mirandized Bart and asked him to recite his name and address. Video and audio equipment recorded everything.

After introducing Martin and himself, Pete said, "We want to talk to you about the events yesterday in the Union Depot parking …."

"Don't say a word, Bart!" the attorney ordered.

Bart didn't open his mouth.

"Before you spend a cool half million taking his advice," Pete said, "you may want to ask him for his success rate in cases where my partner and I conducted the investigation. I'm confident that information will force you to think long and hard before doing as he advises. We'll give you fifteen minutes to decide whether to cooperate with us or pay the price." Pete walked to the door. Reaching for the door handle, he looked back over his shoulder and said, "By the way, it's only fair to tell you our people spoke with Judge Preston." Then he and Martin stepped into the hallway and closed the door.

Bart succeeded in masking his reaction until after the door closed. Then his face reddened, as he uttered a series of expletives.

Pete refused to permit the absence of a reaction to the mention of the judge deter him. Still hoping Lancaster had reason to worry about what Judge Preston might say, he extended their absence by five minutes. If nothing else, maybe it would irritate Lancaster enough to get him to say something he otherwise wouldn't.

With Martin by his side they walked to Pete's office. Once there, Martin said, "Was that his poker face? Your comment about the judge didn't appear to concern him."

"It doesn't look good, but I'm still hoping he has reason to worry. If I told you 'By the way, it's only fair I tell you I spoke with your neighbor,' wouldn't you at least wonder what your neighbor said?"

"Sure would."

"Exactly. Lancaster's failure to react could say as much, if not more, than a reaction."

"Do you think he was Hammond's source for heroin?"

"Hope to find out, if not from him, then from his wife."

"If he was, do you think the judge knows about it and for some reason is shutting up?"

"I'm not fond of her. Still, hope not for her sake."

"I liked the suggestion that he check on his attorney's success rate in our cases. Do you think his attorney has those statistics?"

"Not with him. If Lancaster asks for the facts, I hope his attorney's inability to accommodate makes Lancaster nervous. Really nervous."

While waiting to find out, they worked on their beloved reports. Thanks to the reports, there was never a danger of being bored at times like this.

Judging from Lancaster's red complexion, white-knuckled fists, clenched jaw, and burning stare, Pete thought the guy looked ready to explode when he and Martin returned. Pete took his time, giving Lancaster every opportunity to lose it.

After a protracted pause, Lancaster broke the silence. "What is your batting average when you're up against my attorney?"

"Looking only at his record on our cases," Pete said, "approximately ninety percent of those clients served time in prison."

"Bart, you can't believe a word he says. Stop, before you flush your life down the toilet."

"You say I can't believe him. You, on the other hand, refuse to provide any information to contradict his claim. What are you hiding from me, Harvey?"

Pete took advantage of the opening and said, "If you answer our questions, I'll do what I can for you."

"That and a five spot will buy you a cup of coffee, Bart. If you confess, you're guaranteed a prison sentence. I'm one of the top criminal attorneys in the Twin Cities. That didn't happen by losing ninety percent of my cases. Let's say, for the sake of argument, you answer all his questions. What he wants is a signed confession. If you provide one? Prison! If you suddenly decide being so cooperative is a bad idea? Tough luck! They're recording everything. Would you expect me to get whatever you said disqualified? I've pulled more than a few rabbits out of hats, Bart. That would be like asking me to pull a thousand-pound sow out of a hat. If you follow my instructions, worst case you'll have a jury trial. Do you think an assistant county attorney has a better chance with a jury than I do? If your answer is yes, you need to find another attorney, friend."

"Nice speech, Harvey," Pete said. "You drove the Escalade, Bart. You fired multiple shots out your window. One did this." Pete pointed to his sling. "Do you actually believe this guy can get you off? If not, cooperation is your best bet. You'll still serve a sentence. I can't make that go away, but the woman didn't die. I'm sure Harvey told you that. That works in your favor."

Lancaster put his hands on his head and his head down. He sat that way for several minutes. Then from that position he said, "I don't want to go to prison, not even for a day. I'm going to listen to Harvey."

"We still have a few questions," Pete said.

"Harvey?"

"Not a word, Bart."

Bart listened.

Pete decided not to risk any communication, in passing, between husband and wife. He and Martin detained Bart in the interview room until after Esther arrived at headquarters.

Forty-Two

The two investigators returned in silence to Pete's office. Martin felt relieved when they didn't pass anyone. He knew it would be a lousy time for a cute remark about Pete's sling.

"How you doing?" he asked after they'd settled in Pete's office.

"Disappointed. I need a few minutes to shake that off, then we'll get his wife. The picture of the shoe may rattle her."

Martin's curiosity got the best of him. "What did you put in the note to Doc?" he asked.

"I figure he'll be more likely to do as I ask if he thinks he's helping me, not vice versa. It said. 'Long time, no see. I need your help, again. Please call ASAP.' It included my phone number. He probably doesn't have it anymore."

"When did you get your PhD in psychology?"

"On-the-job training, Martin. I'm working with you."

"Ha, ha. Do you want to go to the pound and rescue a puppy or two before we interview Esther?"

"I want to rescue all the puppies, but they need someone who won't have to leave them suffer with full bladders for hours on end."

Changing the subject, Pete said, "I forgot to ask you. Did you hear the schools are closed tomorrow? The governor doesn't want kids outside, waiting for buses. It's going to be so cold, people can get frostbite in five minutes. I'll make sure Grandma has everything she needs to entertain Marty for a full day without my help."

"You're brimming with cold weather facts, aren't you, Pete?"

"Yes, but I'm very careful not to fill my tank too full. If the facts freeze, they'll expand and cause the tank to crack and leak out all those facts. Then where would I be?"

"Probably in an asylum. I think it's an excellent place for you. There are so many nice, friendly people there. You'd be in your own element and feel right at home."

Apparently Michelle wasn't the only one whose sense of humor was on the rebound.

Standing, Pete said, "Let's see what Esther is willing to share." Before he reached his office door, his phone vibrated. "Hang on, Martin. If this is Doc, I'll take it. We have time. Since Bart Lancaster wouldn't talk, his wife's attorney may not yet be available."

With his good hand, he extracted the phone from his pocket and, demonstrating his dexterity, he answered.

A familiar voice asked, "Pete?"

It had been a long time, but Pete recognized the voice. "Doc, it's been too long. Far too long. I apologize for that. Did any of the guys tell you I dropped in a few times, hoping to reconnect?"

"Yes. I could have called you. I still have the business card you gave me. I've been waiting to hear that you made chief of police. Have you been dragging your feet?"

"No, Doc. They just don't adequately appreciate my talents."

"Obviously not. Why did you want to talk to me?"

So much for the small talk, Pete thought. "Doc, I hope you'll be honest with me …."

"I may not tell you what you want to know. I may refuse to answer your questions, but I'll never lie to you, Pete."

"Yes, Doc, I guess I didn't say that very well. I didn't think you'd lie to me. Based on past experience, I know you may not be willing to answer right away. You may want to spend a little time deciding whether you'll answer."

"Enough of the preliminaries. I'm a busy man. What do you want to know?"

"December was unbelievably cold. This coming week is going to be treacherous."

"Yes. I'm aware of that, Pete. It behooves me to keep abreast of those things."

"Without your help, we'd never have discovered who murdered Brad Winthrup."

"Nonsense. You wouldn't have stopped looking before you knew. Before you found justice for Flash and his family."

"I never succeed in putting aside the unsolved cases, Doc. They're always pushing their way into my thoughts. Needling me to take one more look at my notes, ask one more question. Glad Brad's case isn't in that group."

"I'll bet there's a dearth of cases in that group."

"Here's the thing, Doc. I got to know a bit about you back then. I like you. I care about you. I worry about you. I did then. I still do—now more than ever. I hope this doesn't put you off, but do you have a place to stay these days? Wait, let me rephrase that. Obviously you're staying somewhere."

"That's very insightful, Pete."

"Are you laughing at me, Doc?"

"Yes, but I'm being very surreptitious about it. Don't want Ray to know."

"Are you sleeping on the streets these days, Doc?"

"Yes. Some of the people staying in the shelters aren't trustworthy. My few possessions are dear to me. I want them to remain mine."

"Will you do me a favor, Doc?"

"I have a feeling I'm not going to like the question."

"Can I put you up, beginning on Monday and at least as long as the bitter cold persists?"

"Where, Pete?"

"I'd like you to stay with me."

"Have you thought this through? It's a nice sentiment and a compliment, but I think you should give it some consideration. I don't want you acting on the spur of the moment. I don't want you to do something you'll regret. I like you, Pete. I don't want to take advantage of your thoughtfulness. That would be unconscionable."

"I've thought about it—for a couple of days. I won't change my mind. The only thing I'll regret is you saying no."

"Let me get back to you. You're right. This will take some consideration."

"Will you call me back no later than tomorrow?"

"That's my plan. Thanks for the offer."

FORTY-THREE

Martin and Pete made their second trip of the day to the Ramsey County jail. Every outdoor excursion reminded Pete of the plight of the homeless. He was rarely out for more than five minutes at a stretch and it chilled him to the bone. He couldn't imagine spending hours on end or an entire night trying to cope with this.

After taking Esther Lancaster to a second interview room, Pete arranged to have Bart returned to the jail.

They still had to wait a half hour for Esther's attorney. Then, with the audio and video recording, Pete again went through the drill. He Mirandized Esther, stated the date and location, and instructed Esther to recite her name and address.

Pete's intuition told him he had two wild cards, the shoes *and* the judge. The latter accomplished nothing with her husband. Might Esther react differently?

Pete began with an observation that Esther could interpret in a variety of ways. "You've had quite a year so far, Esther."

Esther flinched.

To Pete's chagrin, her attorney took the same track as Bart's attorney. The only difference was the name at the end of the stand pat phrase. "Don't say anything, Esther," she instructed.

Pete tried an innocuous question. "How was Iowa?"

Esther relaxed a bit and looked at him for the first time since this began. She also took longer than he'd anticipated to respond.

Eventually, she said, "It was wonderful. We celebrated Christmas on New Year's Eve. As usual, the grandkids were unmanageable, until we opened the gifts. Kids add so much to Christmas, don't you agree?"

Pete nodded and continued his efforts to help her relax.

"How many grandchildren do you have?"

"Five. Only three are in Iowa. The others are local. We celebrated with the others on Christmas Day." She smiled.

"You brought her here to ask about her children?" Esther's attorney asked.

"I thought you went to Iowa to celebrate New Year's Eve," Pete said.

"Well, we celebrated both," Esther stammered.

"Many of your friends were surprised Colette didn't invite you to Demetrius's wedding reception. Did it surprise you?"

Her attorney advised against answering.

Esther heeded the warning.

"I'm confused by your unwillingness to discuss that," Pete lied. "Did you buy a new dress and shoes in anticipation of the event?"

Esther's mouth opened just a crack as she emitted a barely audible gasp.

An indication of concern over one of those items? Pete hoped so. "I'll bet you're fashion conscious, Esther," he said. "You keep up with all the latest trends, don't you."

"Esther, don't respond."

"Why not? Yes, I do, and I'm proud of it."

Her attorney smirked and shook her head.

Pete doubted Esther's attorney knew about the shoes he planned to discuss. Apparently she wanted to prevent Esther from answering any questions or had a sixth sense about the direction he was going. Pete would stay the course, until Esther's attorney succeeded in shutting her up.

"You're familiar with Christian Louboutin shoes, aren't you, Esther?"

Esther pulled her shoulders in close to her ears, crossed her arms tightly across her chest, and dropped her chin. This time she didn't require her attorney's counsel.

"My partner's wife has a pair of Louboutin's shoes, doesn't she, Martin."

"She sure does. They set us back seven hundred bucks. They're black patent-leather with a red sole. They have a red line along the top edge of the sole, and another on the heel. Four-and-three-quarter-inch stiletto heels. She looks me right in the eye when wearing them. I prefer her in flats."

Esther squirmed. Each time Martin ticked off a detail, her jaw clenched a bit tighter, her knuckles grew a bit whiter.

"Are you familiar with those shoes, Esther?"

Esther neither looked at Pete nor answered the question.

"You have a pair of shoes just like those, don't you, Esther."

Esther covered her face with both hands.

Esther's attorney leaned over and whispered in her ear.

"How did you know Elizabeth Frost would enter the depot through the parking lot elevators, Esther?"

"Don't say a word, Esther."

Pete thought Esther might save a lot of money if her attorney recorded that statement. Then instead of showing up, her attorney could instruct Esther to hit the play button every time he or Martin asked a question.

Hoping for another break, Pete asked, "Are you aware one of our investigators spoke with Judge Preston?"

Esther's eyes went wide. Her hand shot up and covered her mouth.

Was that a tear forming in the corner of her right eye? Pete wondered. He decided the time was right. He offered to do everything in his power to help her in exchange for her cooperation. He told her she faced a conviction for first-degree murder, if the case went to trial. He explained she might be able to plea bargain down to a lesser offense with the Ramsey County Attorney if she agreed to cooperate.

No need to hit the play button. Esther's attorney delivered the message again.

Pete tried a different approach. "Esther," he said, "you're obviously a well-educated, rational person. I'd like to give you a chance to explain what happened, what drove you to this." Pete didn't specify what he meant by "this." He gave Esther a wide open floor.

Of course, before she could answer, her attorney told her not to say a word.

Esther complied.

Pete knew he and the Lancasters occupied different social strata. He wondered how quickly Esther would discard a seven-hundred-dollar pair of shoes. "Before you or your attorney exits this room," he said, "we'll have a search warrant. If you still have those shoes, our people will find them. It doesn't matter if they have to tear out the sheet rock and flooring in your home and garage. If they don't find them there, they'll rip apart your Escalade and any other cars you own or lease. They'll check to see if you have a cottage, a storage locker, you name it. For each, they'll repeat the process. If necessary, they'll repeat it in the homes and cars of each of your children. They'll find those shoes. Even without the shoes, we have you. Elizabeth Frost saw you go into the ladies room with Colette just before midnight. Now add the information provided by Judge Preston. Do you actually believe your word will stand up against hers? Taking it a step further, you're at least an accessory to the shooting of Elizabeth and me in the Union Depot ramp. Are you gullible enough to believe your attorney can get you off in the face of all that?"

"Whether or not your attorney is willing to admit it," Pete continued, "refusing to cooperate is the worst thing you can do for yourself. I'm making this offer once. If Martin and I walk out that door, it's over. There's no going back. Do you understand?"

Esther bit her lip and nodded.

This time, Pete saw tears, not just a hint of them. "And?" he asked.

"Can I talk to Bart?"

"I can't let you do that."

Esther's attorney repeated her stand pat line.

Esther looked her straight in the eye and said, "Shut up, Charlotte! You're adding nothing of value. Just shut up!"

Pete smiled, but only on the inside.

Turning away from Charlotte, Esther closed her eyes, rubbed her forehead, and breathed rapid shallow breaths for more than a minute.

Pete and Martin waited, wordlessly.

Finally, Esther looked Pete straight in the eye and said, "I want to plea bargain."

"Don't do that, Esther! Bart will be furious."

"Shut up, Charlotte!"

"If you insist on throwing your life away, Esther, at least permit me to get you a decent deal. Allow me to negotiate with the County Attorney's Office."

Forty-Four

Pete contacted the on-call attorney at the Ramsey County Attorney's Office.

An hour later, an assistant county attorney arrived. First, she met with Pete and Martin.

The two investigators outlined the reasons they believed Esther Lancaster was guilty of first-degree murder. They included Elizabeth Frost's description of the shoes and how those shoes fit into the picture. They mentioned Esther's reaction to the reference to both those shoes and Judge Preston. They said those things and her willingness to plea bargain were all they had on her thus far. They explained she was also an accessory in the shooting of Pete and another woman and why they could prove that. They also went over the known and believed areas of participation by Esther's husband.

Thus equipped, the assistant county attorney met with Esther Lancaster and her attorney. She knew Esther had plenty of time to discuss what she had and hadn't done with her attorney. Armed with that, she used her negotiating skills to narrow the possibilities. Esther's age factored into the assistant county attorney's offer. After a half hour of both calm and heated exchanges, Esther and her attorney agreed to a plea bargain of twelve years in exchange for her confession. The assistant county attorney explained the judge must agree to the reduced sentence. That was almost certain to happen.

With the assistant county attorney observing, and after a longer delay than Pete had hoped, he resumed. Unwilling to take any chances, he began by Mirandizing Esther, again. Then he started with, "What drove you to do it, Esther?" He knew the question could be interpreted in many ways, and waited to see what it revealed.

"Colette destroyed my son! He wasn't perfect. Good kid. No saint. Initially, I thought Colette had a good reason for what she did to him. She seemed so liberal, so accepting. For years, I assumed she stood head and shoulders above me in that department." Esther sighed and shook her head.

"My son and I hadn't spoken in years. For much of that time, I blamed him. I blamed his choices. You see, as a small child, he always liked dolls more than trucks. I thought it was a phase. He was our first son. He has an older sister. I tried to tell myself he just emulated her. She was the closest thing he had to a role model. There weren't any boys his age in the neighborhood. I ignored his behavior, even though it was embarrassing when we had friends over. Tomboys are accepted by our society. Boys who are seen as sissies are rejected and tormented. In this case, I'm ashamed to say, even by his mother. I did my best to explain it away. He used to watch his sister put on makeup. I told myself it was because it gave them an opportunity to talk. That changed the day I caught him putting on her makeup. I made him wash it off. I made him scrub his face until there was no trace of the makeup. I was so afraid his father, one of my friends, or a neighbor would see it. His father already complained Raleigh was effeminate. It irritated him to no end. He blamed me. Said it was because I sissied Raleigh. Said I didn't treat him like a man."

Esther grimaced and shook her head. "The next alarm sounded when I caught Raleigh in one of his sister's dresses. I lost it. I demanded an explanation. He said he just wanted to try it on. He wanted to know how he'd look. He wanted to know how it felt. I tried to shame him into normalcy or at least what I thought was normalcy at the time. He was in high school. That didn't stop me from placing a wall between us. From that point until about six months ago, we didn't talk. We gave each other wide berth. Last summer, he called me on the phone. He begged me to listen. He begged me to meet with him. When I agreed, he said, 'Promise, no matter what, you won't slam the door in my face, Mom.' I promised." A stream of tears rolled down Esther's cheeks.

"When I opened the door, I faced a beautiful woman. I looked around her and called, 'Raleigh?' I actually thought she was his fiancée. The woman said, 'Yes, Mom,' in Raleigh's voice. My jaw dropped. 'Please, Mom, I beg you,' he said, 'hear me out.' Bottom line, I did. He told me about working for Read Ink, and his decision to change full time male to female. He explained that was why Colette forced him out of Read Ink. He showed me the proof he'd gathered. He'd survived for three-and-one-half years on the jobs he had to settle for. He lived on a diet of macaroni and cheese. He sold his car and took public transportation. He turned the heat in his house down to sixty degrees and wore sweats and jackets to stay warm. He canceled his Wi-Fi and went to the library to connect to the Internet. Those are just a few examples. By the time he came to me, despite cutting every possible corner, he needed my help. The bank threatened foreclosure. He, I mean she, told me she'd scrimped and saved and bought that house a few years out of college. She started crying when she told me that. It broke my heart." Esther wiped away a tear.

"That's when my relationship with Colette began to splinter. The better I understood him, I mean her, and what she'd gone through, what she's still going through, the more I detested Colette."

"Didn't Colette think you'd be angry when she got rid of your son?" Martin asked.

"No. She never knew we're related. Raleigh and I were estranged years before she launched Read Ink Press. Raleigh's the son of my first husband. I married Bart before I met Colette. Because my relationship with Raleigh disintegrated years before I met her, I never mentioned him. There was no reason for her to form a connection, and she never did." Esther shook her head and shrugged.

"But your other friends knew, didn't they? Wouldn't one of them say something to Colette?" Martin asked.

"None of the friends we had in common knew about Raleigh. Some of my friends date back to his childhood, but none of them know Colette or that group. Do all of your friends know all of your other friends?"

Martin knew that was a definite no.

"Why New Year's Eve? Why the Union Depot? Why Christos?" Pete asked.

"All of our friends knew Colette didn't invite me to Demetrius's reception. I told Rhina Dalton I'd be in Iowa, knowing she'd spread the word. I knew no one would suspect me. The waitress identified me, didn't she? If only I hadn't stepped on her foot. That's what did it, isn't it? That's when she got a good look at my face. I'd seen Elizabeth before, when I ate at Christos with Colette. We loved the luncheon buffet. We were there one day, and Colette asked Elizabeth how she got to work. I was surprised she parked in the ramp. So surprised, it stuck with me. That's how Bart and I knew to wait there."

Esther rubbed the back of her neck and shook her head. "After the two of you came to our house," she looked at Pete, then Martin, "I realized Elizabeth would be a problem. I couldn't let her identify me. I kept wishing you'd leave, so I could call Christos and see if she was working. I hoped she was. I had no idea where else to find her. As soon as you left, I called and she was scheduled to work, but not yet there. I was so afraid she'd be inside by the time we got there. I used GPS to tell us the quickest route. It identified accidents on Marshall and I-94. We took Summit all the way past the Cathedral." Esther stretched and ran her fingers through her hair.

"While Bart parked," she continued, "I called Christos again. Learned Elizabeth wasn't yet there. She'd called and said she was running late. I was so relieved. We sat there, watching the elevators, waiting for her. Needed to see her face, of course, to identify her. Needed to see it, before her back was to us. Just after she arrived, out of the corner of my eye, I saw another car pull in. Never dreamt it was a police car. Why would I?" Esther shook her head and sighed.

"If only I hadn't stepped on Elizabeth's toes. Honest, I didn't want to hurt her. I had no choice. Collateral damage, isn't that what the military calls it? I wonder if soldiers regret it as much as I do. Maybe not. Maybe their collateral damage doesn't have a face." Esther paused and bit her lip.

"At the reception, how did you get to Colette without being seen and identified?" Martin asked.

"Colette needed money. She asked all of her friends, except me. By the time she started asking, I'd stopped speaking to her. Our other friends told me. They also said none of them would loan her the money. I decided that was my opportunity. I walked through the depot and toward the restrooms just outside Christos. I never entered Christos. I waited until I saw an unfamiliar waitress. Motioned her over, gave her a twenty dollar bill, and a note I told her she had to get to Colette ASAP. Told her it was critical, and Colette would be furious if she didn't receive it *immediately*. The note said I wanted our friendship to get back on track. I didn't want to close out the year on a sour note. It said Harper told me she needed a loan, I had the money with me and would give it to her if we could just make up. It said it had to be that night, before midnight."

"Weren't you worried one or more of your friends might catch a glimpse of you or decide to use the ladies room while you were in there?" Martin asked.

"I did everything possible to prevent those things. I waited until eleven-forty-five to give the note to the waitress. I knew that was cutting it close, but I wanted to make it unlikely anyone would use the ladies room, while I was there. I figured they'd all be otherwise occupied that close to midnight. Earlier and later, there are too many women using the facilities. If I did see someone, I knew I'd have to wait for another opportunity. I couldn't think of another time when there'd be so many people, and no one would suspect me. Colette must have read the note and come right over. I waited around the corner. I couldn't see inside Christos. I didn't see Colette until she was almost to the ladies room. I smiled and rushed over to her. I wasn't looking where I was going. I was looking at Colette. That's when Elizabeth must have stepped right in front of me, and I stepped on her foot. Anyway, Colette and I went into the ladies room. I motioned to her to follow me into the handicap stall. She looked confused, but did as I asked. I whispered we should shoot up one more time to seal the deal. She balked. She said she was off the stuff. She said she was no longer willing to do that to her body. I told her one more time wouldn't make any difference. She wasn't buying it. I told her if she wasn't willing to do this with a loyal friend like me, I wouldn't loan her the money. I turned and started walking away. She grabbed my arm and said, 'Okay, fine, if that's what you want.' She might have continued to refuse if she was sober. She was anything but. She said we had to hurry. She had to get back before midnight. I told her it was no problem. I'd already loaded the syringes. I handed her one. She did it to herself."

"Colette wasn't new to heroin, yet this time it killed her," Martin said. "Did you consider that possibility?"

"The heroin was cut with Fentanyl. Between that and the dose, I felt confident of the result. She knew it was heroin, and she self-administered. Technically, I didn't do it. She could have paid more attention. She could have examined the syringe. She didn't. She didn't ask any questions. If she was that careless … I think it qualifies as suicide."

Rationalization at its best, Pete thought. "Why didn't the heroin cut with Fentanyl affect you?" he asked.

"I had a second syringe, but it was empty. Colette was in such a hurry, she didn't even notice. So close to midnight, I hoped that would be the case."

"You ran a significant risk of being seen shooting up in the ladies room, despite the hour," Martin said.

"Two days before Demetrius's reception, when my anger was festering, I began formulating the plan. I went to the Union Depot to check out the ladies room I thought would work. It was even better than I'd hoped. There is a lot of space in the handicap stall, and it's impossible to see the feet of anyone standing in the back of that stall. So, that's where we went," Esther said with a hands-up shrug.

"When and how did you dispose of the syringes?" Pete asked.

"I had a doctor appointment on the second. While waiting for my doctor to come into the exam room, I slipped the syringes into the Sharps disposal box hanging on the wall. I'd been so scared that something would happen when Bart drove home from the depot or on my way to the doctor. I worried I'd be caught with the syringes. The first time I relaxed in two days was after I'd disposed of them. I figured then I was free and clear. It felt like destiny when everything fell into place so nicely."

It might be too late to obtain that Sharps container but, just in case, Pete obtained the doctor's name and office location. Then continuing their efforts both to obtain a confession and ensure that Esther wasn't covering for Roni or someone else, he asked,

"How much money did you give Colette?" He knew there wasn't a large sum in the purse that arrived at the ME's office.

"None." Esther smiled sheepishly. "I told you she was in a hurry to get back to the party. She shot up and rushed back. I only had a thousand dollars on me in case I had to give her something to shut her up."

Pete wondered about the note delivered to Colette. Had forensics found it, it should have raised questions. "You claim you had a note delivered to Colette," he said.

"Yes. She had it in her hand when she approached the ladies room. I saw it, took it, and said, 'Glad you received this.' Shredded it the minute I got home, just in case."

"We talked to the judge. We know about your supplier, Esther," Pete said.

"Esther," Charlotte warned.

Pete considered the possibilities that might cause Charlotte to be concerned about Esther disclosing the supplier. If it was Bart, what was the connection between Bart and Charlotte?

Esther's face grew scarlet at the mention of Judge Proctor. "She swore she'd keep her mouth shut!" Esther screamed. "Was her son arrested? Did she give up on him? I told her Bart never sold to her son. Swore it was true. Said he wasn't that stupid. Did the kid lie to her about his supplier?"

"You're saying Bart supplied the heroin you took to Christos, Esther?" Pete asked.

"Esther!" Charlotte shouted and tightly grasped her arm.

"Why do I have to say it? You already know."

Pete and Martin remained silent.

When the silence became uncomfortable for Esther, she said, "I know you're going to search the house."

"Stop, Esther!"

"They're going to find it anyway," she continued, talking over Charlotte. "Yes, it was Bart. But Bart never supplied the judge's kid. I swear he didn't."

FORTY-FIVE

As soon as Esther signed her confession, the assistant county attorney departed. First, however, she thanked Pete and Martin for asking the questions required to fill in the gaps.

The two investigators escorted Esther back to the Ramsey County jail. Going forward, both she and Bart were now in the hands of the county attorney.

On their way back to headquarters, Pete told Martin, "It's a classic case. It's okay to knock off your brother's block, but no one else better touch him. This time it was a child. The victim dealt that child a blow from which she seemed incapable of recovering, then her mother exacted the retribution."

Back at headquarters, Pete's first order of business was to notify the Narcotics Unit about Esther's confession, Bart's activities mentioned therein, and the expiration of the thirty-six-hour rule as it applied to Bart. Then he and Martin faced reams of paperwork before they could put this case to bed.

"Did your matrix help?" Pete asked.

"Yes and no. The shoes became a critical clue, but until you bamboozled Esther, we didn't know who owned them. The attack on Elizabeth Frost seemed too coincidental to not be connected, but we've seen stranger coincidences. Lots of people had motives. Didn't know Esther Lancaster's until she confessed. Had Raleigh, now Roni, been forthcoming, a lot of pieces would have fallen into place days ago. Wonder if she suspected her mother did it and tried to protect her. The matrix doesn't point a flashing arrow at the guilty party. It does help me keep things organized."

"In other words, Martin, it works. It's a good tool."

Martin smiled and nodded. "I think so."

"We have another case to solve before we attack the paperwork."

"What do you mean?"

"The case of the trip to Rochester. The case of the man who found himself torn between planting himself in front of a computer monitor and going home to spend precious hours with his kids before he left town with their mother. Ring a bell?"

"Are you talking about the guy who was already cutting out early and dumping a load of crap in his partner's lap?"

"No, I'm talking about the guy who recognized that family is the most important thing and responded accordingly."

Martin shrugged.

"I'm talking about the guy who should leave now. Go home, Martin. Pack and relax. Grandma and I will be there by five o'clock. I'll call her and ask her to fix supper. That will take a bit more pressure off you and Michelle. As soon as we eat, you can hit the road. That way, you'll arrive in Rochester early enough for Michelle to get a good night's sleep before you go over to the Mayo Clinic. I'm praying for her, Martin. I'm praying for all of you."

"If everyone had just one friend like you, Pete, the world would be a better place. We might see a major reduction in hostility and anxiety."

"You bet. Problem is you and I would have to find new careers."

"What about the fact your right arm is in a sling? The time required to complete the reports is at least double."

"It's no big deal if they take a few extra hours. If necessary, I'll recruit help."

Reluctantly, Martin headed home.

Before diving into the paperwork, Pete called his grandmother and told her about the revised plans. He also told her he hoped to have a friend stay with them at Martin's on Monday, Tuesday, and Wednesday nights.

"Someone for you to play with after the kids and I go to bed?"

"A friend I'm trying to protect against the bitter cold that's settling in."

"*Hmm.*"

"I understand if you're uncertain. How about if you meet him before answering? If the idea makes you uncomfortable, we can make a minor modification to our plans. He can stay at my house with me. It would only affect the sleeping arrangements."

"Hotdish or pork roast for supper tonight?"

"Whichever you prefer. Whichever is easiest."

"Your grandfather's favorite hotdish then. I'll get going on it right now. How is the case coming along?"

Pete said he'd tell her all about it that night. He had to take another call. Per his caller ID, Reaching Out was the source.

As he'd hoped, it was Doc.

"Why would you offer to open your doors to a homeless man, Pete?"

"Because you're a human being and my friend. A friend who happens to be homeless. In my mind, homelessness does not define you. Where and when can I pick you up? I have to put in some time at headquarters, but anytime after four tomorrow afternoon will be fine."

"How long did it take you to prepare that speech, Pete?" Doc smiled. Without waiting for an answer, he continued, "I gave your offer a lot of thought. It's exceedingly generous, but I must decline."

"Why, Doc? We have several options. I'm confident I can make you comfortable."

"I'm confident you can make me physically comfortable. Frankly, that's the least of it. The place where I sleep is my home. It isn't the Hilton and it's outside, but my things and my friends are there. If I'm not there, I'm uncomfortable. The ambient air temperature can't affect that sense of security. Eighteen months ago, when I first met you and wound up in the hospital, the air conditioning felt heavenly. Despite that, it was the stay from hell. All I wanted was to go home. I didn't sleep a wink. I live in a close community, Pete. It's a community created by my homeless friends and me. We look out for one another. If I cut out on my friends in order to escape the cold and something happens to one of them, I'll blame myself. We can handle the Arctic front, Pete. We'll withstand it."

"Is there anything I can say to change your mind?"

"Nothing. Again, I appreciate your kindness and your concern."

"Will you do me a favor, Doc?"

"Depends."

"Can I take you shopping tomorrow? I'd like to buy you a few things to help make the next few days more bearable."

"Seriously, there's no need."

"It might help soothe my conscience."

"What time?"

Pete selected four o'clock. It gave them time to shop, and he'd still arrive at Martin's in plenty of time for supper. He wondered if an afternoon in the deep freeze might change Doc's mind. "Shall we meet at Reaching Out or someplace else?" he asked.

"How about at Seventh Place and Minnesota Street? There are usually parking spaces available there."

"Seventh Place and Minnesota at four o'clock tomorrow. Looking forward to seeing you, Doc."

FORTY-SIX

Pete grew impatient with the amount of time the paperwork demanded. He thought about recruiting administrative support, but decided against it. His methodology, composing as he went, made it difficult to perform as a team. Dictation was not his forte. He reminded himself he was at work, not in a hospital or morgue, and plugged along.

At four twenty, with many hours still required, he called his grandmother and said he was on his way.

When he arrived at her apartment, he helped pack the food. "If it tastes half as good as it smells," he said, "Martin and Michelle may not be willing to let you go."

"I'll be glad to share my recipes. My life is another story." She smiled.

On the way to the Tierneys' Pete explained everything was up in the air with Doc. "Looks like a definite no, but I won't know for sure until I see you late tomorrow afternoon."

"You seem disappointed, Pete."

"Worried and disappointed, despite this friend's assurances."

Martin lay on the floor, playing with Marty and Olivia, when they arrived.

By all indications, Michelle was asleep in the Barcalounger.

Marty jumped up and ran to Pete. Rather than giving Pete the usual hug, he stayed back a few paces. "Uncle Pete, Dad told me what happened. He said you're fine. Are you? Does your arm hurt? How long do you have to wear the sling? Will you still be able to help me build robots with my LEGOs Mindstorms?"

"Where's my hug? I won't break, you know. You just need to steer clear of my right arm for a few days. LEGOs are no problem. In a couple of weeks, I'll be skiing."

The last remark seemed to relax Marty. "You wouldn't want to ski this week anyway. Did you hear they canceled school for tomorrow? I thought maybe I could go running with you. If you shouldn't run, we can walk."

"That would be great. I have to spend some time at headquarters, but I'll also spend part of the day here with you."

"Really? Awesome!"

"While Uncle Pete's gone, can we make cookies, Grandma Jackie?"

"I'm planning on it." She smiled and excused herself to dish up the food.

Marty jumped up and followed. "How about if I set the table?"

While Marty and his grandma were occupied, Pete filled in Martin and Michelle on Doc's rejection of his offer.

Both seemed disappointed.

Martin and Michelle raved about the hotdish. They ate quickly and headed out.

The corners of Marty's mouth sagged as he stood at the picture window watching them back out of the garage and down the driveway.

Olivia didn't seem to notice their departure. She was occupied, playing peek-a-boo with Pete's grandma.

"Want to talk?" Pete asked when Marty returned to the table.

"Will she be okay?"

"Your dad is taking her to the best place to achieve that. It may take a while, Marty. You have to be patient. A lot of people are hoping and praying. Are you praying for her?"

"Every night."

"That's good. Me too."

"Really? You're praying for my mom?"

"For sure. She, your dad, you, and Olivia are all important to me. For now, that's the best contribution I can make."

"That and staying here. Mom and Dad are so glad you and Grandma Jackie are doing this. Me too. Uncle Pete, Dad said you being shot didn't mean he's more likely to be hurt. Is that true?"

"I've been a cop for sixteen years, Marty. This is the first time I was shot. The chances are better that I will not be hurt like that again than they are that I will. A hundred injuries like this one will not stop me. I know there is always a danger of being hurt. That's why your dad and I continue our training. That training reduces the chance of a serious injury. There's one thing I can tell you for sure. Every time your dad goes to work, he does everything in his power to insure he'll come home to you at the end of the day."

Marty nodded. "He's a great dad, Uncle Pete. The best!"

FORTY-SEVEN

Pete got up at five thirty on Monday morning. His night was a testimonial to Doc's claim about sleeping better at home. He'd walk today. Based on the pain, a run seemed inadvisable. He pulled on his sweatpants and sweatshirt, keeping his right arm in the sling and inside his sweatshirt. *Three days and counting*, he thought and made a mental note to make an appointment with his doctor. He'd do that much to comply with the emergency department doctor's instructions.

Tiptoeing, he made his way toward the living room where he'd wait for Marty. Glancing in Marty's room as he passed, he saw the wave and the holding up of a finger.

Reaching his side, Marty whispered. "Are you going to work?" A frown clarified the boy's reaction.

"For a walk," Pete whispered.

"Can I come?" The question lit Marty's face in the predawn darkness.

Pete nodded. "Planning on it."

A minute later, Marty joined him. "Let's take Benji. He loves to go outside with me, even when it's cold. I'll get his leash."

Once outside, Pete asked, "How do you like having a dog, Marty?"

"I love it. Benji is super. I'm sure Dad told you we got him at a shelter. I wanted Benji the minute I saw him. He's perfect, don't you think? I take him walking every morning, every day after school, and every night. Sometimes I have to stop working on a robot to do it. I don't mind. He's worth it! At first, Mom didn't want a dog, but she changed her mind when she saw Benji. Dad and I were so glad."

They'd walked about a half mile, and Benji communicated his desire to return home. They yielded. Pete had the zipper on his jacket halfway up. That's as far as it went with his right arm in a sling and across his chest. Hoods and Thinsulate gloves did little to fend off the cold for Pete and the boy.

Marty occupied himself with LEGOs while Pete worked for a bit.

At ten to seven, Olivia made her presence known. Despite Pete and Marty's efforts to reach her before she roused Pete's grandmother, his grandma reached her first. She exited the nursery, baby in arms, a smile on her face, chatting away. "You slept right through the night, didn't you, Olivia. How about a bottle?"

After breakfast, Olivia went down for a nap, and Grandma Jackie pulled out the mixing bowl and asked Marty if he was ready for some serious baking.

"Sure am!"

Pete decided that was his cue. He changed and drove to headquarters. Defensive driving was paramount. If black ice sent him into a spin, responding adequately with one hand would be tricky.

Settled in his office, his first order of business was contacting Esther Lancaster's doctor. He wanted to know if they'd disposed of the Sharps container in the room Esther occupied. Turned out she would have been in one of two rooms, and both containers were still in use. Pete sent an investigator to the doctor's office to collect them and drop them off at the Forensic Services Unit.

That accomplished, he tackled the paperwork.

At noon, he called Martin's house to see how things were going.

"One batch down, one to go," his grandma said. "We're moving from chocolate chip to peanut butter. Any idea when you'll return?"

"Five? Five thirty at the latest. Sound okay to you? Will you be fine until then?"

"Sure. Marty's helping with Olivia. Said he helps his mom a lot. He's going to make me something or other with LEGOs. The names are all Greek to me. He also promised to help assemble the meatloaf I'm fixing for dinner. He's a real prize, Pete."

Pete returned to the paperwork until three forty. Then he left to pick up Doc. He didn't want to risk being late. He didn't want Doc to think he'd changed his mind or that something else took precedence.

Pete arrived at the designated location ten minutes ahead of schedule. The early stages of downtown St. Paul's rush hour barely hindered his progress. He pulled into a diagonal parking space a short distance west of Seventh Place and Minnesota.

Pete checked the north and south sides of the block. He saw no sign of Doc. Downtown lacked the throngs of people that might block his view of an approaching Doc.

Pete didn't worry. He waited. He watched the north and south sides of Seventh Street to the east and west. At four fifteen, he began to worry.

Did Doc agree to meet just to get him off the phone? Did something happen to Doc? He wished he could turn St. Paul upside down and inside out, looking for the man. The only thing was, he had no idea where to look. Pete's mind raced, searching for any resources that might help with the effort. He drew a blank.

When Doc refused his invitation for a place to stay, he found consolation in the opportunity to provide provisions to help make the next few nights more bearable. Now it looked like that effort had failed too.

His right bicep had been a minimal distraction today. He had Oxycodone, but took only Tylenol. Now, sitting here and growing frustrated, the pain began gnawing at him. He thought about taking an Oxycodone without water and decided against it. Ditto for taking Tylenol dry. He decided cold air might reduce the pain. He opened the car door, got out, and leaned back against the car.

After he'd been there long enough to crave some warmth, he did a three sixty, looking without much hope for Doc. He'd almost completed the circle when a voice said, "Would you zip up that jacket and put on a hat?"

"Doc! I thought you stood me up."

"I've been assessing your resolve. Been watching you from that window." Doc pointed to a second story window in the Golden Rule building. "They say that building's haunted, you know. You got my attention when you got out of your car, didn't zip up your jacket and just stood here. I read about the Union Depot. Didn't realize it meant you couldn't zip up. Get back in the car, for God's sake. I don't think Regions Hospital wants to see you twice in three days."

Both men welcomed the warmth the car provided.

"Where would you like to go shopping, Doc?"

"How about St. Vincent de Paul's Thrift Shop on West Seventh? They're wonderful. If you don't have the money, they give you what you need. It'll be an opportunity to pay them back for some of the help they've provided for me."

Doc found a fiber-fill jacket, wool sweater, thermal underwear, thick socks, boots large enough to accommodate a few pairs of socks without cutting off the circulation and freezing his feet, flannel-lined slacks, a new hat, three pairs of mittens, and a half-dozen blankets. He'd have settled for a new jacket, but each time he said he had all he needed, Pete added to the pile.

Pete paid an unbelievably small sum for all of that. After they hauled the stuff to the car, Pete said, "There's one more thing I'd like to do. I'd like to buy you a throwaway phone. One where you just buy the minutes. I can get you an inexpensive one, so no one will want it bad enough to take it away. Could you charge it at the library? Some place like that?"

"I could, but I have no need for one."

"I'd like you to take it as a favor to me, Doc. I'd like you to keep it charged, so you can call me if you ever need help. If there's ever something I can do. It would ease my conscience, Doc."

"Pete, you owe me nothing. On top of that, twice in the last year and a half, you've gone out of your way to help me. Tell your conscience to get a grip."

"My conscience is more likely to listen if you take a phone … and keep it charged. You can call anyone you want. I'll buy a thousand minutes. If you prefer, just call me each time you're running short on minutes."

"A thousand minutes will last me at least ten years, assuming I get some use out of the phone by calling for weather reports. I'm not destitute, Pete."

"Glad to hear it. That has no bearing. Tell me you'll accept this investment in my emotional health."

"If you must." Doc threw up his hands in resignation.

Pete took Doc to Target, bought a phone, minutes, and thirty packages of thermal heaters that Doc could shake, put in his gloves, boots, wherever, and they'd emit heat for four hours. They got the phone service activated and a partial charge on the phone while at Target.

Pete hoped to get an idea of where Doc lived when he dropped him off with his new acquisitions. Didn't happen. Doc asked to be dropped off where he met Pete. Nothing in the vicinity could serve as a domicile for a homeless person.

FORTY-EIGHT

Pete glanced at his watch as Doc walked away. He smiled when he saw he'd reach Martin's a little before five.

Thoughts of Doc occupied Pete on that drive. He regretted Doc's unwillingness to let him do more. He wondered, and not for the first time, how an educated man like Doc became homeless. He hoped Doc would keep the phone charged. He hoped Doc would trust him enough to call if he needed help. He wanted to stay in touch. How would Doc react if he called every few months? Would Doc consider it an invasion of his privacy? He had to think about that. He wondered if at some point Doc might trust him enough to share his story. Pete hoped so. It wasn't prurient interest. Pete wanted to help the man find peace. Resolve whatever tormented him.

Marty talked nonstop at supper. He told Pete about baking cookies and making dinner. He said he changed Olivia's diaper—twice, and gave her one of her bottles. "I built a First Order Transport and the X-Wing Star Fighter. Both are from *Star Wars*. I'm sure you know that. I took Benji for two walks. Will you go with me when I take him tonight?"

"Wouldn't miss it."

Pete looked at his grandmother. She looked like a day full of action took no toll. In fact, she wore a broad smile.

After everyone else was in bed, Pete called Katie. It was still early. Marty had school tomorrow.

"Hi stranger," she answered.

“Two days and you’ve forgotten who I am? I’m crushed. I decided I want to adopt, Katie.”

“Really?” she asked and followed it with a significant pause.

“Yes, I think it’s a great idea. Martin and Michelle adopted, you know.”

“I know they didn’t adopt Olivia. I didn’t think they adopted Marty.”

“Correct on both counts, but they did adopt Benji.”

“Benji? Are you talking about their dog?”

“Yes. I think we should adopt a dog. He or she could run with me and protect me.”

“That’s a great idea. I’ve always wanted a teacup poodle.”

“A teacup poodle couldn’t run with me. I’d have to carry it.”

“Exactly. We could get two. You could carry one in each hand. It would be like running with a five-pound weight in each hand. They will be an excellent source of exercise.”

“True, but a couple of teacup poodles won’t provide much protection.”

“Sure they will. If you have them in your hands, they will lick any attacker to death.”

“That’s not exactly what I had in mind.”

“Okay, what kind of dog do you want?”

“I’m broad-minded. A German shepherd? A golden retriever, a black lab? A mix that’s about that size? You name it. How about if we go to a shelter and see which dog we fall in love with?”

“I’ll vote for that.”

ACKNOWLEDGMENTS

My thanks to Tom Motherway, retired Hibbing police chief; Don Gorrie, retired chief investigator, Ramsey County Medical Examiner's Office; Dr. Mark Contrato, emergency medical physician. Errors in any of those areas are the result of my misinterpretation or misapplication of the information these people so generously shared.

Thanks to Jennifer Rose, Chris Joyce, Pam McCord, Jackie Merlehan, Lynn Maiers Paulson, and Dale Smith for their research assistance.

Thanks to Ruth Krueger, Rick Winter, Deb Harper, Gale Hawkinson, Tara Kennedy, Arlene Carpenter, and Marly Cornell for proofreading and editorial expertise; and Christopher Smith for being quick to share his computer expertise.

Made in the USA
Lexington, KY
27 July 2017